THE LONG JOURNEY OF A PROMISE

GARY CUSHNER

outskirts
press

The Long Journey of a Promise
All Rights Reserved.
Copyright © 2022 Gary Cushner
v3.0

This is a work of fiction. Names, characters, businesses, places, events, locales, and incidents are either the products of the author's imagination or used in a fictitious manner. Any resemblance to actual persons, living or dead, or actual events is purely coincidental.

The opinions expressed in this manuscript are solely the opinions of the author and do not represent the opinions or thoughts of the publisher. The author has represented and warranted full ownership and/or legal right to publish all the materials in this book.

This book may not be reproduced, transmitted, or stored in whole or in part by any means, including graphic, electronic, or mechanical without the express written consent of the publisher except in the case of brief quotations embodied in critical articles and reviews.

Outskirts Press, Inc.
http://www.outskirtspress.com

Paperback ISBN: 978-1-9772-5192-3

Cover Photo © 2022 Jason Cushner. All rights reserved - used with permission.

Outskirts Press and the "OP" logo are trademarks belonging to Outskirts Press, Inc.

PRINTED IN THE UNITED STATES OF AMERICA

ACKNOWLEDGEMENTS
There have been many that have added to the writing of this book. Every person who has spent the time to write, draws from their past and the people they have met. It is no different in my case, but a few have stood out or added to this writing.
My daughter Stefani Hartsfield, who has been counselor and sounding board, and supporter throughout the effort. Also Judie Cotton for being there and adding comments. There were Doc and Doris Palencia, who really started things off. There were Pat Spitzmiller with Tess, Pam Bent with Katie, Deb Fort with Midge. Jim Boula for his clever eye and knowing the sea. Scott and Lynn Schenck, Roland and Bonnie Spell Glenn and Tillie Blocker, Dorene Carle, Bob Haller. Dr. Arnold Cushner and many others who added their support. A special thanks to Anna Ely of Outskirts Press, who guided and advised along the way.

Ancestral Line: *Elsa to Lacey*

	1700s	1800s	1900s	2000s

Heinrick Gufsterson
Dorta Gufsterson
　Daughter　Katrina
　Son　　　　Lutwig
　Daughter　Elsa　　adopted by　Thomas　Vanderbeck
　　　　　　　　　　　　　　　　Ruth　　Vanderbeck
　　　　　　　　　　　　　　　　　Adopted Daughter　Elsa　Levine
　　　　　　　　　　　　　　　　　　Married　　　　　Harry　Levine
　　　　　　　　　　　　　　　　　　　　　　　　　　Daughter　Sarah　Married　Joel　Binski
　　　　　　　　　　　　　　　　　　　　　　　　　　Daughter　Ethel　　　　　　　　Daughter　Valerie　Married　Josh Lockhart
　　Daughter　Lacey

1

THE LATE 1700S

A cool wind blew across the island as the little dingy slid onto the sand in front of the wall surrounding the white house. The only sound was from the small waves lapping on the shore with twinkling stars and a bright moon above. Three men stepped over the side of the boat and silently dragged it further onto the beach above the water line. The tide was receding and the line of sea grass and kelp that had washed up smelled of salt and iodine from the decaying mass. A fourth man was still in the dingy and now stepped out onto the dry sand.

They moved toward the low wall made of blue bicht stone, which led to an entrance and pathway to the house. The house was dark except for the light from a cooking fire and a single lantern which shone from a window with no covering. The house had a red tile roof, and the walls were made of the concrete from crushed coral and wood framing. The windows had wooden shutters that could be closed in case of storms but on most nights were left open for the breeze to flow in.

Three of the men wore heavy cloth trousers which were cut off above the ankle, no shoes and dark shirts of a heavy cotton fabric. The leader, who had stepped out last, had more formal attire with dark trousers and socks and leather shoes with brass buckles. He was of medium height and build with a small face and long brown hair. He had small squinting eyes over a bookish like nose and was clean shaven. His face had an angry expression stressed with tension.

Approaching the front door, the leader had the three men stand on either side of the entry out of site. The leader knocked once on the door loudly and reached for the door handle. There was no lock on the door as was custom in this time. He said loudly, "inside." As was the custom in these days to have the person outside say "inside" and if allowing entrance, the person inside would say "outside."

Without waiting the man pushed open the door and barged into the main room. Sitting in a chair by a little table sat Heinrick Gufsterson. His wife Dorta was sitting in a wooden rocker with knitting yarn on her lap. Both had looks of surprise on their faces and were too stunned to speak. Heinrick regaining composure first shouted "Brother Frederick, what is the meaning of this!"

Heinrick was slightly older than Frederick and was mostly bald with a grey fringe around the scalp. He was muscular from hard work but had started to show a late age paunch. He started to stand.

Fredrick sprang across the room and pushed his brother back into his chair, "Where is the deed to the island" demanded Frederick.

"It is at my counsel's office along with my will. The will gives the island to any of my immediate family and then to my closest living relative," Heinrick stated. "So, don't go blustering about getting any part of this island or what you may think is buried on it." The brothers had disliked each other for a long time. Heinrick was favored by their father for his industrious nature and skill at managing the boat cleaning business. His brother was lazy and used manipulation and treachery to get out of working. That is why the father had sent him to live on a different island altogether.

At this point Dorta jumped up realizing something bad was about to happen and fled into the hall leading to the bedrooms and servants' quarters. She didn't stop until she reached the door entering the maid's room and burst in startling Letisha the 14-year-old housemaid. Without hesitation Dorta took Latisha's arm and pulled her from the bed. "Get Elsa, Katherine, and Lutwig and get out a window and run." "Do it now!" Dorta was nearly hysterical.

Dorta left the room and headed back to the main room where loud voices were shouting and cursing each other. She walked in and saw the three other men circled around Heinrick. Dorta screamed at what she saw.

Heinrick swung his head around at the scream and the fellow on his left swung a machete into Heinrick's left side rib cage. Blood spurted out but Heinrick spun around with his right fist trying to hit his attacker. The next fellow then stabbed out with another knife catching Heinrick just under the sternum. This pierced the heart, and the fight was over, Heinrick collapsed. Dorta was in shock but blocked the doorway to the hallway and bedrooms. The 3 men turned toward her. She was frozen with fright. At that time, she was struck across the neck by the man with the machete which severed her aorta. Blood spurted out like water from a hose, and she crumbled to the floor.

By then Letisha had run into Elsa's bedroom and woken the 6-year-old little girl. Letisha picked up the little girl and motioned for her to keep quiet. Preparing to go into the hallway, she heard the screams and changed direction and went out the window with the girl in her arms.

Creeping low along the side of the house she went to the next bedroom window. Peeking over the sill she saw a large man enter and go straight to the bed with a knife in his hand and thrust downward into the sheet covering Lutwig. Letisha fled in panic with little Elsa in her arms with screams trailing behind her.

Over the wall, down the beach to where there was a shallow channel that crossed to the main island where Letisha ran. Water in the channel was only a few inches deep at low tide and sometimes no water at all. Maybe 100 yards wide, she crossed to the mainland and into the fishing huts that were built along the dirt streets there.

Three little streets over, she turned right and up to the 3rd little shack. She pushed open the door with her shoulder and collapsed on the dirt floor with the little girl in her arms.

The little girl was wearing only a white nightshirt with an open collar. She was a pretty little girl with rosy cheeks a bright smile that seemed to sparkle in her eyes. She had a gold chain around her neck with a gold locket about the size of a half dollar and a clasp on one side. The locket had a face engraved on it and ornate filigree around the face.

Into the room walked an older woman with dark hair and deep-set brown eyes above high cheek bones. Slumping shoulders as if weighed down by time. She wore a faded night dress which was frayed around the collar. She spoke, "My god, child what are you doing?"

Letisha, crumpled and sobbing on the floor, looked up through watery frightened eyes and said, "Terrible things are happening." "Masta and Missus are dead and men with knives were killen everyone in the house.' Still sobbing Letisha began to shake with fear, tears streaming down her face and could only say "terrible, terrible" through trembling lips.

The little girl was whimpering on the floor and calling "Momma, Momma." Large tears swelling in her eyes and a look of panic in her face. The little girl crawled to Letisha and cuddled in her arms.

Letisha hugged the little girl and finally looked up at her Aunt. "Dey done killed them and the screams were terrible. I run with little Elsa and run straight here." "Aunt Tina what we gonna do?"

Tina stepped across the wood floor which creaked with every step. She reached down with heavy arms and lifted Letisha and Elsa off the floor and moved them to the old rickety bench sitting against the wall. In a soft calming voice Tina said, "You gonna stay here tonight and then in the morning we go see Captain Williams, he'll know what to do"

2

HIGH COUNTRY - 2017

Lying in bed as the sun's rays were creeping down Buffalo Mountain and a new day was dawning; Lacey could see through a partly opened window all the majestic beauty and grandeur the Rocky Mountains offered. She was deep under the covers, because in July at 9,000 feet the temperature was still in the 40's.

The room was a large square and the walls were made of hewn wood in a reddish-brown color with all the knots and imperfections showing beneath the lacquer. The king size bed was covered with blankets and a quilt in muted blue. Several throw rugs covered the wood floor. The bed faced west allowing the panoramic view from the hump in Buffalo Mountain and on to the Gore Range with all the ragged intimidating grey/brown peaks barren above timberline.

There were several dog beds scattered on the floor in different sizes. Lacey closed her eyes quickly knowing it would start any moment. First the flapping of the ears from the golden retriever standing next to the bed. Then the pacing of the blackish-brown mixed breed with deep brown eyes, on top of the covers on one side of the bed, whose collar tags clinked as she walked. Then the spring from the floor to the bed of a small beagle mix who loved to lick Lacey's face right after getting up. They were always happy to get up and start the day. Tails wagging and making weird little noises to make sure Lacey got the message.

The air was alive with their energy and excitement. "All right, all right I'm up and you can all go out and pee" Lacey slid her feet out from under the covers and stood up. Wearing a T shirt and flannel pajama bottoms and around her neck a gold chain with a gold locket given to her by her mother. Crossing to the door and opening it, there was a mad scramble of paws to jump from the bed or race around it to be first out the door and down the steps with tails wagging, except for the blackish brown mix, which only had a bob for a tail so her whole behind wagged instead. Chaos ruled every morning with the delight of starting another day. Lacey walked down the stairs and down a hallway to the back door to the backyard and lifted the slide covering the doggy door. Flap, flap flap as the plastic covering the opening was hit by each dog as it went out.

Lacey turned and went back down the hall and turned left to enter the kitchen. Opening a cupboard on her right she took out a large bag of dry dog food and a can of wet dog food. Going back into the hallway and picking up the three dog dishes and setting them on a counter in the hall. One dish had the prongs in it to slow down the eating process. She measured out the amount she wanted in each dish of the dry dog food and returned the bag to the cupboard. Then, peeling back the lid from the wet dog food, she measured out amounts wanted in each dish. Having dogs of different sizes meant different amounts for each dog. Then came the pills each one would get and the pill pockets that with the different pills. The whole process only took a few minutes. By then the sound of the dog door flapping meant they were back and hungry for breakfast. All three standing in the hallway and watching intently. Katie, the little beagle, was making a squealing sound while the other two were shifting from one front foot to the other.

"Sit" Lacey commanded. Three fury butts hit the floor. Lacey put the bowls on the floor in positions that would not be close to one another. "OK" was all Lacey needed to say as the 3 dogs sprang up and headed for their individual bowls. Tess, the golden retriever, was the quickest and was a chow hound to boot. Her bowl was red with the prongs because she inhaled the food instead of eating it. The prongs slowed things down a little but not much. All that was heard was the lapping of tongues and the crunch of kibble.

Lacey headed back upstairs to make the bed and get a quick shower and dressed. As she stepped into the shower, she began to ponder her life. Having a degree in psychology and a master's degree in criminology, she had spent 3 years with the FBI in the Miami Office. But after 3 years of dealing with the low lives of today's society, she wanted to smell clean air and not constantly be stressed by the demands of other people. She wasn't antisocial but needed to get away from the underbelly of crime, and criminals. In just a couple of years, she had seen rapes, stabbings, mutilations of all types and enough shootings for a lifetime. An 18-year-old boy had pulled a gun during a surveillance in Tampa, and she had to shoot him or he could have killed her or her partner. Like it was said in the movie La La Land, people seemed to worship everything and value nothing. She was cleared immediately because the whole incident was videoed by the dash cam in the car. But killing another person stays in the brain like a virus and eats at you mentally, unless you're a sociopath.

It just so happened that she had volunteered at the Humane Society and took a course in pet first aid. By chance she had been looking online for something that would get her out of the Bureau and she came across a house and pet sitting job in Silverthorne, Colorado. Just the break she needed. She responded by e-mail. The owner responded and said that she would be gone from November to July and needed someone to watch the house and 3 dogs. They had talked on the phone and although Lacey had never been at 9000 feet, it seemed just a perfect fit. The owner was warm and honest to talk too and had been a high school teacher and coach. They had talked on facetime. Because of her FBI training, Lacey knew that the kind face and no-nonsense personality fit the profile of an honest person.

   Now coming to the end of nine months she was going to leave the high country. Since Colorado had passed the legalization of marijuana, crime hadn't increased and only gave new meaning to the term "high country." Lacey, like most, had experimented with weed at a younger age and didn't like the effect of not feeling in control of herself.

   Lacey was about 5 foot 5 inches tall with a good figure. Her shoulders were narrow and although she had ample breasts they were not oversized or out of proportion. She had a narrow waist but always thought her hips and thighs were too big. Shoulder length brown hair, wide green eyes and a straight nose, with medium to full lips that fit her face. More like Julia Roberts and Keira Knightly than Sandra Bullock.

   The water in the shower brought her back to the present. She had just responded to a caretaker position for a Villa in, of all places, St Thomas. She didn't think the people would accept her; however, she got a call back and a request for a phone interview. Inwardly it sounded like a great way to see the Caribbean and she was excited. Something within her said it was the place to go, almost like she had a connection to the island. Thinking about it gave her a feeling of calm and warmth.

   Lacey knew that her great-great grandmother had some connection to the islands, but little was said when she was growing up. Her mother and grandmother never spoke of the past Her mother had married and had the last name of Lockhart. Her grandmother's name was Binski by marriage and her maiden name was Levine, So Lacey's great-great grandmother's last name was Levine by marriage. She did not know her great-great grandmother's name, but she had some connection with a family in the islands. There were old photographs of a Dutch family but none of them had a resemblance to Lacey's great grandmother. She did know that her great-great grandmother's first name was Elsa. Not much else was ever mentioned. Knowing that with DNA you can find out a great deal of your family tree, someday she would have to check it out. Right now, she could hear the dogs in the bedroom and knew she better get out of the shower before they got into something they shouldn't.

She shut of the shower and pulled back the curtain to grab a towel off the wooden rack. Since she left the door open the deep brown eyes of Midge were peering up at her. "What are you looking at, "She chided the dog." The butt began to wiggle as she spoke.

She dried quickly and stepped out and over to the mirror. Since she left the door open, no steam had covered the mirror and she could see the 32-year-old face looking back at her. Body lotion to keep the skin moist in the high country was a necessity, minimal make up, teeth brushed and a brush through the hair and she was ready for clothes. Panties, bra, jeans, t-shirt, light pullover yellow sweater, socks and light hiking boots and she was ready to go.

Six eyes staring at her the whole time. The golden had the most beautiful face. The eyes were rimmed by a brown line that looked like the dog was wearing mascara. This was due to an infection that would not go away and would create a brown streak from the inside corners of the eyes at times. The streak needed to be wiped away, every so often. Tess was a British white golden and had a glow to her coat which was clipped short, so as not to pick up every twig and bramble. Her mouth had the continuous smile that all goldens have. She was more than pretty, she was beautiful, but she was the princess rogue. If there was trouble to get into, she would find it or be rolling in Elk droppings. Tess also was a kitchen counter surfer for food.

As Lacey headed for the door, all three brushed past her, hitting her leg in an effort to be first down the stairs. At the bottom of the stairs was a small room that that had hooks that held all sorts of leashes. Short, long, red, blue, print and the retractable kind for a smaller dog, which is the one Lacey selected. It was blue plastic with a handle that had the button to stop the leash from extending. This leash was for Katie the youngest, who hadn't learned not to walk in front of cars and was easily excited by almost anything.

Snapping the leash on Katie's collar, Lacey headed for the front door. Tess and Midge were well trained and listened to commands. Lacey opened the front door and all four together headed down the three steps to the driveway. The driveway was about 150 feet long made of cement and covered with a black sealant to keep the cement from cracking in the harsh winters. The air was clean and crisp, and although the temperature was probably in the high 50's, in the direct sunlight it felt 20 degrees warmer.

At the end of the driveway, she turned right on the street, which had no sidewalks, and went about 60 feet to an empty lot with a downhill trail made from many tramping feet. The Forest Service calls them social trails because the people walking creates them. At the bottom was a sidewalk, which continued for a quarter mile to the bike and hiking path at the Blue River. She took the dogs down to the ponds at the north end and then walked back about 3 miles in total.

Down along the ponds was a housing development with willows and cattails growing from the water. There was a wooden fence on both sides of the path and houses started on the south side of the path. As she turned around to head back, a moose sprang from the willows and went over the fence and landed upright on the path. Katie, the little beagle, squealed and tugged on the leash. The other 2 dogs froze in their tracks and stared. Lacey's heart pounded as her adrenalin started to spike. Moose are not friendly creatures and they think dogs are a threat. At 1200 pounds this one could stomp a person or dog into the ground in no time. Lacey regained some composure and started backing back down the path toward home. The moose was only 20 feet away and she could smell the odor from the mud on the fur.

The moose stood watching for maybe 15 to 30 seconds. Lacey had noticed it was a young female and only looked curious. After a few steps back with Midge and Tess backing away and Katie being pulled, the moose from a standing position flew over the fence on the other side of the path and started eating the leaves from a tree in a house's front yard. Lacey kept backing and pulling until all were around a corner and out of site of the moose. Tension eased and she gave a sigh of relief. Twenty minutes later and 3 poop bags filled and deposited in the trash, the group was back at the house.

Lacey plopped on the couch and opened her laptop. Midge was next to her trying to cuddle, Tess was in a dog bed ready for a nap and Katie was out the backdoor in the yard seeing what birds or critters she could terrorize. Opening her e-mails, she saw that she had one from the owners of the villa in St Thomas. Clicking on the e-mail line the screen had a message with an attachment. The message read, "We would like to offer you the caretaker position for the villa, if you are in agreement with the terms and conditions in the attached agreement. We think your qualifications and resume are outstanding and you would be a great fit to take care of the villa, as well as the guests, who come there. Please read the attached agreement and let us know that you will take the position.

Lacey clicked the attachment by moving the cursor using the touchpad. A new screen appeared with the word "Agreement" in caps and bold print at the top. She read through the attachment by scrolling down. It was about 3 pages and not really an agreement but a disclosure of what was to be paid by the owners and generally what the villa and island were like. Food was expensive but rum was cheap. There was no place for a signature, and she thought, there was nothing in the document that she couldn't live with. Starting date was to be July 30th, and that would work well with her current schedule. The owners expected her to stay a year and then they would pay her return airfare.

She closed the attachment and clicked reply. She typed in, "The Agreement looks fine, and the starting date will work out with my schedule. Looking forward to meeting you at the Villa."

Putting the computer to one side, she went to the kitchen for a glass of water. Now to checkout airfares, she thought.

3

STAYING HIDDEN - 1700'S

As the sky started to lighten over the harbour, Aunt Tina, Letisha and Elsa left the shack and headed down the dirt street toward the main part of town. Staying in the shadows of the little houses they moved quietly toward the main street where buildings and houses started and then moved up the hills. Crossing the main street and heading north to the next street back. There were no sidewalks, and nobody was on the streets yet. Not even cooking fires were lit yet and the buildings and houses were dark.

Approaching a white two-story building with a red tile roof Tina turned and motioned for the other 2 to be quiet and follow her up several steps at the side of the house. Peering in through a side window, she could see the kitchen table and bricked out fireplace. The room was empty. There was a solid wood door next to the window and Tina turned the handle. The door began to open inward and as quietly as she could she opened it all the way. The door did creak on its hinges but not loudly. All three entered the kitchen and stood listening. They could hear creaking from the floors above signalling the sounds of movement.

Then heavy steps from someone walking down the steps in the hallway outside the kitchen door leading into the main dining room and the front of the house. The three stood just inside the back door. Letisha and Elsa were frightened and silent their faces filled with fear. Tina was focused on the doorway and seemed to be calm, with one hand resting on Letisha's shoulder to stop her from bolting out the door.

Entering through the kitchen door was a man about six foot two inches tall with broad shoulders, dark hair, blue eyes, square face and the calm expression of someone not easily excited. He had a full beard and a bushy moustache that seemed to match the thick eyebrows.

Tina spoke first, "Morning Captain Williams, sorry for the early disturbance."

Still looking calmly at the three, Captain Williams spoke in a calm but purposeful manner, "I'm sure there is a good reason you are here at this hour and will tell me what it is soon enough." Still looking at the two young girls he continued, "but first light the kitchen fire and get some water boiling for coffee."

Tina moved across the room and started a fire in the cooking oven. Taking a round pot with a round handle she went to the far wall and poured water from a large pitcher into the pot. She then took the pot back over to the oven and rested the pot on a metal grate above the fire. She put a loaf of bread on a plate and set it on the table. There was a metal box setting on the counter and she took out butter and a jar containing jelly. The Captain pulled a heavy wooden chair away from the table and sat down. The chair creaked from the strain. Tina brought him a heavy knife with a wooden handle and set it next to the Captain. He sawed back and forth thru the bread until he had cut several slices. Taking the first slice and cutting in half he spread butter and jelly on it and handed to Elsa. He did the same with the other half and handed to Letisha. Both girls were silent and staring at the Captain.

"Go ahead and eat, you both look like you need something in your belly's," the Captain said. By then steam could be seen coming from the pot and Tina took a large thick ceramic mug from a hook above the counter. She pulled a jar setting in a cupboard and took the top off. Pouring about 2 cups of coffee grounds into the pot on the oven. She then got a cotton cloth out of counter drawer and laid it over the top of the cup. Grabbing a heavy woven pad, she wrapped it around the pot handle and carefully poured the steaming liquid into the mug. She placed the pot back to the side from the fire and turned and leaned against the counter.

"Now tell me the story of why you're here?" asked the Captain.

Tina spoke with a strained frown on her face. She related the story that Letisha had told her and what had occurred at the Gufsterson's house. "Little Elsa is in terrible danger, if they killed all the others."

Elsa and Letisha were now sitting on the floor with jelly and butter on the corners of the mouths. Elsa's eyes weren't frightened anymore and her mouth was relaxed and calm.

The Captain looked directly at Letisha and said, "Did you see anybody being killed? Tell me what you saw."

"I done saw a man with a knife, stab poor little Lutwig and there were terrible screaming, terrible." She was remembering something that caused her breath to quicken, and her eyes had a blank far off stare. Latisha passed out.

Tina stepped to her and cradled her against her chest. She started stroking Latisha's head and murmuring "alright, its' alright."

The Captain stood and pushed the chair back. "You and the kids stay here; I'm going to get dressed and go to the fort to speak with the Governor." He turned and went out the door and up the stairs quickly. In a matter of minutes, he was back down the stairs followed by an elderly woman with grey hair and a kindly face, obviously Mrs Williams. The Captain didn't bother to go into the kitchen, he went straight to the front door and left the house.

Mrs Williams entered the kitchen. The sun was up now with sporadic clouds over the eastern mountains and over the ocean to the south. The harbour was turquoise to dark blue or gun metal where a cloud blocked out the sun. There was noise in the streets as the town came alive with people going to work or opening shops.

Several hours had passed since the Captain had left and the sound of the door handle turning and the door being pushed open startled the four women alert. Letisha and Elsa were sitting at the table. Mrs Williams and Tina were getting the noon day meal ready. Red beans and rice, ham shank and papaya chunks. The captain entered the kitchen, his face was serious and slightly flushed. Greta, his wife, handed him a mug with water in it. He sat down and looked at Greta, "It is bad, they are all dead." He had been across to the Gufsterson's home. and "The army is digging graves for the family. They were murdered and there was blood all over."

"Let's not talk about it, right now," said Greta looking from her husband to Elsa. Elsa was sitting at the table fidgeting like a child would and pulling on her hair. This was obviously a way of calming herself. She really had no idea of the situation but knew that things were not as they should be.

"Ah yes", we will discuss it later," said the Captain. Let's have lunch and talk about plans for Elsa. "We need to decide what would be best for her"

Greta Williams gave a knowing nod at her husband and turned to the cabinets for plates. She put bread and some butter on the table. This bread was already sliced.

Tina was placing a plate of mango, papaya, starfruit and bananas on the table with a silver serving fork. She looked at Letisha and then to the Captain. The Captain nodded and said to Letisha, "you sit next to Elsa and keep her company." Letisha responded immediately.

He then stood and looked at Greta and Tina. "Why don't we go in the living room for a moment." Leading the way, he walked through the door into the dining room, which had a formal dark mahogany table with a white linen runner down the whole length and 10 high backed cushioned chairs. There were two silver candelabras on the table with white long stem candles in them.

They all walked past the table into the entry way and into the far side of living room. The walls were all white with an overstuffed couch sitting in front of a large window. The window had heavy shutters on the outside and beige drapes hung from an iron bar on the inside. There was a dark mahogany coffee table in front of the couch and several large, cushioned chairs on the other side of the coffee table facing the couch.

The Captain had long dark mouton chop sideburns that stuck out from his cheeks. He pulled at his beard in agitation. "We can't let Elsa be seen in town and we can't let her be stuck here," meaning the house.

Greta was quiet for a moment and spoke, "Can we get her on a ship to the Colonies?" "My sister Ruth in Charles Town could take care of her and see to her upbringing" We could send a letter with a little money and explain the situation." Her husband has done well growing rice and they have never had children. Ruth has expressed to me in letters that she regrets not being able to have a child." Ruth was 5 years younger than Greta, and they had stayed close.

"That is a possibility", said the Captain, "but what about Letisha? She may be in danger too."

Tina spoke, "I'll keep her with me and she could help here at the house for now. If, that would be all right with you folks." They looked at the Captain.

"It would be fine with us," spoke the Captain. "But for a short time, she only comes and goes when it is dark, and few people are about. And definitely do not go to the harbour or the docks. Till I can arrange for passage, she and Elsa should sleep in the house. That way Elsa will not be alone and Letisha will not be seen."

Greta smiled a little because she knew under a gruff exterior her husband was warm hearted and caring. They had had a son and a daughter, who were grown up and lived back in the States. Tina also knew his character and liked the idea of having Letisha around.

"Settled then, I should go down toward the harbour and see what ships are in." He said, as he went to the front hallway and picked up his hat and went out the front door and down the steps. Greta and Tina smiled at each other and headed back to the kitchen.

Sometime later as the sun was setting over the Western hills and the moon could already be seen in the East. Noise on the street had quieted down and only the sound of a donkey pulling a cart could be heard creaking on the dirt street.

The front door opened, and the Captain stepped in. Taking off his hat and setting it on a polished wooden sideboard. The calm face showed no emotion and he listened for sounds in the house. He heard, pots and pans being moved in the kitchen. He walked through the dining room and into the kitchen. There was Tina, Letisha and Elsa. Tina was preparing the evening meal and the two girls were at the table playing a game with their fingers. He was just about to turn around and look for Greta when he heard her footsteps on the stairs. Walking back through the dining room, he saw Greta coming down the stairs and motioned toward the living room.

She followed him in and as the late afternoon shadows crept along the walls, he went to a sideboard and poured himself some sherry. She lit several candles and an oil lantern setting on the coffee table. He turned and said, "we are in a bit of luck." There is a cargo vessel heading up to the Carolinas to deliver arms and slaves to the Colonists." Captain Hamlin owes me a favour and for a small sum will take Elsa to Charles Town and see she gets to Ruth. "He leaves day after tomorrow with the morning tides." "We will need to get her aboard tomorrow night."

Greta was silent for a moment as consternation covered her face. "Will she be safe with him," she asked? Greta felt nervous for the first time and it was clear she was bonding with Elsa.

He looked straight into her eyes, "safer than with most." He knows that if anything happens to the little girl, he will be hunted and killed and no place on this earth will be safe for him." "Plus, I told him on his return, he will have to have proof of her safe delivery by letter from Ruth, and I would make available to him the land he wanted to buy at a very reasonable price."

Still concerned Greta said, "I will pen a letter to Ruth to go with Elsa that specifies how to state that Elsa was safe and unharmed." The dimming light outside was almost gone and they headed back to the dining room.

There were three places set at the table in the dining room and several steaming plates of pork, boiled potatoes and squash. The water glasses were filled and wine in a decanter was on a side table next to the head chair. The Captain took the head of the table and waited till Greta sat down on his left before sitting down. Elsa sat on his right. He poured a dark ruby coloured wine into his glass and looked at Greta. She nodded and he filled her wine glass. There were places set in the kitchen for Tina and Letisha,

The Captain bowed his head and said, "thank you lord for the food we are about to eat, amen." He took a sip of wine and reached for the plate with the pork on it. Light danced off the crystal wine glasses as the candles flickered.

Elsa was pulling on her hair and had a very serious look on her face. She looked straight at the Captain and didn't smile. "Will I see mommy soon," she asked in a timid small voice?

The Captain looked at Greta and wasn't sure how to answer the question. There was silence for several seconds. He realized that she didn't really understand the situation and his heart was in turmoil. Keeping a compassioned look on his face he said, "Mommy is going to be away for a long time." He didn't have the heart to tell her never.

Greta jumped in to try and help the situation, "We have been planning a wonderful trip for you to visit my sister Ruth. She lives in the colonies and has a big house and ponies for you to ride." Greta put some food an Elsa's plate and started cutting it up, quickly.

Elsa kept the serious look on her face and pulled at her hair. "When am I going on this trip and when will mommy come see me?" Her little face was in a frown and she was on the verge of tears.

The Captain spoke, "You're going to have a great adventure and see lots of wonderful things and a new country. It will start with a voyage on a big ship, and you'll see creatures you have never seen before out in the ocean. Have you ever seen a dolphin?"

The frown was gone but the serious face was still there. "No, I haven't, will they hurt me?" She was not convinced that this was going to be alright, but she was trying to be strong.

"No, they won't hurt you, "said the Captain. "They will jump in the air and blow air through a hole in their head and always have a smile on their face."

Silence had come over Elsa as she was trying to think of the dolphin. She took some yam and put it in her mouth and began to chew.

The Captain poured himself some more wine and looked at Greta. Greta was smiling at him and continued to eat. Noise from the kitchen could be heard as Tina and Letisha were finished eating and were cleaning up.

The next day, the Captain came down right after dawn and Tina was back already boiling water for coffee. She brought a cup into the dining room for the Captain. He looked and could see Tina wanted to speak.

She spoke softly in almost a whisper, "when does she need to leave? Her round face was almost to the point of crying."

"We need to get her on the ship tonight," said the Captain. "I'm going to send Greta into town after a while and buy Elsa some clothes for the trip. The rest Ruth can buy her in Charles Town."

Are Elsa and Letisha still upstairs in the guest room?" Tina just nodded. "Good, as soon as Greta comes down, I will speak to her and then head down to the docks to arrange for a skiff tonight."

Greta came down the stairs a few minutes later and sat in her normal chair just to the right of the Captain. Tina brought in a plate with fruit and cup of coffee for her. "Thank you, Tina." She said.

The Captain finished his coffee, which was strong and had a burnt smell of nuts to it. He looked at his wife and spoke, "You will need to get a carrying bag, and clothes for Elsa to travel in. Even in the summer it can get cold at night when you're on the ocean and we want her to be safe as possible." He got up from the chair and pushed back from the table a few inches. The chair legs made a screeching sound as they were pushed across the wooden floor. "I'll be going down to the harbour and arrange for a boat to take her out to the ship."

Tina walked in and said, "See my cousin Lamar. He got a fine boat and is a man, who don't talk about what he is doin."

Captain Williams just nodded and walked toward the hallway. He put on his 3-pointed hat and opened the door. He walked out the door and down the steps and was gone.

Greta Williams finished her coffee and nibbled on a slice of bread. Finished, she went back upstairs to see what the girls were up to.

Later that day, as the sun was setting, and the clouds were turning orange and pink around the edges in a robin's egg blue sky. Elsa and Letisha were sitting in the kitchen, playing with Elsa's stuffed doll. Tina was getting a dinner of black beans and rice with chunks of pork in a coconut water sauce ready. The sweet smell of the coconut water and pork filled the air.

Greta walked in with cloth bag with handles on both sides. It was coloured with blue and white stripes and had a strap across the top and a buckle on the other side. It was puffed out from whatever was inside. Under Greta's arm was a dark mauve wool coat with black buttons. The wool looked heavy, and the coat had a collar that could be turned up and buttoned. It had deep pockets on each side with little flaps that covered them.

She set everything down in the living room and went to see what the others were doing. Entering the kitchen, Tina looked questioningly at Greta, who smiled and nodded Tina's way. Looking now at the two girls, Greta said, "What have you been doing today?"

Elsa blurted, "We've been playing tag and hide and seek." Her face went serious for a second and she pulled at her hair. "But we didn't break anything," she exclaimed, as her mind tried to process what Greta might be thinking.

"Well good," Greta said. "I wouldn't want to have the Captain know; you have been breaking up the furniture. Why don't we all go into the living room and I'll show you some new things, I bought for you?"

Tina moved one pot to the side of the fire and followed the other three into the living room. Several paintings and a mirror hung on the living room walls. They all circled around the bag and the coat, which was lying flat on the arm of a chair.

The front door suddenly opened and in walked the Captain. He spotted the four of them standing in the living room. There was no smile on his face, and he looked a little stressed about something. Greta picked it up on the look immediately and so did Tina, but neither of them said anything. "What is going on now?" said the Captain.

"I was going to show Elsa her new things," said Greta. "Come in and take a seat and watch. Tina, why don't you bring the Captain a little port." Tina turned around and went into the dining room. She was back a few moments later with a glass of port on a silver tray and set it down in front of the Captain. He picked up the glass and sipped a little bit and leaned back in the chair.

Turning to Elsa, Greta motioned to her to come closer. Picking up the coat, Greta opened it and held it for Elsa to try on. Elsa slipped her arms in the sleeves and looked up at Greta. "A little large for now, but she will be able to grow into it," said Greta, pulling the coat shut and buttoning it, giving Elsa and admiring look.

Elsa pulled at her hair and said, "The coat is hot to wear."

Greta said, "I know but it will keep you warm when you are in Charles Town." Greta then unbuttoned the coat and let Elsa slip out of it. She then opened the bag and took out two dresses in pastel colours and some little cotton white underwear. She then took out a pair of pants and beige cotton blouse. Finally, she took out a couple pair of sox and leather shoes. "These are all for you Elsa", Greta proclaimed.

"Thank you." said Elsa. "But why do I need all these new clothes?" Can't I have my old ones?" The small face on the verge of tears and the hand pulling on her hair.

"Well," said the Captain with a soft smile on the gruff face, "you are going to a new place and will have to go on a ship to get there. We want you to have a wonderful time and we want to make sure you are dressed well."

The tears finally came down her face and her little body trembled. "I want my mommy," she panted between sobs.

Greta bent down and picked her up. Greta patted her back softly and hugged her close. "It's alright, it's alright," Greta repeated as she walked toward the stairs with Letisha and Tina following.

An hour later, they all were standing in the hall. Elsa was dressed in the new pants and beige blouse. The Captain said.

"It is time we be going. There was a sadness in the air as Elsa said "goodbyes" to the women. She was pulling at her hair and carrying the coat under her arm. The Captain opened the door and put his hand gently on Elsa's back and looked directly at Greta and nodded. He checked the street and then he and Elsa went out and down the whitewashed steps to the street.

Greta watched as they went down the street and closed the door.

At the beach by the side of the harbour, Lamar was waiting with the boat resting partially on the sand. You could hear the waves lapping gently on the beach.

There were some clouds high above partially blocking the moonlight. The breeze was coming from the south, and probably less than 10 knots. Waves were rolling across the water that was black except for the white foam on the little waves hitting the beach.

Lamar was not a big man about 5'5" with grey hair cut short. He had a lean body from years of hard work. The muscles in his arms and shoulders were carved and little fat shown except around his waist that comes with age and a starch diet.

"Captain ready", was all that Lamar said as they got within hearing distance. The Captain nodded and lifted Elsa into the rowboat. He helped push the boat off the sand and stepped into it. Lamar gave it a final shove and jumped in. Grabbing an oar, he lifted from the lock and used it as a poll to push the boat farther off the sandy beach. He replaced the one oar and grabbed the other to start rowing into the dark harbour.

With little light to go by, Lamar rowed with dead reckoning and a few minutes later the black shape of the ship appeared directly in front of them. There was one deck lantern, but the rest of the ship looked like a black hole against the night sky.

Pulling up along the starboard side a line dropped over the side and the Captain grabbed it. A face appeared above them over the rail and a voice said, "Captain Williams."

"Aye" responded the Captain. Then a little rope ladder came over the side. Lamar was holding the rowboat in place and lifted Elsa on to it. She climbed about 3 rungs when an arm reached over and under her arm. She was lifted the rest of the way and set down on the deck. The Captain tied the coat and bag to the line that had come over the side. It was lifted up onto the ship. The captain looked up and said, "You take good care of her now." We expect a good report." "Fair winds Captain."

The rowboat pushed off and started back in the direction to the beach.

4

HEADING TO THE ISLANDS - 2017

Bags were packed and sitting in the downstairs entry way waiting for the shuttle. Lacey walked into the kitchen with a sad look on her face. Alice, who had come back, was at the island cutting up some carrots with a small knife with the standard glass of chardonnay next to her. Alice didn't like stemmed glassware, so the wine was in a 6-ounce tumbler with small coloured raised dots on the sides. "I'm going to miss you and the dogs," Lacey said.

"Alice stopped cutting and looked up, with those happy brown eyes. The dogs will miss you, I'm sure." Alice smirked. Alice's way of saying I will miss you too.

The sound of the shuttle van coming up the driveway could be heard before the brief beep of the horn. Lacey walked over and hugged Alice, scratched three furry heads and turned to the door. She knew she was going to miss the non-judgemental affection given by the dogs and the bonding she had done with Alice. Walking to the door she turned and said "Stay" loudly and opened the door. Three dog butts hit the floor. Grabbing the backpack, purse and the two pieces of luggage, she walked out.

The driver walked up and picked up the luggage and walked back to the van. Lacy turned and waived to Alice, who had come to the door. Alice's foot and leg were stopping the three dogs from heading out. Alice waived back and mouthed "Good Luck."

The driver had stowed the luggage and had opened the side sliding door so Lacey could climb in. He held out his hand to help her in, but she just grabbed the seat back and pulled herself onto the first grey vinyl cushioned bench seat behind and to the right of the driver's seat. This way she not only had a side view, but a front view also. There were windows all around the van, so everyone could lookout when traveling. There were three other passengers in the van, two young girls about thirteen or fourteen and a forty-ish woman wearing an expensive looking pant suit. The two girls were dressed in designer jeans and t-shirts with cute sayings on them. Probably sisters with the same dish blonde hair and brown eyes.

The driver came around opened the door and climbed into the driver's seat. He reached across with his right hand and pulled the safety harness across to the latch by his right hip. Lacey could hear the click as he strapped in. As he backed down the driveway, Lacey noticed that the two girls had phones or some device out and were either texting or playing some sort of game. She started to relax and look out to the face of the Dillon Reservoir earthen dam. She could see the cars crossing over the top and heading for Frisco about 2 miles to the west. The driver having pulled out to the street, and was now heading for I-70 and the interchange. She looked up at Buffalo Mountain and Salt Lick trail at the mountain's base, just below the Wilderness Condos and homes. She knew she wouldn't be seeing the elk and moose that live around the Salt Lick Creek. She came back from dreaming when the driver got in the left lane to turn on the entry ramp and head up to the tunnels.

The light turned green and van started up the on ramp, gaining speed to keep up with the traffic that is constant on I-70. He slid into the right lane ahead of a tractor trailer with "FEDEX" painted on its side. Trucks run this route 24/7 because it is one of the main links for supplying the Midwest from the West coast and vice versa. They were now doing about 65 to 70 mph, heading up to the tunnels. Rounding the second turn Lacey could see red traffic lights about four miles up the twelve-mile distance to the tunnels. Delays were constant on the trip from Summit County to Denver some eighty miles away. Nobody had figured out how to handle the sheer volume of traffic that comes up from Denver and the plains everyday to get to the mountains. She could see there were some snow on the tops of Grey's and Torrie's, which are two of the mountains over 14,000 feet in Colorado. She thought, that is something I won't be seeing in person for a long while.

The van was now in the middle lane. The driver was trying to position the van so he could get around the traffic as quickly as possible. The traffic was stop and go and would probably take thirty minutes to reach the tunnels at the summit, some five to six miles away. The Interstate went from three lanes to two just before the tunnels and this caused the backup.

The driver turned his head and started talking to use up the time, "the Eisenhower Memorial Tunnel is approximately over 10,013 feet in elevation and one of the highest road tunnels in the world and it also crosses the Western Continental Divide. In 2016 approximately 12,395,195 vehicles went through the tunnels."

The traffic started to move but he kept on talking. "That equates to about 24 cars per minute going through the tunnels." "The tunnels are about 1.7 miles long, so if a car in each lane hits their breaks, it slows up all the cars behind." "So, all the cars start slowing down and just like a wave effect traffic starts backing up." Thus, we get what they call the I-70 corridor problem. I've seen this ripple effect stretch from the tunnels all the way to the onramp in Silverthorne. You can have a two- or three-hour delay during ski season."

Lacey could see we were now approaching the entrance to the tunnel Eastbound. Which was actually called the Edwin C. Johnson Tunnel, but nobody ever called it that. Traffic was picking up speed as they entered the tunnel, which reminded her of a very large white tiled bathroom. There were lights in the tunnel, but vision was dim. Speed was up to about 30 and she could see sun light on the other end of the tunnel ahead.

Breaking out of the tunnel the van had accelerated to 60 mph as it started down toward Denver. She sat back and hoped she see some of the rocky mountain big horn sheep that grazed near the freeway. They were approaching the steep downhill stretch to the Georgetown turn off. She could taste the sweet meat from roasted chestnuts that venders sold around Christmas in the town. They were keeping a steady 70 mph and the scenery was rushing past. She began to doze as her eyelids got heavy.

She came back fully awake as they braked again entering the stretch past the town of Idaho Springs and spotted the waterfall and waterwheel on the right side. Another set of smaller tunnels up ahead and the climb up Floyd Hill. Then on to the turn off to Evergreen. The evergreens were giving way to the dried-out tan/brown grassland. This was the dry time of year and the ground was hard and cracked. As the van came over the last hill, Lacey could see the plains all the way to the horizon. The city of Denver laid at the bottom and the brown cloud from, and inversion layer laid over the City. The flatirons and Red Rocks amphitheatre were off to the south. I-70 was three lanes wide, the van stayed in the middle lane. They should reach the DIA turnoff in about fifteen minutes.

Reaching the turnoff and making the sweeping left turn to get on the airport approach road she could see the white tent roof of the terminal. She smiled at the idea the roof was supposed to represent the mountains in winter. It didn't really look like that thought Lacey.

The van pulled up on the East side of the terminal and the driver came around and opened her door. He then went to the rear of the van and unloaded her luggage and backpack. She reached in her pocked and took out some cash and gave the driver a $5.00 bill as a tip. She pondered just a second, if she had over tipped. The saying is that Americans tip well, and the Europeans and Canadians don't. Didn't matter, the driver was upbeat and was trying to give good customer service. She turned and walked with the backpack over her shoulder and the two bags rolling behind her. One was a hard-sided roller from Samsonite and the other was blue nylon, Eddie Bauer with a hard bottom storage that was good for shoes. People were going in all directions and she was hoping that the line would not be too long at security. She went to a kiosk and used her phone to get the boarding pass to St Thomas.

She turned and looked for a departure gate screen. Spotting one she went over and found her gate on the C concourse. Then she walked into the maze that led to the security checkpoints and was thinking "cattle in a que."

She had checked in the one hard sided suitcase, but the nylon bag was small enough to be a carryon and the backpack was also. Traveling was always stressful she thought. After clearing security and seeing a fat guy's plumber butt crack when he bent over to take off his shoes, disgusting, she headed to the escalator that would lead down to the tram that would then take her to the part of the terminal, where and her gate was. Crowding into the tram with others she hoped not to stand next to a person who smelled. The constant background chatter of people discussing plans or business was constant. The doors closed and she heard the women's voice, who cautions to hold handrails and which part of the terminal A, B, C was next.

She made it to her terminal and gate and saw she had about an hour to wait before boarding. Looking at the different restaurants, bars and fast-food places to choose from, she decided on a place with tables and waitresses and a bar. Why not, the airline won't have anything but stale nuts or pretzels for the flight. Sitting down, a dark haired waitress in a uniform showed up with a tired look and set down a plastic coated menu. The waitress asked, "Can I get you something to drink?"

"What the hell thought Lacey, "I'll have a Corona with a lime and a glass of water." There was a time that a glass of water was served automatically when you sat down, but not today. The waitress turned and left. Lacey slid the suitcase next to her chair and put the backpack on the chair next to her at the table for four. She looked at the menu and selected the Cobb salad with an oil and balsamic vinaigrette dressing.

The waitress was back and set the Corona and the glass of water in front of her. The waitress took a pen and pad out of her apron and said, "What would you like to eat?"

"I'll have the Cobb salad with oil and vinegar dressing, thank you." The waitress just nodded and left. She obviously had a rough night last night or was totally bored with her job. Lacey scanned the rest of the restaurant, which had couples at two other tables, a family across from her with two little girls and a lone fellow near the bar with a burger with fries, and a Heineken in front of him. He had a handsome face with deep brown eyes, heavy dark eyebrow's a strong chin medium length black hair. He saw her looking at him and she dropped her gaze to the table slightly embarrassed she got caught checking him out. She did not want to meet anyone right now.

The waitress showed up with the salad and placed it on the table. She said," Can I get you anything else?"

"No thanks, "Lacey responded and gave a polite smile. Looking around the waitress, she noticed the dark haired man approaching. He was about 6ft 2 in with broad shoulders a small waist. Definitely someone who worked out. I don't need this right now, Lacey thought. I'll just blow him off and be done. Remembering from her training, she believed he wasn't a serial killer or a paedophile because he had no predatory look about him. In fact, he had a goofy cute smile.

"Hi, where are you headed?" He asked. He was wearing a blue cotton polo shirt and khaki slacks with a brown belt. He had sandals and no socks, so he was going to warmer climates.

I'll be polite, she thought and said, "the islands."

"Which one?" he responded. He was watching her face and she was not showing any warmth or smile.

"St Thomas," she said.

His face still in a goofy smile, "I'm going there too, but I can see you don't want to be bothered." He turned to leave.

Lacey realized that she was being rude and childish. She realized she could get some firsthand information from him about the island. She hadn't learned his name. "Wait, she said, "What is your name? I'm sorry, I was being rude, and it would be nice to know someone on the Island." As an excuse, she continued, "I haven't been around people much lately, only dogs."

"Are you going to tell me to sit and stay next?' He joked. "My name is Daniel Williams and whom do I have the pleasure of being commanded by?"

"Lacey Lockhart and if you would like, please join me." She now was smiling impishly and to her astonishment a little flustered. She hadn't flirted in a long while and pondered if that was what she was doing. "How long have you been on St Thomas or is this your first time?"

"I've lived on Island for about 3 years and go back and forth from New York about once a month."

Lacey looked a little puzzled, "If you go back and forth from New York, why are you flying out of Denver?"

"I came out to see an old roommate, who lives in Boulder. We used to share an apartment on the Island. He went to work with NOAA, so he moved here to be close to work."

They announced the first call for boarding people with small children and those needing extra time to board over the loudspeaker.

"We better pay up and get in line." Daniel said.

"Now who is being bossy?" She said and signalled to the waitress for the checks. She liked being in control.

They paid separately, she grabbed her backpack and slung it over one shoulder and took the handle of the carry on and started to the exit of the restaurant. He had picked up his carry on made of green nylon and waited by the side as she went in front to him. Lacey wondered if he was checking out her backside or just being a gentleman. She glanced over shoulder to see where his eyes were looking. Straight ahead at the moment, so he wasn't being lecherous.

The first class passengers or those with special privileges were being called to the gate. The crowd for economy class was gathering in anticipation for the boarding call by number. They both had their tickets out and she boarded with section one and he boarded with section 4. This has nothing to do with where your seat is but keeps the crowding to a minimum at the entry to the boarding walkway.

"Where are you sitting?" He asked.

"36 C, and you?"

"24 F." I wanted an aisle seat also but was to late to get one." "I settled on a window hoping that a small person will sit next to me." If someone with large shoulders sits next to me, I have to lean sideways, just to keep from feeling like an accordion."

"They announced Section one could board at this time." She walked with the crowd trying to be polite and not bang into anyone with her carry on. She handed the ticket taker her boarding pass and had it scanned and handed back. She walked down the entry way rolling the carryon behind her and came to a stop in line to wait for people to get seated on the plane. The noise and talking on the entry way was upbeat and jovial because people were looking forward to an adventure, but not the plane ride.

The line started moving again and she made it to the doorway of the plane. Two flight attendants were working in the forward galley. A middle aged woman with premature grey hair and a smiling face welcomed her aboard as she lifted the rollers of her carryon over the doorway. She began to turn right down the aisle, when the person behind her banged into her suitcase, in a hurry to board and not paying attention. She had to stop, so she wouldn't bump into the person in front of her, but the person behind seemed agitated and was not paying attention. There was no apology from the man behind her. Another jerk from America, who is caught up in himself to be polite. The ugly American still exists in multitudes, she thought. The pathway in front of her had cleared and she continued down the isle, only to have to stop after a few feet to let someone up in front jam an oversized carryon into the overhead compartment.

She looked back at the man behind her, who was red faced and needed to cut down on salts and alcohol to reduce the chance of a stroke. Sandy brown hair with a receding hairline above a round face and little grey bloodshot eyes. He breathed heavily through his nose which made a wheezing sound. There were 3 rows in first class with 2 larger seats on each side. He couldn't get his carryon into the overhead on the left side, so he pushed the small bag on the right overhead to one side and jammed his carryon into the compartment. Hopefully there was nothing breakable in the other person's small carryon. He then took off his jacket and crammed that into the overhead. Then he proceeded to squeeze his large flabby body into the seat.

Just then Daniel entered the plane walking partially sideways toward his seat. She could see he got lucky with an elderly small woman in his row. For just a moment she thought about trying to change seats with the woman, but having to sit in a middle seat for a 6 hour flight was too much. He found his row and luckily a space he could slip his bag in the overhead. At his height, he couldn't fit anything under the seat in front of him and have room to unbend his legs. The elderly woman stood and came out of the row to let him get to his seat. He looked back at Lacey and smiled, which caused a slight stirring in her stomach. It had been a long time since she had felt attracted to someone.

What the hell, she thought and stood up. She took her backpack with her and walked down to wear the woman was standing. "Excuse me, but would you like to exchange seats with me? I have an aisle seat and it may be more comfortable for you." Daniel had paused with his head pushed up against the overhead and one hand was resting on the seatback.

The elderly woman smiled and spoke with slightly raspy voice. "That would be wonderful, you are such a dear. Let me take my purse." The woman took a black leather purse with straps and a gold clasp from the seat and walked back to where Lacey had been sitting. Neither she nor lacey tried to shift their stowed carryon's. It would have been too much trouble with the plane as crowed as it was.

Daniel stepped back into the aisle . "Would you like the window or the center seat?"

Lacey looked into his sparkling eyes . "I prefer the window, if you don't mind?" She thought she was being forward, but his smile appeared genuine and she knew that he was going to be good company for a long flight. Nothing more than helping the time pass more quickly or was she kidding herself and trying to start something. Nonsense she thought, this isn't going to be a chapter out of "Fear of Flying." She sidestepped over to her seat and sat down with the backpack on her lap. She slid it down under the seat in front of her.

He waited until she was comfortable and fastened her seatbelt. Then he picked up an end of his seatbelt in his left hand and slid into his seat. He searched with his right and found the other end to his seatbelt and snapped the silver ends together.

A middle age man in a grey knit polo shirt and blue jeans came back down the aisle after putting his carryon in an overhead further back and sat in the aisle seat. His hair was starting to turn grey and there was a bald spot starting. He had a fabric black briefcase stuffed with papers and a computer. He squeezed the briefcase under the seat in front after taking out a laptop computer and resting it on his lap. He appeared preoccupied and kept his gaze down the aisle at the behind of a teenage girl in short shorts trying to get her carryon into the overhead. The bottom of her butt checks were exposed.

The flight attendants were checking that the overheads were closed and seatbacks and tray tables were in the upright and locked position. Plus checking that people had their seatbelts fastened. One went to the microphone in front and the others stood in the aisle holding the laminated folders about the aircraft safety instructions. The flight attendants went through the normal speech and with very few people paying attention. The pilot came on and said "flight crew, please prepare for departure."

The plane's engines began the whining sound of ramping up and there was a slight jolt as the plane was being pushed backward from the gate. Lacey and Daniel looked at each other and he said. "Do you get nervous on take offs?"

"Nope." She replied. "I find it more exciting, than anything else."

"Aren't you worried about crashing?" He continued, trying to keep the conversations going.

"Would it do any good to worry? Are you?" She asked.

"Nope, I agree with you. Worrying does no good at all." He saw the tarmac out the window and some hangers in the distance, as the plane started taxing toward the runway. She was looking up into his face which appeared relaxed.

"Tell me more about St. Thomas?" Lacey asked. Her gaze still looking into his eyes.

"Well, it is a volcanic island, so it is pretty hilly. Roads curve a lot and are narrow. People drive on the left there, but most cars are made for right hand driving with the steering wheel on the left. That puts the passenger on the right side, looking directly into oncoming traffic. Can be a little scary at times. Driving is definitely a challenge. They have a few stop signs and stop lights, but I believe the locals don't obey the rules and the tourists are all looking around." "So, drive defensively. You'll need a car to get around, because with the steep hills and few sidewalks, walking is not a good idea. Will you have a vehicle?"

She thought for a moment. "Yes, the Villa has a vehicle to get around. I was told that part of my requirements, was to go to the airport and have the guests follow me in rental cars."

The plane was now first in line to take off. The engines were getting louder and the plane was being held back by the brakes. The pilot released the brakes and the plane sped down the runway. She could feel the wheels leave the runway and the plane's nose rise into the air. She glanced out the window and saw the mountains bathed in sunlight and the white tips against the light blue skies. There were no clouds to break the view, so it appeared endless outward.

She turned her attention back toward Daniel, as the plane climbed and headed southeast across the vast planes. "What do you do in your free time?" She asked.

"There isn't a lot of free time during the day or days off, but I SCUBA dive or just hang out at a beach. When I can, they keep us busy getting the cruise ships in an out of the harbour. The island has some of the best, white powdery sandy beaches in the world." There are a great many bars and restaurants there, so, if you want entertainment, you can find it."

She noticed his eyes light up, when he talked about the ocean. What was so fascinating about the sea to some people. The old poem by Samuel Taylor Coleridge about the ancient mariner and the mysteries of the deep. Does it evoke fear or curiosity or adventure or is it the mystery? Does it represent the adventure of the unknown? Could be all or more. Anyway, she liked the excitement that showed in his voice.

Daniel smiled and said, "I'll show you around the island if you'd like?"

"That sounds like a date?" Lacey replied.

"Oh no, just being a good tour guide. A smirk appeared at the corners of his mouth. "Remember, I do have a captain's license, this allows me to show people the world."

"Hmmm, let me get settled first and then I may take you up on it." Lacey now had a smile on her face and she could feel a little heat coming up in her cheeks. Yes. I'm flirting and I haven't felt like doing that in a long time. She always felt a little uneasy around men, but with Daniel, something was different.

The sound of the engines was in the background and people were moving around the plane. The guy in the aisle seat was engrossed in his laptop and wasn't paying any attention to them. She felt slightly drowsy and her eyelids started to feel heavy. She looked over at Daniel and he was watching her face.

"Why don't you take a nap with your head against the window for a little while. We can start the documentary of the island later." He suggested.

She shifted in her seat and rested her head on the window frame and tried to get comfortable. She felt better than she had in a long time and the shooting of the boy was fading into other parts of her mind. She could never get rid of the vision completely, because it stayed in her memory like a scary movie. She drifted into a restless sleep with the constant humming of the engines in her ears.

She woke with her head resting on Daniel's shoulder and the announcement to prepare for landing. She noticed that she had drooled a little bit on his shirt. "Oh, I'm really sorry." She blurted. "I hope I didn't snore." Daniel had that goofy smile still on his face.

He was looking into her face. "Just a slight buzzing sound, not anything like sawing logs. Don't worry about it, you look like an angel when you sleep."

She was now blushing and trying to get control of the present. "Well now, you know, I came from heaven." She could feel the plane turning and then lowering the flaps.

"We can get to our histories later. When I give you the tour."

She thought he was being a little controlling, but let it pass. "How are you getting to your place?"

"I take a taxi to it. It's not far, but you haven't given me your cell phone number, yet. So let me put it in my phone now If that is OK with you, of course."

She smiled because he was backing off the control thing. She gave her number, area code first. She had purchased the phone in Colorado and that was the reason for the 970 area code. She felt the wheels touch down and heard the screech of the rubber on the runway. The nose dipped slightly as the breaks were being applied.

Daniel was looking at her throat. "The coin you're wearing around your neck, where did you get it?"

"It is an heirloom passed down in the family, my mother gave it to me. She told me that it was originally my great great grandmother's. So, it's been in the family a long time. It actually gives me some peace of mind and has a calming effect when I hold it."

"Have you ever had it appraised?" He asked.

"Never, it means too much to me to part with. The chain it's on also came with it." The chain was braided gold and appeared fairly thick. "Why do you ask?"

"Well, in the shops in town they sell old coins and artifacts from the old days of the pirates I've seen similar pieces on display and in books and they are valuable. "You may want to insure it."

The plane was nosing up to the terminal and stopped. As if someone threw a switch. People were getting up and opening the overhead bins. Grabbing and hoisting their luggage and in the process bumping and hitting others on the plane. As if they were going to get off any quicker.

Daniel watched and said. "don't rush, it takes about 10 minutes for the offloading stairs to get moved up to the plane. There is absolutely no reason to try and stand up, till the doors are open and people are getting off."

She watched the other passengers squeezing into the aisle and looking like cattle in a loading shoot. The fellow in the aisle seat was still sitting and putting his laptop back in the nylon briefcase. A rather large woman in some kind of stretch pants had her butt toward him and he was leaning toward Daniel trying to stay out of an uncomfortable situation. The aisle was packed and no one was going anywhere.

Finally, the doors opened and they could see the shuffling of passengers getting off. They waited until the rows in front cleared and then the man stood up, grabbed his carryon from the overhead and started down the aisle. Daniel was next and got up and reached in the overhead for his bag. Lacey moved sideways next to him with her backpack in hand. She had to go back several rows to get her carryon. "She looked up and said, you go ahead, I've got to wait to get further back for my bag."

He glanced backwards and then looked down at her, pondering if he should wait. "OK, I'll see you outside."

She waited for the rows to clear and the elderly woman she had traded seats with came and stopped to get her carryon. She paused and said. "Thank you again."

Lacey just smiled and nodded. The woman went on down the aisle with her rolling suitcase. Bumping into armrests every few feet.

Lacey could get back to her bag then and went back to get it. Lifting it out of the compartment, she set it down and extended the handle. She rolled down the aisle and picked it up to get down the steps. Daniel was standing at the bottom looking up at her.

"You made it." Daniel smiled.

She smiled back and thought that was very nice that he waited. They walked together, heading for the terminal. The sun was out and there was a breeze. as they walked. It was warm but not oppressive. She felt the humidity, not like Colorado.

The sliding glass doors were opened at the terminal with the line of passengers going in. As they entered, they could see a man standing back by a wall, next to a kiosk which was giving samples of different flavoured rum in little plastic cups. He had a yellow sign in a clear plastic sheet cover saying, "WELCOME LACEY LOCKHART."

Daniel said. "Looks like your ride is here. I'll give you a call later." He veered to the right to head out a set of doors leading to the parking area.

"Thank you for being a pillow on the flight." She watched him leave and wondered would he call.

She approached the man holding the sign. He was in his late 60's or early 70's. Around 6 feet tall with all white hair cut neatly and a round face. He reminded her of pictures she had seen of Earnest Hemingway. His eyes were a light blue and looked a little anxious. "You must be Stan" she said.

"I am and you must be Lacey Lockhart." He had a deep voice, and he was talking loudly to overcome the noise in the terminal. She could hardly hear over the noise in the building. There was a fellow playing a steel drum next to the rum kiosk. "Do you have any luggage to pick up?" Stan asked.

"Yes, I have one bag"

He turned toward the baggage area and said, while looking over his shoulder." How was your flight?"

'It was fine." "Like most flights today, it was crowded, but no turbulence." As they approached the luggage conveyor, she noticed the heavy set man with red face waiting for the conveyor to start and the luggage to come through the flaps. The man was still breathing heavily and wheezing slightly. He looked up as they approached and there was the look of recognition on his face as he saw Stan. The man had his jacket over his arm and his shirt sleeves were turned up.

Stan spoke first. "Hello Harry." Stan didn't make an effort to extend his hand to shake. It was clear to Lacey that the relationship was one of mistrust.

"Hi Stan." The man replied, and glanced at Lacey, with curiosity and an open leer in his eyes He had sweat stains and some other food on his shirt. His eyes were looking at her blouse without rising to look her in the eye. He wasn't leering at her breasts, but looking at the locket hanging in front of her blouse. The man's breath reeked of liquor and garlic. She definitely did not like this person.

"This is Lacey Lockhart; she is going to be taking care of the Villa." Stan stepped slightly in front of Lacey to come between her and Harry." Harry responded, still staring at her locket. "Nice to meet you. Where did you get that locket?"

Clearly uncomfortable she said. "From my mother." She then noticed that he had a similar looking coin on a gold band around his wrist. Just then the conveyor started up and unlike other airports, no alarm sounded before starting.

They all looked at the flaps as the luggage came through. Stan, "nice seeing you Harry," and rested his hand on Lacey's elbow and moved away. He looked down at Lacey.

Lacey walked with him to nearer the conveyor. Lacey's bag came around and she reached down to get it. She set it on the floor and raised the handle.

Stan said. "I'll get this one." She lifted the backpack and took hold of the other suitcase and followed him out the doors and along the walkway to the parking lot.

As they walked side by side, she said. "You don't like him very much?"

"Not at all." Stan replied, "He has been on island as long as my family, but there is something creepy about him, he spends most of the year in New York doing something in finance, his name is Harry Gufsterson and he has a house on the island in the harbor."

They approached an older brown Jeep station wagon. Stan clicked open the doors with the key and the click of the door latches could be heard. He stepped to the rear tailgate and opened it. He then reached in and picked a wooden bar about 4 feet long and used it to hold up the tailgate. "It's old but it runs and down here cars wear out due to salt, sun and pot holes." You'll get used to driving in a couple of weeks." He then placed her bags in the back of the car, removed the wooden bar and placed it in the back. Then closed the tailgate and walked to the driver's door.

Lacey walked to the passenger door, opened it and got in. She noticed that the leather seats were cracked from wear and the sun. There was a slight smell of something, which was probably mold.

They backed out of the parking spot and started for the exit. There was a toll booth and Stan paid for parking and turned on to the road on the left side. This is creepy she thought, with the traffic coming at you. It will take a little getting used too.

Stan was approaching a traffic light and spoke. "We are going to go through town and you'll get a good view of the harbor. I'll take you around later and show you the rest of the island."

"That would be great." She replied. She was watching out the window and trying to see landmarks that would give her bearings to get around. They had turned onto a four lane street with a median down the middle. She noticed that people would cross the street anywhere and traffic made erratic turns to get where they wanted to go.

Stan was focused on the traffic in front. "I have a statement. I say to all the guests. The locals don't obey the laws and the tourists don't know the laws. So, you really need to drive defensively. You'll also notice that most people don't use turn signals down here. The good thing is that the roads are curvy and speeds are relatively low."

She thought Daniel had said almost the same thing. Best to take heed.

Just then the harbor came into view and Lacey could see just how beautiful the harbor was. Navy blue and emerald green with dark green hills in the background covered with dense vegetation. Long stretches of white buildings with red and green roofs. This is truly magnificent, she thought. "You said your family has been on the island for a long time if you don't mind, tell me about it."

They were turning left and heading up the hill. The street was 2 lanes and narrow for the larger trucks and SUV's on it. Stan had stopped at a sign that read Stop here on Red light. "No problem. The family goes back a long way, my great grandfather was an officer that served with the British Navy. He was stationed here, while the Danish were still in control of the island. He settled here and had a house in town. He had 2 kids, me and my sister. My sister married a guy from England and lives there, my father was an attorney and developed the property and built the house I got a degree in accounting but didn't practice. I liked the investment business better."

She could see he was reflecting on his prior life. His eyes were focused on the road, which was twisting up a steep hill with several switchbacks and blind turns. A large water truck came around a 180 degree turn and she held her breath until it passed.

"Anyway, the villa was partially destroyed in hurricane Marilyn and my wife and I rebuilt it. My father moved up to Florida for better healthcare, than he could get down here. I'm developing some property up in the states, so my wife and I can't spend a whole lot of time here, but I still consider it my home."

She could feel the depth of his statement. He obviously loved the villa and the island and there was a distant look in his eyes. As if he was already regretting having to leave the island. It was touching and showed the depth of his character.

They had gone around several more turns and then turned into a gated property. He hit a clicker that was in the center console and the gate in front of them opened slowly.

Stan said. "If the power goes off, the gates open and stay open until the electricity is restored." They went through the gate and the street got even narrower. In Colorado this would be a bike path, she thought. Just then a lizard appeared, it was about 3 feet long with a stripped tail. A grey body with spikes running along the tail and back all the way to the head. It got spooked by the car and started running into the undergrowth. It was dense just off the road with large trees and plants of all sorts. The creature ran with a waddle like a drunken sailor. It was comical to watch it run.

"Iguana crossing." Stan said. "They are harmless and normally afraid of humans, unless they have been fed by people." "They are vegetarians and don't bite. They do whip their tail, if you get too close. If people have fed them, they can be a real nuisance." He continued down the street and turned into a driveway that had a steep grade and was circular, so you could drive out the other side. There were beautiful yellow flowers growing on the embankment next to left side of the green cement villa with a white roof showing black mold growing in spots. He stopped in front of an arched portico and said. "We're here."

She opened her door and felt the sun, heat and humidity hit her face. She walked to the rear of the car, where Stan was opening the tailgate and got the biggest suitcase out. She grabbed the other suitcase and backpack. He walked around her to the front door, which was louvered with wooden louvers and screens to keep the insects out. He opened the door and walked in.

She followed and stopped in her tracks. Looking across a wide living room that was 3 steps down from the foyer that she was standing in. The room was large which had a dining table to the left, but it was all one great room. The foyer had a planter along the left edge made out of a blue, black and grey rock. The floor of the foyer was Spanish red tile in foot squares that ran about twenty feet. Then it was dark hard wood for about another thirty to forty feet.

Looking across the living room were archways with pillars made out of the same rock as the planter. There were five arch ways each about 15 feet wide. Outside of the first archway on the left was a patio of red Spanish tile matching the floor inside. At the start of the of the second arch way was a glimmering swimming pool with clear blue water reflecting the sunlight back up to the cloudless blue sky. On the other side of the pool was more decking and a lower patio overlooking the brownish green yard with multiple bougainvillea bushes with ruby red flowers. Beyond the patio she could see that the hill with dense foliage started. Beyond that lay the city of mostly white buildings with red, green and white roofs and beyond that was the harbor with emerald green and various shades of blue water. The water changed color whenever a cloud was blocking the sun's rays. There were white patches beneath the water, where a boat had stirred up the bottom. Out in the harbour was a small island in shades of dark green and little hills sprouting up from the beach edge. There were a few white buildings on the island. Maybe three or four at most. Behind the first island there was another island, however from this view they looked like they were one. After the island was the ocean a greyish blue to dark blue all the way to the horizon. She could feel the waves more than see them as she stood there. Is this paradise, she thought? Is this what people imagine when they picture the perfect place to live in their mind. She knew there were beautiful places throughout the world, but this had to rank right up there in the top three.

All of a sudden, there was a feeling of coming home. Maybe she was just reacting to the beauty of the view. She felt little goose bumps on her arms and a warm wave moving inside of her. She was lost in the feeling, when with a start, she realized someone was talking to her. Shifting her gaze with effort. She saw Stan and a woman standing in the dining room.

"This is my wife, Lynn." Stan was saying. The woman next to him was about 5 foot 3 and had a lean build. She had brown hair cut short over brown eyes and swept back from her neck. She was wearing blue jeans and a light green blouse.

"Hi," Lacey replied. "This is such a beautiful place. I can see why you love it."

"Thank you "Lynn said. She had a soft medium pitched voice. "Let me show you where you will be living and give you a few minutes to freshen up from the trip, we give you a complete tour of the villa before we have dinner."

There was a partial wall on the left of the dining table which stopped after about 15 feet. Lacy had moved about three feet into the foyer, she was just inside the wall near the set of three steps that led into the kitchen. The kitchen was large with a center island made of dark wood with a cement counter top. There was a double sink in the middle of the island on the far side. Across from the island was an area with a stove, more counter with cabinets below a matching brown cement top. This was all fitted in an archway of the blue, black and grey stone. There was a microwave and air vent above the stove with a recessed light next to the vent. At the far end of the kitchen there was a doorway that led to another room. Next to the door on the right side was a wall and passage way leading out to an alcove. On the left side of the door were two stainless steel stand up refrigerator/freezers. Above the refrigerators were cabinets that ran to the corner. She could see glasses inside the glass panels on the front of the cabinets. Lynn was walking up the three steps leading from the kitchen with a smile on her face. Lacey thought she appears to be a happy person. Why not to live in a house like this.

"Follow me." Lynn spoke as she reached the top step and headed under the portico.

Lacey slung the backpack over her shoulder and grabbed the handles of the two rolling suitcases. "Lead the way." She then looked up and saw a coconut palm up ahead where the driveway curved left and up back to the road. There were several groups of coconuts hanging over steps that led down. She had only seen the nut itself in the grocery stores.

Lynn had noticed her stare and said. "When you walk under the coconut palms always look up. You could get injured if one of those hits you in the head. We like having them there, because the quests get excited about seeing them."

Lacey thought I'll have to remember that. There was a delightful breeze blowing and the palm fronds were swaying in the breeze. The sun was behind her, she couldn't feel the heat on her back because the villa blocked it, thus she wasn't overly hot. She followed Lynn down some cement steps that turned right at a small landing and went down further. There was a doorway with a black iron screen door. Lynn opened the door for her and she entered a studio apartment in a short hallway with a door to what looked like a bathroom on the right.

There was a good sized room at the end of the hallway. The walls were all cement painted in this a pastel light green. colour. It was a dark place, even with sliding glass doors across the far end. There was a porch on the other side of the doors with a white painted railing. The view was of the harbour. But there was a large tree blocking part of the view. She could see the water and a scattering of boats rocking at mooring balls. Sunlight was dancing off the water and small swells could be seen rolling in from the open ocean.

There was an area set aside for a living space with a big screen TV sitting on a credenza of black painted wood. Two stuffed chairs and a white wicker cabinet setting in front of the TV. There was a small little table with little print tiles inside of a wood frame of blonde wood. To kitchen chairs made up the dining area. An old white refrigerator and a cement counter with cabinets underneath and above in an L shape made up the kitchen area along with a white stove and oven on the long part of the L.

Across the room was a short wall and dividing a king size bed with an orange and yellow duvet covering it. There were two screened louvered window on either side of the bed. The louvers were opened and she could feel the breeze cooling the room.

On the wall from the hallway were white wire shelves with a table, filing cabinet and old black cushioned desk chair with multiple torn spots from wear. There was a walk-in closet on the right side of the bed with a little fan running inside. It was liveable, she thought.

"Do you think you'll like it?" Lynn asked. Her eyes were studying Lacey's reaction.

"I think it will do just fine." Lacey was thinking it would be fine for a year to collet her thoughts and plan for her future. Did she want to go back to law enforcement or venture into something new? She kept a smile on her face not wanting Lynn to think she was unhappy or had second thoughts.

"Good" Lynn said. "We want you to be comfortable here, I'll be heading back to the Villa and you come up when you're ready." Lynn was a warm person and there was sincerity in her voice. She turned and went back out the door and up the steps.

Lacey couldn't see the island in the harbour because the tree was blocking her view, but she could feel its presence. It seemed there were voices calling from beyond the tree or from the tree itself. A chill came over her. and She was aware of mixed emotions about what was happening. The wind grew stronger coming thru the windows and a chill swept over her. Standing completely still, she thought she heard soft whispers all around her. She shook off the feeling and tried to focus on her surroundings. Get a grip, she said to herself mentally. It is just the wind coming through as goose bumps ran up her arms.

5

BOSTON – 1800'S

It was 12 years later and Elsa was standing in her room in Boston. America had won its' independence and was starting to move into the great nation it would become.

She was thinking back on how she had gotten here. It was like yesterday, walking down to the rice barn and meeting Thomas Vanderbeck. The Captain handing my satchel to him and asking for a letter to go back to Captain Williams. Thomas took a white envelope with a red wax seal on it and handed it slowly it to Captain Hamblin.

Thomas looked the Captain directly in his eyes and said. "Make sure the seal isn't broken, when you give it to Captain Williams."

"Most certainly." Was the reply. The Captain then turned and left sticking the envelope in his coat pocket.

Thomas with a warm smile said. "Come, Ruth has been anticipating this day and will be so delighted to see you." Taking my hand he picked up the satchel, and we walked over to a wagon behind a horse tied to a post. Thomas lifted me up and put me on the seat. He then untied the horse and climbed in beside me.

"It's not too far to the house." He made a clicking sound and snapped the reins.

We headed down a road lined by various trees with green leaves. Not one palm tree among them. She remembered being afraid and confused. She was in a new country without all the people she knew and relied on. She fought back the tears and stared out at the countryside. It was green and lush with fields in every direction. They were going along a river and the road was rough as they bumped along. The horse was trotting and it seemed like Thomas was anxious and had a focussed but relaxed expression on his face. The land spread out in every direction. and She could not see the ocean. Something she hadn't ever experienced before. She tried to hide the feelings of being alone and show courage and strength to these people. They turned left onto another road and there was a large house in the distance. It had large pillars and a long porch along the front. Double doors were in the center under the overhead roof, which held a patio above it. The patio didn't run the full length of the width of the house. It was humid and she remembered feeling sweat running down the back of her neck behind her ears. She could see several figures standing in front of the door. Coming closer she could see a tall woman in a beige and white dress with a high modest bodice that buttoned just below her neck. She had dark hair swept back into a bun. Her face was round and kindly with high cheek bones leading to full lips and an upturned mouth. Her hands were at her sides and she was staring directly at the wagon. We were too far away to see the colour of her eyes. Behind her and slightly too each side stood a black man and woman. The man had on something of a uniform, like a butler she had seen once. The woman had a black dress with a white apron. Each had a anxious expression on their face. There was a large cleared area Infront of the porch to allow wagons to turn around. There were several large trees on either side of the house on cleared lawns. Beyond that were more fields where something she didn't know what was grown.

I remembered she thought the woman must be Ruth his wife. He pulled to a stop in front of the porch, and Ruth was already coming down the steps in a hurry with a huge smile from ear to ear on her face. I thought, I'll never forget that moment. Thomas walked around and lifted me out of the wagon. Elsa's heart was in her throat amid all the fuss and confusion, fear started to tear at her thoughts. Suddenly Ruth scooped Elsa up in her arms and hugged Elsa to her chest and practically smothered her. Ruth held Elsa underneath both arms and swung her around. All the time, saying her name, "Elsa, Elsa, Elsa"

"My god, Ruth don't terrorize the poor girl." Thomas said. "Give her a moment to catch her breath. "

Ruth set the her down and Elsa pulled at her hair, reminding herself to be brave. Her eyes were cast down and her insides were in turmoil but no she wasn't going to cry.

"This is George and Mary our servants." Ruth said, and they both just nodded at Elsa.

"Nice to meet you." She wondered if she would see Letisha again.

"Let us go in the house." Ruth said and took her hand and they walked up the steps and through the double doors. "Are you hungry?" She continued. "I'll bet some bread with sweet jam and some milk would be good right now?"

Actually, it sounded very good to her because the food on the ship was not that good, except for the apples. They had come into a large foyer with a hall straight ahead and a large living room off to the right and a study or library room off to the left. There were wide stairs going up the left wall just after the library door. The inside was all off white with a big chandelier hanging in the middle and candles along the wall every few feet. They continued down the hall to the next set of doors. There was a formal dining room on the right and kitchen was behind it. The kitchen had a pump over the sink and big windows along the back wall. The room was large with a big wooden table in the center that could sit eight people easily. The kitchen was also white with cabinets above the counters and a big stove of black iron with two sets of doors in the front. One set of doors probably held the fire for cooking. There was a closet room with the door open and Elsa remembers she could see shelves with all sorts of items stacked on them.

Mary was getting plates out of a cupboard and setting them on the table. She went into a pantry and came back with a dark slice of bread and a glass of milk. She then took a jar from a wooden like cabinet and placed it on the table. Elsa could still smell the sweet berries of some kind she had never smelled before. Strawberry jam was what Ruth called it.

Elsa remembered she was daydreaming, but everything seemed so real. She remembered the palomino pony with the golden mane Thomas and Ruth had given her to celebrate the 2nd year she had arrived. She loved the pony and rode it through the fields.

She remembered the serious meetings at the house on the outskirts of Charles Town the men used to have at night in the library. Stern looks and constant hushed talk. She couldn't hear what they we saying, but something was about to happen. And then, Thomas announces that they were moving to Boston. The next day a wagon was loaded and they were off.

She had heard that the day after they left a group from the colonist army attacked the British soldiers, but were defeated. This was all part of the Revolution that happened many years before.

She looked around her room and realized she didn't know what happened to her Mother, Father, Brother and Sister. She had grown to love Thomas and Ruth, but was determined to find out what had happened to her family.

BACK TO THE PRESENT IN 1800 ???

She walked out of the room and down the stairs to the drawing room, where Ruth was reading. The room was square with mauve walls. It had a window looking onto the street below, with a small couch in front of it. The window had curtains that were drawback and muted grey light was coming through. It was a dull grey day in Boston. There were stuffed chairs and tables in other parts of the room. Ruth was in one of the chairs with a little table next to it. She had a cup of tea sitting on the table. Ruth looked up as Elsa entered and smiled warmly. They had grown very fond of each other over the years and to say Ruth had doted on Elsa was an understatement.

Ruth spoke first, "tonight Captain Williams is going to join us for dinner he wants to see you." Ruth's brother in law moved to Boston after his wife had passed away. He didn't want to stay in the islands anymore and had left his adopted son the home there.

"That would be wonderful," Elsa said. She never forgotten the strange and terrifying circumstances that brought her to America. 'Which brings up a point that I would like to talk to you about." She continued, "You know I love you and Thomas very much." It has been bothering me that you never said what happened to my parents, sister and brother. I can vaguely remember screams and being carried in someone's arms, but not much more. It keeps me awake some nights and I lay awake hearing the terrible sounds in my ears." Elsa's face was very serious and a wrinkle was formed above her eyebrows. She was looking into Ruth's eyes. She could see some pain in her eyes and for a moment, she was sorry she had asked.

Ruth sat frozen for a moment and then spoke. "It is better that you hear it from Captain Williams. He has first-hand knowledge, Thomas and I would be just repeating what we were told. We love you as our own child and that's why we had you legally adopted, when we got to Boston. As far as we are concerned your last name is Vanderbeck." Tears were forming in her eyes and a small sob came from down in her throat.

Elsa immediately threw her arms around Ruth and hugged her tightly. She was about to cry also but, as was her nature she held back. She was sorry that she had given this wonderful person any pain.

They stayed in that position for a few seconds and then Elsa said, "What time will the Captain be coming."

"About 6, I assume. Thomas will pick him up." Ruth was getting back to normal.

Elsa stood and said, "I will go see what Guthrie is doing and be right back." Guthrie was a young fellow from her school who lived only a few blocks away. Before she left the room, she turned and smiled and said "I love you." Then went out the front door.

She was back an hour later and went up to her room to freshen up for dinner. It was about 5 PM, the shadows were getting long and the sky was dimming. She had a smirk on her face and a little bit of a blush in her cheeks. She went to her wash basin splashed some water her face looked in the mirror; then quickly headed for the door.

She could hear the grandfather clock in the foyer chiming as she walked down the stairs, just as the front door was opening and Thomas walked in. Thomas was showing the years now and moved a slowly. He hadn't gained any weight, and walked upright as ever, but his hair was all grey now and bags had formed under his eyes.

Right behind him was Captain Williams. Showing a lot more age and limping slightly. He walked stooped and used a cane for balance. His life on the sea showed in his weathered face, still the eyes were clear and strong. Spotting Elsa a smile came to the corners of his mouth. In his deep penetrating voice, he said, "Who is this lovely young woman that is in your house, Thomas?"

Elsa bounded the last few steps and hugged the Captain. "You know good and well, who I am and why don't you come see me more often?"

"Well let me get my coat off and look at you," said the Captain, not answering her question. "My god, you get prettier every time I see you." He struggled out of his coat and hung it on a hook in the foyer. He still had the strength in his features that showed his authority around people. "I don't get out much anymore or I would be over every day."

Thomas said, "Let us all go in for dinner, I'm hungry." Smells from the kitchen of roasted turkey and spices were permeating the house. Mary the cook was still with Ruth and Thomas. She was setting platters of food on the table. There was a silver candelabra in the center of the dining room table. The table was set with wine glasses, silverware, several china plates with a matching china bowl on top of the plates and a linen napkin on the side. The table was big enough for six people easily.

Thomas sat at the head of the table with Ruth on his right and Elsa on his left. The Captain took the seat at the end of the table. They all bowed their heads and Thomas said, "Thank you lord for the food we are about to eat and giving us the opportunity to all be together, Amen." Mary came in with a soup tureen and ladle, stopping on the left side of Ruth first. Each in turn took a small amount of soup. Thomas reached out and took a plate with bread on it and tore off a piece and passed the bread to Ruth. She just past the bread plate to the Captain, not wanting any bread. The Captain tore off a chunk and past the plate on to Elsa. Elsa put the plate down, knowing there was more food than she wanted still to come.

The Captain dipping the bread into the soup with his left hand and picking up his soup spoon with his right, started to eat the soup. Dipping bread in the soup and took a bite. He chewed and swallowed slowly and looked at the others as he spooned the soup. Mary came in and was pouring wine into each of their glasses. "Well Elsa, what are your plans now that you are finishing school?"

Elsa's eyes lit up and she brought her head up to speak, as if to say as proudly as possible, "I think I will go to college and study medicine." She sounded very determined and her eyes flashed on Thomas's face.

Thomas was not a man to start confrontations, especially not at the dinner table. He remained silent, but there was a undeniable frown showing from his eyes and mouth. He really didn't like the idea of Elsa leaving the home she had grown up in. He cared so much for her.

Ruth looked a little uncomfortable after seeing Thomas' face. The Captain, who didn't miss much looked at Elsa and said, "is there a man on the horizon, also?" He was trying to change the subject, which was obvious.

Elsa caught the drift and said, "There is one fellow that I have been friends with for some time." Now all eyes were watching Elsa. "But nothing is serious," she added. "Plus, I want to graduate college, before ever thinking of settling down."

"Is he a Christian Reform member', the Captain asked? Thomas's gaze dropped to the table, and Ruth spoke fast, "we are not sure what church he belongs too." She was quick to avoid any further discussion, knowing it would only cause more tension.

The Captain just grunted and pushed back his chair a little. He had finished eating Mary had come in to clear the plates. Thomas asked, "would you like some port?"

The Captain said, "yes that would be delightful." Mary was already setting new glasses in front of Thomas and the Captain. She got the decanter from the credenza and filled the Captain and Thomas's glasses.

Ruth turned to look at the Captain and in a calm voice said, "Elsa would like to know what happened to her parents, brother and sister?" "I have told her that only you know the story and she should hear it from you."

The Captain's face became serious, and all softness seemed to have vanished. He looked at Elsa, who stared back and was just as serious. Her eyes had a penetrating gaze looking for any sign of not telling the truth. "Well', he said and paused. "It is about time you heard the whole story, you're old enough to understand."

He related how her parents, brother and sister were all brutely murdered. She started to recall the nightmare. He went on to tell her how she was saved by Letisha and brought to his house. She knew his servant at his current house was Letisha and tears started to form in her eyes. Her lower lip trembled as the night of her escape came flooding back to her mind. The screams resounded in her ears. She had buried the memories for so long and thought her nightmares were not reality. But now she knew it was not fantasy. Her hand came up to her throat and she felt the gold chain and pendant around her neck, giving her a sense of calm. She didn't want to speak for fear of starting to cry again. She looked at Ruth, who had been sitting quietly, with a sad look on her face. Finally, she spoke, "this is my family now and I am a very lucky person to have them as parents. This brought tears to Ruth's eyes.

Elsa continued, " Sometime I would like to come and talk to Letisha about my lost family. She might be able to give some details about them. If that would be alright with you?" She was now looking at the Captain.

"That would be fine with me, if Thomas and Ruth don't mind," said the Captain.

Thomas finally spoke in a soft caring voice. "We have no problem at all with you talking to Letisha, we both love you as a daughter and want you to know about your biological parents, we knew you have had nightmares and maybe, just maybe this will help put them to rest."

"Thank you", Elsa said. "Did they ever catch the killers?"

Just then Mary came in from the kitchen with a tray with 4 pieces of her special rhubarb pie and a smile on her face. She moved slowly now, slightly stooped over, and she knew this was Elsa's favourite. She set the tray on a side table and started setting the plates down in front of everyone.

"By the heavens above, you are going to spoil me, Mary" The Captain blurted out." I won't want to leave!" He winked at Thomas. "I will just have to take you home with me."

"Captain fraid I can't do daht." Mary exclaimed. "Cause I still got to take care of this family. An you got Letisha to spoil you. An see 'n how tight your pants are fitten, she be doin a good job of it."

This brought laughter to the table all around.

After desert was finished the Captain stood. "Thank you for the wonderful meal, but I should be getting back. I have stayed out past my bedtime."

The Captain walked over and kissed Ruth's cheek. Ruth said, "see you again real soon, OK."

The Captain just smiled and nodded.

Elsa was up and came around to him. "Thank you for telling me, and if it is alright with you, may I stop by tomorrow?"

The Captain paused for a moment to think and said, "Tomorrow would be fine. The neighbours will be curious, who the pretty girl is."

"Well in that case, I must wear my best dress, to get them all talking," replied Elsa.

Thomas was standing holding the Captain's coat. He helped him put it on and opened the front door. "I'll walk him down to the carriage," and they both walked out.

The next day Elsa was at the Captain's door about 11 in the morning. She tapped the brass knocker and heard footsteps on the other side. This is the first time she had come to the Captain's home since he moved up to Boston.

The door was opened by a tall black woman with long black hair green eyes and a serious expression on her face. Upon seeing Elsa, a broad smile came to her face, and her eyes lit up and she gasped. "Dear God, it's you Miss Elsa." She hugged Elsa and nearly knocked her off the steps.

Elsa was trying to recognize the person realizing this had to be Letisha all grown up. Letisha was barely a teenager, when she left. She hugged Letisha back and then put her arm around Letisha's back and stepped through the door. She held Letisha at arm's length so she could get a good look at her. "I wouldn't have recognized you after all these years," she gushed. "We were just little girls all those years ago."

Letisha's face was radiant with happiness and she kept staring Elsa straight in the eye. "Da Captain has told me all about you and how pretty you are." He is right, you is the prettiest thing I's ever seen. "Come in dah kitchen and tell me all about what you been doin?"

Elsa was just as excited and couldn't keep the large grin off her face. Flashbacks of Letisha were going through her mind. Suddenly she remembered and asked, "How is Aunt Tina?"

Letisha's expression went serious for a moment. "Aunt Tina done passed about five years back. " Dahts when the Captain started making plans to move. Dey had an adopted son, who been to a good school and become a lawyer. Dah Captain said that he could have the house and dey would move to Boston, so Greta could be near her younger sister."

They were standing in the kitchen, which faced a courtyard and a carriage house. The room faced southeast, and light was coming through the kitchen windows and you could see the tiny dust particles floating in the air. There was a small garden at the back of the courtyard. Elsa thought, so the Captain has an adopted son. Elsa turned to Letisha and said, "Please tell me about my parents, I have trouble remembering them."

"What you want to know", Letisha asked?

"Everything you can remember" exclaimed Elsa. "Everything, also about my brother and sister."

This brought a look of pain to Letisha's face. "Tis was a horrible night. I done got you as I heard you momma scream and went out the window. Then I went to your brother's window and saw a man with knife cut you brother and blood was all over the sheets and your brother was screaming. I done run with you in my arms and carried you to Aunt Tina's. She den take us to Captain William's house." Letisha paused to stop the memories and calm herself.

Elsa could feel the anguish in Letisha. She knew the truth as the memory of that night came flooding in. It was 15 years ago, but the memories flooded in and she shook with a feeling of total terror. She remembered her mother being kindly and loving. She remembered her brother, who teased her and pulled her hair at times She remembered her sister, who played with her and combed her hair. But most of all she remembered her father. His twinkling eyes and loving way with her. He never raised his voice, but always discussed things when she had been naughty. There was pain in her heart as the memories came flooding back and tears came to her eyes. She knew if she started crying it would be worse for Letisha. She looked up and hugged Letisha and with a soft voice said, "thank you for saving me."

That brought more sobs from Letisha and they continued to hug for several seconds. There were slow footsteps coming from the hall and the Captain appeared. He looked tired and old, but seeing them hugging brought a small smile of affection to his face. He spoke in a patient tone, "well I see you both have been chatting. Isn't she pretty Letisha?"

"She be the prettiest woman, I done ever seen."

Elsa blushed, her cheeks turned pink, and the tears stopped. She felt a great warmth for the island woman and the Captain.

6

THE ISLANDS - 2017

It had been a week, since Stan and Lynn had left. The Villa had been cleaned and Lacey had a good idea of her duties. She had also met some other people on the Island. She was sitting out on the pool patio looking down on the harbour were musing at the two cruise ships tied up at the cruise ship dock. She was thinking of what she wanted to do, as no guests would be arriving for another week and half. Seeing the ships, her thoughts turned to Daniel and what he may be doing, picking up her cell phone she tapped his name in the address book screen.

"Hi there", came his voice over the speaker. "I was wondering when I would hear from You."

Kiddingly she said, "Since I have tons of friends on the island, I didn't have time to give you a call. You know I'm a socialite. Actually, the owners just left and I've been busy learning how the Villa needed to be cleaned and where things are kept. Although they have some help, this place is a lot of work." "Just knowing where all the switches are takes time." "What have you been up to?" I can see two cruise ships in the harbor."

Daniel said, "I brought the early one in today and will have to take it out at about 4:30." "That takes about an hour and a half due to paperwork and clean up." But after that I'm free. "What are you doing for dinner tonight?" There was an anxious tone in his voice.

Lacey could tell that there was a hopeful wish implied. It brought a smile to her face and her voice sounded bright and cheerful. "Well I will have to cancel several other engagements, but I may be able to work you in."

"That sounds great." How about I pick you up about 7 tonight." That will give me time to clean up and put on a tuxedo."

"I left my jewels at home, so I must come informal. Actually, how should I dress?" Knowing he was kidding about the tux.

"Shorts, T-shirt and Flip flops, the standard . I know the best pizza and wing place on the island, with lots of different beers. It's a little noisy but you can still have a conversation."

"Sounds just right ", Lacey said. It would be good to be in an open forum, she thought. Keeping things light

"Great, see you at 7."

"Wait," she said before he could hang up." I need to give you the gate code and directions to the Villa." The gate code is #1974 and it is the gate on your right. Then follow the road down to the third house on the right." "There is a pile of rocks at the start of the driveway." "And the driveway is circular, so you can drive down without having to turn around. Do you know where Brad's Bar and restaurant is?"

"Yes, everyone knows where Brad's is. It used to be and probably still is one of the most popular spots on the North hill."

"Good', she said. The gate entrance is just up the street at a stone round about. Across from the cemetery."

"I know exactly where it is", he said in an upbeat voice. "Fair winds" and he hung up.

She smiled to herself and felt a little giddy. You're not a little teenage school girl, she reprimanded herself. Still, it feels good to be wanted and what is the harm in a little flirtation. She turned and looked at the statue of David at the end of the pool. It was a replica of the original and even had one hand larger than the other which is the same as the original statue. Since the base of the statue was covered by water, she thought that the comments about shrinkage were true.

Turning to face the harbor, she looked down on the island in the middle with the white house down from where they had dredged a passageway for small boats. To the left of that were the two rails for dragging boats out of the water, up the ramp to the old steam furnace. In those days ships were mainly sail, and still had to be dragged up to have their bottoms cleaned and repairs done. Slaves carried baskets of coal up to the furnace. It was hard work for little money. Down the beach from the rails was the little white house with the red roof.

As she gazed at it from above there came a strange breeze and goose bumps covered her arms again. She felt a little dizzy and her face flushed. What was going on? It was like something was trying to take over her body. All of a sudden there were voices all around her. Some were screams, other were curse words and then as she covered her ears to block out the voices, there was a calm deep but soft voice that said, "come and you will find peace." She must be hallucinating, she thought. Maybe she got stung by a wasp or mosquito or I'm getting sick. Then the voice came again, "come and you will find peace."

It was a man's voice that she did not recognize. Her hand instinctively started tugging at her hair and the other hand reached up and touched the charm around her neck. Everything seemed to calm down and the strange breeze diminished. It seemed to go back toward the silk cotton tree and disappear. The goose bumps were gone and her breathing went back to normal. Maybe I've been out in the sun to long, she thought. She turned and headed into the villa to get out of the sun.

A few hours later she had showered and put on a light green pair of shorts with a white collared blouse and white sneakers. She was ready to be picked up in fifteen minutes. "Come and you will find peace" had slipped from her mind and she was thinking about Daniel. What kind of a person was he and did she really want to find out? She walked up the steps from her studio to the driveway and looked up at the coconut palm. Several large, about a foot long, green and brown husks were hanging on the right side just above the steps. The constant breeze was blowing, and the moon was bright in the sky.

Just then she could hear a car's engine and turned to look up the steep driveway. Coming down was a Dodge Dakota pickup with red sides and a faded grey hood with most of the lacquer gone from the sun. It had to be twenty years old, she guessed. The engine sounded strong but the lights were a little dim. It made squeaks and groans all the time as if the springs were complaining from old age. The driver's door opened and Daniel with the goofy grin jumped out. The truck was still running, but he must have put it in park, because it wasn't moving.

"How do you like Brutus," He said. He had a joyful gleam in his eyes and the energetic step that comes with excitement to a young boy. He was wearing a turquoise green sport shirt with a collar, khaki shorts and sandals. He had strong legs with well-defined calves and a narrow waist. He had the Brad Pitt boyish face and the hair that flopped in his face at times.

"Like is not the question", Lacey replied. "Is it safe is?"

"Safe as can be. It is an island truck and I get offers from people who want to buy it every day." He grabbed the door handle and as he opened the door there was a scrapping groaning sound of metal on metal. As she went to get in, she noticed that the panel below the door was rusted leaving a four inch hole. Stepping up she gingerly jumped in.

He went back around the front and climbed into the driver's seat, brought the seat belt across and buckled it.

He looked over to make sure she had her seat belt on. She thought he cares about my safety at least. He put the truck in drive and there was a slight jerk as the transmission engaged and then they started forward. She said, 'feels like Brutus's transmission is slipping."

"He needs a little work and I haven't been giving him enough attention."

Daniel didn't try to make an excuse and took the blame, she thought. Not one to shirk responsibility is another good trait. "OK, where are we going to get the best pizza on the island?"

"A place called Coyote's. It's not much to look at, it is more of a local's hangout. It's not very far, but nothing on the island is very far."

It was disconcerting having headlights coming straight at you, because of the left hand driving and the steering wheels on the left also. As they drove along, she noticed that there were green road signs with airplanes and the word "airport" painted on them, but she knew the airport was in the opposite direction. "What's up with all the airport signs pointing in the wrong direction?"

"They just had signs, so they put them all over the island, I guess." He was looking straight ahead and concentrating, because on twisting narrow roads at night you did it to survive, the steep hills on the sides of the road would be fatal if you went off. They came down a hill and turned right onto another street, which led to a shopping center at the top. Turning right into the parking lot, she saw the neon lights spelling out Coyote's in four foot letters.

They parked in an open space and walked in. There was a large wooden bar of dark wood on the right. Behind the bar was a bartender mixing drinks and opening beer bottles. Behind him was a large mirror with shelves on either side stacked with all the usual alcoholic beverages in an organized fashion by type. The shelves were about five feet long and ten to twelve inches deep. One shelf had nothing but different types of rum. Every island seemed to produce their own rum and thought it was the best. A type of brand loyalty in the islands. The tables were typical diner style with Formica tops and the tube chairs with plastic seat cushions. All were in a dull red color. There were two booths along one wall with the same seat covers and Formica tables. The place was three quarters full and the noise level was fairly high. There was a pop tune playing over a sound system, it was muted by the other noise. At least it was turned up to go over the talking. They found a table by the front window and sat down.

Immediately a waitress came and said, "what can I get you to drink?" There were plastic covered menus on the table in a holder, but on the wall was a blackboard which listed fifteen beers and the specials from the island brewing company. Daniel looked at lacey and saw she looked a little puzzled. "Would you prefer wine or a cocktail," he said?

"Beer sounds good, what do you suggest?"

"I like the Island Summer Ale." He replied.

Lacey said "sounds good."

Daniel just nodded at the waitress and she left. There was a background noise from the people talking in the room, so he leaned toward her so he would not have to talk loudly to be heard. He obviously liked her and was making no effort to hide it. He kept his eyes level with her as he said. "What do you think you'll do after taking care of the villa?" His voice reflected a casual tone, but she knew it was a leading question.

Lacey kept her eyes on his face trying to discern how casual the question was. "I really don't know at this point, she responded. That's what I want to figure out in the next year. What about you, any plans for the future, or are you going to stay as a harbour pilot?"

"I want my own boat that I can charter or not as I desire, I want to cruise down island for a while. I like the freedom cruising gives you."

"I am monarch of all I survey
My right is none to dispute
From center right round to the sea
I am the Lord of the fool and the brute"

"He had a smirk on his face and a twinkle in his eyes. So, you like poetry," she said. "But are you saying you like to control things?"

"No, no, he sputtered, I just like the freedom the sea brings." I probably qualify as the fool and certainly not the brute." He was flustered, because he said something that could be taken all wrong.

"Relax, William Cowper was not intending the statement to be offensive. And by the way, it was, I am the lord of the fowl and the brute, not the fool and the brute. Let's not get to deep right now. Keeping things fun and light feels a lot better to me."

She could see he was embarrassed and not his casual self, to break the moment she said, "how big of a boat do you want?"

"Oh, somewhere between 40 and 50 feet. That gives enough room for comfort, but is still feasible to single hand. It should have 2 staterooms and 2 heads. It doesn't have to be luxurious, but have a decent aft deck for fishing."

"Sounds like you've given it some thought," she said. The waitress showed up with the beers, which caused them to both lean back and realize they haven't looked at the menu.

He looked at the waitress and said, "give us another moment, thanks" He looked at Lacey with a thoughtful expression, "what do you like on your pizza or would you like something else?"

"I'm pretty much a vegetarian girl, and the Margarita looks good. But you also mentioned something about wings."

"Sounds good to me with an order of their rum flavoured wings on the side." How would that be?"

She took a sip of her beer and smiled at him. The waitress came over and he ordered. The waitress left and the music through the speakers was John Denver's "Rocky Mountain High." A look of sadness came over her face as she remembered how much she liked the mountains.

He was looking at her and said "is there something wrong?"

"No, just thinking about Colorado. Seems far away now." Changing the subject, she said, "so when are you giving me the deluxe island tour?"

The goofy grin sprang to his face. "I have a cruise ship tomorrow, but how about the day after, if you are available?"

She paused thinking of her calendar and said, "I don't have guests coming till the following week so that should be great. I have been so busy getting the villa ready, I haven't had time to do much sightseeing. Should I bring anything?" She was looking into his face and thinking how handsome he was.

"Bring a bathing suit and a towel, just in case we want to go swimming. The island has so many great beaches and no sense in passing them up." Just then the waitress showed up with a metal tube frame to set the pizza on and the pizza. White cheese with red slices of tomatoes and sweet basil leaves on the top. The smell of the cheese mixed with the fragrance of the basil was mouth-watering. There was a metal spatula sticking from one side of the pizza tray, and Daniel scooped up a slice and offered to put it on her plate. She held the plate up so he could slide it on. The waitress came back with a plate of dark brown wings with a sauce over them but no breading. They had the smell of BBQ and rum. Sort of a sweet tangy fragrance with a smidge of chilli.

She decided that she should at least try one. Picking a drumstick up with her fingers she sniffed, then took a bite.

She realized he was watching her. She chewed and swallowed. "These are delicious, you're right." Then took another bite.

He just smiled and took a bite of a pizza slice. Both sat there enjoying the food. A short muscular fellow came in through the door with a small blonde woman with thin lips and large breasts pushing out her dark blue T-shirt. Daniel waved and said "Joe, Brenda." They walked over and Daniel pushed his seat back and stood up. She just sat there as Joe and Brenda grinned at her. She realized she had sauce on her face. Lacey grabbed her napkin and wiped her mouth.

Daniel said, "Joe and Brenda this is Lacey." She just got here a couple of weeks ago.

They both said "Hi" in unison. So, this is the fabulous lady that has stolen Daniel's heart." Joe said.

Daniel gave Joe a look that could only be interpreted as shut up. Joe trying to get out of the mistake said, "Only Kidding." Then trying to obviously change the subject said, "What pizza did you have?" Brenda was rolling her eyes the whole time and had given Joe a friendly nudge in the ribs. This man was still immature, and it showed. You would think he was still a teenager.

Daniel was quick and responded by saying "a Margarita. Same as always." There were a few slices left on the tray and Daniel said, "would you like some?"

Joe's eyes lit up and said, "certainly." Brenda said, "no thanks, already have eaten."

He could see I wanted to leave, so he stood and said, "We are going to take off, I've got an early morning tomorrow."

Lacey stood and said,"It was great meeting you and we should get together soon. Looking at Brenda, who was watching Joe eat, she said, "it would be great, maybe we can work out together?"

"I would love that I haven't been able to in a long time." I'll give you a call tomorrow, if that is OK?"

"Good, Brenda said, see you.

They walked to the door and Daniel held it opened for Lacey. The man was making points again. Outside the air was humid and the moon light illuminated the dark hills across the parking lot. There was a shadow about twenty feet away across the walkway. Lacey's senses went into alert mode and a touch of adrenalin shot through her body. She tensed and Daniel could recognize her stress.

"Hi Sonny," he said casually.

"Hi Mon" the man replied. "You have a good night, now."

"Who was that", She asked? They were at the truck now and the passenger door made the creaking, scraping sound as he opened it for her.

"Just a friend who works here."

He started the truck and they headed back up the mountain toward the Villa. It was a little nerve racking having cars coming at you with their lights on coming directly at you on a narrow road, also about every third vehicle had its' high beams' on." This will definitely take some getting used to, she thought. Trying to keep the conversation light, "The wings were fabulous tasting. I could get addicted to those." She was watching his face as he concentrated on the road. He had a smile on his lips and twinkle of happiness in his eyes.

"You are getting the island fever. It never goes away, and will always bring you back." This place has a way of getting into your soul and causes people to get attached. I think you have already been smitten."

We had gone through the gates and he was pulling the truck down the driveway. He passed the portico to the Villa and pulled to a stop by the steps leading down to my apartment. He left the motor running and jumped out to come around and open the door. Obviously, he wasn't going to try and spend the night. Which took a little of the first date tensions away. The door creaked again as he opened it and Lacey jumped out. She looked into those beautiful eyes and said,

"I had a great time, thank you." He was standing close and looking down at her face. She was getting that warm feeling when people feel more than just casualness to each other. He brought his lips close to hers and paused, waiting for her acceptance or rejection. She didn't hesitate and pressed her lips to his. They embraced and stayed that way for several moments. Both needing to breathe a little. Feeling his body so close brought sensations she hadn't felt in a long time and a warmth was spreading through her body.

"I'd love to stay longer but I really do have to get up early tomorrow. I had a wonderful time tonight and we have a date in two days to see more of the island. I'll pick you up Wednesday about nine, if that OK and bring a towel and swimsuit."

"I'll be ready," She said and gave his hand a squeeze. The hand was strong and a little rough from doing some kind of work, but not overly calloused. He quickly bent forward and pecked her lips and went around to the driver side of the truck. Probably to hide his erection, which noticedwhen he kissed her. He waited till she walked down the steps and then heard him get in the truck. The sensor light over the door had come on and Lacey opened the door. Warm wonderful feelings were floating through her body and the mind was creating some sensual stirrings that were very pleasant. It had been a long time since these types of sensations had been awakened. She flipped on some lights and walked across the room and pulled the sliding glass door to the patio open and then opened the screen.

A wind came through the silk cotton tree and swept over her body. It seemed to penetrate her skin and possess her being. Lacey's mind was being taken over as she looked out on the harbor below and across the bay to the dark little island . She tried to think was I bitten by some mosquito or was the food laced with a narcotic. The voice inside her mind said "relax and I will lead you." For a second, she thought that someone was in the room speaking, but she had shut and locked the door.

The voice inside her head was calming and the breeze was gone. She wasn't chilled or had a fever. She felt the inner spirit talk again. "You are here to right the wrong and find what is yours."

Out loud , "What is mine and what wrong?" She was thinking I must be losing my mind and need some sleep. This is crazy. She went to the bathroom and splashed water on her face and decided she needed to pee to get rid of the beer. It didn't make her feel any better, except relieving her bladder.

She went to the refrigerator and took out a bottle of water and took several gulps. The voice said, "feel better now?" Don't be afraid, I am part of you and will guide you along the journey. More as a guide, so you don't get mislead. We share the same blood. There is good and evil waiting for you at this time and I will help. You have strengths that I did not possess. But the locket you wear is also a way I can communicate with you. If it feels warm and soothing, then you will know you are on the right path, if it vibrates or trembles then you are in danger or something bad may happen. Now I suggest you take an Advil PM and go to bed. Quit worrying about what you don't know and focus on what you do."

That is not a bad suggestion, she thought and went to the bathroom, to take an Advil PM and went to bed holding the locked that was around her neck. It was warm and gave her comfort. This is silly, she thought. I must have eaten something strange. But I don't feel sick or dizzy. In fact, I am feeling peaceful, relaxed like cuddling up in a warm blanket on a cold snowy night. She started thinking about the last comment, "we share the same blood." What does that mean? She dozed off then.

7

MEDICAL TRAINING – 1800'S

The Captain had left a lot of unanswered questions. Elsa was thinking. Who murdered my family and what was left of my family's property? Nothing I could do about it now. I wanted to get into college and make something of myself. Elsa took a carriage back to her house. Still thinking, so, my last name wasn't Vanderbeck but Gufterson and I lived in the islands. Arriving at the house and she paid the carriage driver. Went up the steps to the white painted front door. "Ruth", she called out as she entered.

There was a noise from the kitchen, as a pan was set down and Ruth said, "Here."

As she walked down the hall, she saw mail was sitting on the side table. There was a letter addressed to her from a Doctor Earnest Blackwell. Ruth had entered the hallway and was looking at her. She had a wry smile on her face and her eyes twinkled in anticipation. Elsa smiled back with all the affection she felt for this woman. "Looks like I have a response to my letter requesting apprenticeship." In America at this time there were no formal medical schools that accepted women and had poor training for the men they accepted. The only actual formal education system was in Europe and mostly England, Scotland, Ireland and Italy, that she knew of. There was a medical school in Pennsylvania, but the training was for four or five months and had no hands on training. It wasn't until 1821 that the first women received a medical degree in the US. Her hands were shaking as she opened the envelope and read the letter.

> Dear Miss Elsa Vanderbeck
>
> It was with great pleasure; I received your request for apprenticeship with my medial practice. I have known your mother and father for some time and find it an honour to have them consider me their friend. I have spoken to both of them and they give you the highest of attributes when it comes to dedication and focus to your endeavour's. They say you have very astute intelligence and grasp understandings quickly. This being said, I would be willing to accommodate your apprenticeship
>
> Under the following conditions. You would have no salary for the preliminary period of six months to one year, at my discretion. I would provide lodging at my home and meals. It would be expected that you work a minimum of 6 days a week and 10 hours per day.
>
> I must say, there will be times when you will experience various forms of carnage and people with various wounds and problems. If you have a problem with the site of blood, please do not accept my offer.
>
> If you desire to accept my offer, I would expect you to be at my residence at 4:30 PM two Sundays from now. Please respond as soon as possible, so I can make further arrangements.
>
> Thank you for your considerations,
> Dr. Earnest Blackwell

Elsa was delighted that she could work with a respected doctor, who had studied at Edinburgh and had credentials from England and America. America had a shortage of trained physicians and this could be an opportunity to do good for humanity. Ruth was still smirking and smiling at her. She obviously shared my delight and probably knew in advance what his response to my proposal said. Elsa said, "he said yes."

"Well it doesn't give you a great deal of time to get everything together," Ruth said. She now had a sombre face realizing that her adopted daughter would be leaving soon. "Wait till your father hears the news."

"I will only be a little way from here and will come to see you every Sunday." Dr. Blackwell's office was about 2 miles from where they were and not a long ride. She said this to settle some of Ruth's feelings of loss and to brighten her spirits. This woman had been a guiding light and friend to her growing up and Elsa felt a little pain for leaving her.

Dinner was at 5:30 and as usual Thomas walked in just prior with the Captain right behind him. Thomas turned and said to the Captain," let us have sherry before diner.

"Good idea," was the Captain's reply.

"Well, you are making a habit of coming over," Ruth said seeing the Captain standing in the hallway taking his coat off.

"I couldn't resist seeing your beautiful face again and of course it has nothing to do with Mary's cooking."

Ruth gave him a wary eye for the flattery and said, "some of your favourite's, callaloo soup, Cornish hens, red beans and rice, and flan for dessert." "Mary will make sure you don't starve. She always has a way of knowing when you're going to appear."

"Enough of your flirting, let's go into the parlour," Thomas said and they moved into the parlour. The room was getting dark, so Ruth went about lighting whale oil lamps. Captain Williams sat in an overstuffed chair and Thomas went to a dresser with a silver tray, a decanter of sherry and several glasses. He poured the amber liquid into three glasses and handed one to Ruth and the Captain.

Picking up the last filled glass he turned to the other two and said, "what shall we toast?"

Ruth's eyes were on Thomas when she spoke. "Well, I've got news but I don't know if it merits a toast. Elsa has been offered an apprenticeship with Doctor Blackwell. She will be leaving in two weeks and will be living in his residence. She got the letter today."

"Why not toast to her good fortune, this is exactly what she wanted," the Captain said. Always wanting to promote Elsa to the highest level he continued, "this will be a great opportunity for her to do as she pleases, by helping others. Why the concerned look Thomas?"

"It was not that I don't wish her to fulfil her dreams, but it will leave a void in our house and hearts that cannot be replaced." His eyes saddened. "But you're right, this is what she desires and as you know, Elsa gets what she desires."

Just then Elsa entered the parlour with a flourish of green taffeta and a bounce in her walk. She looked at all three and spoke," Ruth must have told you, because you all have dower faces." I'm not leaving the City, so you aren't getting rid of me that quickly." With a smirk she said, "I intend to practice my blood drawing techniques on all three of you." "So, beware."

In his false gruff voice and smiling, the Captain said, "come anywhere near me with a needle and I'll put you over my knee and give you a few whacks!" They all chuckled at this point. Elsa was relieved and the tension, which had been there departed. Plus, the news was out there and didn't have to be stated. "So, how much will you be earning?" the Captain said. He was always concerned for her welfare.

Elsa, "nothing for at least the first six months, but room and board are included."

"This will not do," spouted the Captain. "He would pay a man to be his assistant." The Captain always looked for equality in things. "I'll have to have a chat with the Doctor."

Elsa was not certain that this was a good idea, but she knew once he had his mind set it was hard to change. She said, "seeing how red your face is right now, you should see him more for an examination, than for my compensation. In fact, if you should stop by his office, I might give you the examination myself. "

The Captain grumbled something to the effect of, "that will be the day."

By now, Ruth and Thomas were laughing. Mary appeared at the parlour entrance and said, "dinner is now ready." The Captain stood up and they all followed her into the dining room. The table was set with the white table cloth, four place settings, including wine glasses at three places and water glasses. Each place had a dinner plate, a soup plate and a soup bowl already filled with brown liquid that had vegetables and meat floating inside.

Thomas sat at the head with Ruth on his left, Elsa on his right and the Captain at the other end. The aroma coming up with the steam from the bowls was of Indian seasonings and Indian beef broth. Although there was no beef in the soup. "Smell's delicious, the Captain exclaimed.

They all bowed their heads and Thomas spoke, "thank you lord for the food, which we are about to eat and allowing us to be together, Amen."

Elsa was excited but she wanted to keep the tone of the conversation more factual, so as not to disturb Thomas and Ruth any further. "In talking with Dr Blackwell before he had mentioned that he does some surgery at Mass General over in the west end. That would bring me closer to the Captain's home and I could drop by now and then, if he didn't mind," Elsa said before bringing the soup spoon up to her lips.

The Captain, who had just put a spoonful of soup in his mouth, grabbed his napkin and blotted his lips. "Mind, I think that would be wonderful." His moustache was still a little damp from the soup, and he took a sip of wine that Mary had just poured. "Maybe you could come by for lunch sometime, when of course you are not seeing patients." "The nosey neighbours will have something to talk about. "

Thomas looked at Elsa and spoke, 'West End, how will you get there?"

"The trolley goes right there and I can ride it the whole way." "It really works out well," Elsa responded.

Dinner turned to general conversation and everyone seemed to be more relaxed now.

Two weeks later Elsa arrived punctually at 4:30 at the residence of Dr Ernest Blackwell, which also served as his office. There was a large porch with wide steps and 2 front doors separated by a small space. The door on the left had been painted in white letters Doctor Ernest Blackwell and the door on the right had no markings. The doors were part wood and part glass starting about half way up. Elsa could see light coming through the door on the right, but the door on the left was dark on the other side. She had two suitcases with her, thinking she could always go back and get more of her belongings. The carriage driver who had brought her had brought the two suitcases to the front door and set them down. She paid him and he had left. She turned to knock, when the door was opened before she could by Dr Blackwell.

Dr Blackwell was a about 5' 6" with short, messy black hair, ruddy complexion, square face and a bushy moustache under a substantial nose, normal looking mouth and intent brown eyes. "Thank you for being punctual and how was your ride over?" He said.

He didn't say "welcome" she thought but that seems to be his nature to be straight forward. "Just fine and it is great for me to be here" "Thomas and Ruth send their regards."

"Please come in and let me help with your luggage." He stated.

She picked up one suitcase and he got the other. He allowed her to enter the door first and she walked into a lighted hallway with beige walls and wainscoting about 3 feet up from the bottom. A Chandelier hung from the ceiling and there were stairs with a brown banister leading to the 2nd floor on the left. There was a wood framed arch way on the right leading to a living room. At the end of the living room was another wood framed archway leading into a formal dining room.

There was a table set for 2 in the dining room. She was surveying the rooms, when she heard him say, "just leave the luggage here for now and I will show you around, but first let me hang up your wrap.

She had worn a light grey jacket over a plum colored blouse and a reddish brown skirt and cordovan high top shoes which covered her ankles. "Thank you," she said as she handed him her jacket. Is your wife at home? She asked.

Dr. Blackwell was in his late 40's and she had just assumed he was married. "I have not met that woman yet, mainly because I have been married to my work," he said. "But I have met a nurse at the hospital, that may be the one, I'm hoping"

This brought relief to Elsa, who had not realized about living alone in a house with an unmarried man. She was not certain however. She was not a prude, but did not want to ward off unwanted advances.

Dr. Blackwell recognizing the concern in her eyes, said, "but we are not alone.' My housekeeper Olivia lives here also." She is preparing dinner as we speak and you will meet her momentarily." "Please follow me and I will introduce you." With that he turned and walked into the living room and turned toward the dining room. Elsa followed behind.

An elderly woman in her late 50's or early 60's came through a door at the far end of the dining room. She had grey wiry hair, stocky built about 5' 1", round face and pug like nose, which held a pair of wire rimmed glasses and magnified a pair of flinty grey eyes. "Olivia Stewart this is Elsa Vanderbeck, the assistant I told you about."

Olivia set the plate of food she was carrying on the table and wiped her hands on her apron. She held out her hand and said, "Nice to meet you Elsa."

"Nice to meet you also, Olivia." Both women were sizing each other up, but being very polite about it. Elsa said looking at the 2 place settings at the table, "aren't you eating with us?"

"Not tonight", Olivia responded. "I had a bite earlier and this will give you and Dr Blackwell time to talk." Tomorrow, I will join you."

Elsa was noticing that Olivia takes control around the house or at least when she is with the Doctor. Probably, she is the type of person who attempts to control most situations. The table had the food already on it.

Olivia said," I'll be going now and don't worry about cleaning up, I will get to it later, when I get back" With that she turned and went through the door, she had come in. Elsa thought that must be where the kitchen is.

Dr Blackwell held Elsa's chair for her and after she sat down, he went and sat at the head of the table. "How long has Olivia been working for you", Elsa asked? Curious about the people she would be around and trying to gain insight into Dr. Blackwell's and Olivia's relationship. There didn't appear to be any animosity or stress about them.

"Oh, she has been with me for several years and I can rely on her to take care of the house and make sure there is food available. "It works out very well, because a Physician cannot always keep regular hours." He passed the plate of salad to Elsa. "I never have been able to have babies arrive on regular hours. They seem to be on their schedule not mine." He had a slight smile and a twinkle in his eye, so Elsa knew he was kidding with her.

"Terribly inconvenient of them", Elsa replied. She was beginning to feel comfortable with Dr Blackwell. He seemed to have a fun side to him and was not quite as uptight as he appeared. She also felt that they would get along and be a good teacher for her.

Dinner of meat loaf, salad, rye bread and beans went smoothly with her doing a little more prying into his life. Afterwards, he pushed back his chair, wiped his mouth with his napkin and said, "let me show you the house."

She put her napkin on the table and stood up. She walked around the head of the table and followed him to the door that Olivia had come through. He held it open for her and she walked into a kitchen with bright lights and for all standards very modern. It had a large wooden refrigerator on the far wall. There was a wraparound counter with steel double sinks. On the far wall there were windows looking out to the back yard with blue curtains pulled to the sides. There was a tea kettle on the stove and a drip coffee maker setting on the counter beside the stove.

Dr Blackwell stated, "this is Olivia's domain but you're free to prepare anything you would like to eat here. I usually have coffee in the mornings about 6:30 and Olivia has a pot ready when I get down." "She will show you where everything is stored." "You can find out more from her tomorrow." With that he turned and held the door open for her to exit. She went through and waited until he could lead her through the dining room and through the living room back to the hallway. He paused and pointed to a door at the end of the hallway, "There is a closet there and it has enough room if you need to stow luggage." She just nodded and he turned to go up the stairs, picking up one of the suitcases she had brought. She picked up the other suitcase and followed.

The stairs were wide with carpeting down the middle. As he started up the stairs, he spoke over his shoulder. "The upstairs has 3 bedrooms and 2 bathrooms. Hopefully you will find it comfortable." "You and Olivia will be sharing a bathroom." At the top of the stairs, he turned left and walked down the corridor, which had matching carpet as the stairs and opened the door on the right. This was a bathroom with white tile floors and white walls. There was a mirror on one wall with a pedestal sink below it. At the end of the room was a white tub with short legs holding it off the floor with an orange rug in front of it, so you wouldn't slip when you got out. There was a narrow white vanity with doors on the front and shelving holding towels on the inside wall.

Elsa was thinking that it was clean and bright and would do fine. The Doctor closed the door and continued to the next door on the right and opened it and went in. Setting the suitcase, he was carrying on the floor next to a night table with an oil lamp on it. Elsa stepped in and looked around. It was not as big as her room at home but big enough to move around without feeling cramped. There was a closet on the far wall and a dresser with a mirror above. The far wall had 2 windows with shades drawn and a small desk and chair in the corner. The bed next to the night table was a double with 2 pillows a blue comforter and an extra white blanket across the foot. The bed had an iron headboard and footboard. She set the suitcase down next to the dresser and turned to look at Dr Blackwell. His expression was showing some apprehension and his eyes were asking if she approved of the room. She smiled and stated, "this will do just fine." Answering the unspoken question.

"Olivia's room is across the hall and my room is down on the other side of the stairs," he said. "I will leave you alone now, to unpack and will see you tomorrow morning." If there is anything else you should need, please don't hesitate to ask." Good night"

Elsa said, "good night and thank you again." She could tell he was uncomfortable standing there and wanted to leave quickly. He went out the door and closed it behind him.

She stood for a moment and slowly gazed around. I can be happy here she thought. Not having Ruth there to talk to was a little depressing, but she was looking forward to learning and what might be ahead.

Six months later, she was standing outside one of the examination rooms at Mass. General Hospital.

She had just helped the doctor set a little boy's broken arm. The boy had fallen off a swing, so the boy had said. She was a little sceptical of the story and so was the boy's mother, she had noticed. The boys screaming, while his arm was being set, brought back the memories of that horrible night, when her brother was screaming and she could do nothing to help. The resolve was that she would never again run away from screams of someone in pain, and some time somehow, find a way to right the horrible wrong done to her family.

"Good morning" a deep voice said behind her. She turned and was looking at Dr. Harry Levine. A man about 6' 3" tall, reddish blond hair cut short, wide set blue eyes with reddish blonde eyebrows and high cheek bones which offset a small nose. He was ruggedly handsome with a short beard and firm thoughtful mouth. "Sorry to startle you", he said." You looked like you were in deep thought."

Her thoughts went into overdrive and she felt a flush coming to her face. Something primal stirred every time she got near him, and her heart rate started to accelerate. Good morning, I was just going over the resetting of the boy's arm and what might have made the procedure more comfortable for him. "Maybe an anaesthetic.

"Well, I'm sorry for disturbing you, but the look on your face was more of terror than of concentration. "I was wondering if after you're done today, would you like to go out to dinner?"

Elsa thought for a moment and said," I need to ask Dr. Blackwell what plans he has and to let him know I won't be back at the residence for dinner." Can I let you know later this afternoon?"

"Most certainly", he replied. "I have surgery in about an hour, but leave a note at the front desk and I will check it afterwards."

I have to go, but I hope to see you later." Elsa spoke as she headed down the hall where Dr. Blackwell was standing. Her heart was leaping and slight smile came to her lips. He wants to take me out to dinner. She was walking fast knowing that Dr. Blackwell did not like tardiness and her spirit was flying.

Later that day, she had left a note for Dr Levine at the front desk, and had said in it that she could meet him at 6:30 at the Hospital entrance. She had spoken to Dr. Blackwell and he said that he was delighted that she had been asked out by Dr. Levine. In his opinion Dr Levine was one of the best and brightest doctors at the hospital. He had assured Elsa that he would talk to Olivia and not to worry about missing their dinner. She had finished the rounds with Dr. Blackwell at about 5:45 and went to the ladies' room to wash up and take off the white coat that doctors wore when seeing patients. She had a locker there and put the coat in it. She put on a little lipstick and brushed her hair. She had seen Dr. Levine several times over the last 2 months at the hospital, but he seemed shy and turned away if she caught him looking at her. A final look in the mirror and she was ready to head to the front door.

He was standing at the front door talking to another doctor. He noticed her walking up and smiled. He said goodbye to the other doctor and turned to her. His look was so intense she started to blush.

"You look beautiful," he said and held the door open for her.

She was nervous now. "Thank you, where are we going?" she asked to start the conversation. She was aware of her blushing and tried to walk while looking straight ahead, so she wouldn't stare at him.

"A little Italian restaurant I know of downtown." It's quiet, but the food is good and the wine is delightful."

"Sounds very romantic, she said. His turn to blush and she realized that her bluntness, had taken him by surprise. But before he could say, if you rather not, she added, "I would like that very much." She now wondered if she had gone too far and he would think she was easy. They came to the street and he hailed a carriage. It was a cold night so, they sat close under the blanket. The ride took about 15 minutes and they made small talk about the hospital gossip.

At the restaurant, he paid the driver and opened the door for her. It was warm inside and a cheery small man with a moustache that stuck straight out and slick back black hair came up and said" Doctor, good to see you!"

Luigi, it is good to see you too, how is your wife?" Harry said.

She is better now and getting around without the pain." Luigi replied, "who is this Bellissima lady?"

"Luigi this is Elsa and she is studying to be a doctor at the hospital.." Harry answered.

"Wonderful," Luigi exclaimed and unexpectantly hugged Elsa. "Come let me show you to a table and bring you an antipasto." He led the way to a table by the back wall with a candle on it and pulled out the chair for Elsa. He also helped her off with her coat and took Harry's from him. Luigi hurried off and a waiter in a white apron appeared with a plate of olives and prosciutto, cheese and brochettes.

There were little white plates on the table which the waiter poured a little olive oil into and a few drops of balsamic vinegar. Then he disappeared and Luigi was back with a bottle of chianti with a straw wrapper and filled a glass for each. He set the bottle on the table and dashed away. There was an identical chianti bottle on the table, but it had a wax coating at the top and a candle. Elsa's heart was pounding and every fibre of her being was tensed.

The restaurant was filled with wonderful aromas. Harry picked up a brochette and dipped into the olive oil and vinegar. Then placed a slice of cheese and slice of prosciutto on top and handed to her. She looked around, there were about 6 other tables with people at them and they were all involved in their own conversations and food. She took the brochette and said, "thank you." He was watching her, so she took a bite. It was delicious, all the flavours came together like a symphony in her mouth. He smiled, and said,' truly a wonderful restaurant. "

"This is really delicious and to be honest, it's my first time having Italian food." He probably thought she was extremely sheltered or immature. Elsa was loving every minute of this including the company.

He picked up his glass and said, to a beautiful evening with a beautiful woman."

She swallowed the food, picked up the glass and nodded agreement and took a sip. The wine was peppery but also smooth and filled her mouth with a tingling sensation. It had a bouquet all its own and made the food seem even better. Harry took a brochette and made for himself what he made for her. He seemed relaxed and enjoying the atmosphere. She took an olive and another sip of wine. The flavours blended again and it appeared that all her taste buds were enjoying themselves.

The waiter appeared and cleared off the plates and brought new ones. Then the waiter brought a platter of some kind of noodles in a red sauce with pieces of clams in it. He served portions of the noodles and sauce to both of them and brought a basket with warm bread with a hard crust. Harry said, "Thank you" to the waiter and he was gone.

Elsa watched Harry's handsome face as he broke off a piece of bread and handed it to her. He then broke off a piece for himself and picked up his fork. He spun the fork in the noodles and put it in his mouth. She said, "thank you", for the bread and followed with the fork rotation. Again, the flavour was outstanding.

She took another sip of wine and the pepper seemed to make the sauce come alive. They ate quietly for a little while and Harry refilled their glasses with wine. He took the bread he had broken off and dipped in in the sauce and took a bite. She followed with the same action.

They both took another sip of wine and he said. "Are you enjoying working in medicine and at the hospital?"

Elsa had to gain her thoughts and thought for a moment before answering. "I love helping people and relieving pain." The hospital is the only place where so many people are trying to help others." "I can say that hearing the anguish and seeing the pain that some people are in does bother me at times, but it comes with the profession." How about you?"

"I wouldn't want to be doing anything else." What are your other interests", he asked? His eyes showed a calm glow, paving a pathway to his nature and the personality that was patient and didn't show any signs of ulterior motives or guile.

"I love the symphony and for some unknown reason, I have an attraction to the sea." Probably because of the Captain, who was my benefactor." Sometimes it is, as if it calls to me." She replied. "What about you?"

"Other than work, which takes up most of my time, I also like the symphony and the literature, some of the old texts."

Luigi appeared at the table. "Tonight, you must try and old favourite of my family." The desert is called tiramisu and it is my gift to a beautiful couple," She was thinking this guy must have been prompted in advance. Elsa smiled and said," can we share the dessert? "I've eaten more than I normally do already."

"Most certainly," he replied "and may I suggest, coffee with a little amaretto. It would add to the meal."

"Whatever you suggest sounds wonderful," she replied. He then vanished again and the waiter appeared with the coffee and a small plate with what looked like a white cake with chocolate running through the middle and shavings of chocolate on top. He placed to small forks in front of each of them and set the coffee cups next to each of them. Then he set the dessert in the middle of the table, so both could reach it. Harry turned the plate a round, so she could have the first bite.

She took a small fork full of the cake and put in her mouth. Again, the flavours burst into her mouth, blending dark chocolate and some type of pudding into a palate pleasure that she had never experienced before. She resisted grabbing the plate and shovelling it into her mouth. After swallowing she said, "this is heavenly."

He was just smiling at her as he took a bite himself. "Your right", he said. Knowing that no agreement was necessary. He picked up the coffee and took a sip.

She did the same and the sweetness of the amaretto and nutty flavour of the coffee only added to the enjoyment. The feeling was almost euphoric. She realized that the wine and the liquor was giving a slight dizzy feeling. She said to herself go slow, your losing control and that was something she didn't want to do.

They had finished eating and Luigi was there again. Harry was thanking him and wanted to pay more than the bill that was presented, but Luigi refused because of the care Harry had shown Luigi's wife and was refusing anything extra. She came around the table and hugged Luigi, who smelled of olive oil, garlic and tomato paste. "I will be back for more of this delicious food and I'm going to bring lots of friends", Elsa exclaimed. "This meal was simply wonderful." I can't thank you enough."

I think Luigi was blushing which was hard to tell with is dark complexion.

"You are welcome anytime, he said and I think you add beauty to my little restaurant." Harry held her coat and as she put it on Luigi hugged her again.

"I called a carriage for you and he is waiting outside."
"Ciao," Luigi said.

We walked to the door and Harry waved and said "Thank you" for about the third time. The night air was cold and Elsa was glad because she was still feeling the effects of the wine and liquor. Harry helped her into the carriage and put the blanket over them. He put his arm around her shoulders and she snuggled in close to him. Her feelings were that this night could go on forever. She felt safe, warm and thought she could feel the passion rising inside of her. He was looking down at her as the carriage started moving and she looked up and kissed him deeply on the lips. There was fire on her insides and she had to pause and let her breathing quiet down or her heart could be heard a mile away. She said, "this has been one of the best nights of my life."

"Mine too and I don't want it to stop, but tomorrow is another day and we have to be at work early." He replied with a small frown on his face.

Elsa reached up and put her hand on the side of his face and looking into those beautiful eyes, she said, "your right and Dr. Blackwell will be waiting up for me, but I want to do this again real soon." Was I being too forward she thought, I wasn't sure, but I didn't really care that much? Is this what love feels like, forgetting caution and being irresponsible. This time he was kissing me and I could feel his pulse rising and his breathing becoming shallower. Elsa had lost track of time. It was nearly 10 PM and she needed to be up for a meeting at 7 to go over the case load for the day. She wanted to stay in the cab and hold this wonderful man next to her. They pulled up in front of the house and the driver did not turn around, trying to be discreet. Harry kissed her again quickly and opened the carriage door. The driver got down and helped them out.

Harry took her hand as they walked to the door. He said," I have patients and surgery all day tomorrow are you going to be at the hospital?"

Dr. Blackwell and I have patients here all day tomorrow, but the following day we are going to be there for my first appendectomy, That will be Saturday and we can do something that night, if that is OK with you? She realized, she was being forward.

Harry smiled and said," I will count the minutes."

Just then the door opened and Dr. Blackwell was holding it open with a serious look of annoyance on his face. Harry spoke up immediately, "sorry for returning so late, but we had a wonderful dinner at Luigi's. Elsa just looked sheepish, but she thought I shouldn't have, I'm not a little girl.

Dr. Blackwell then grinned and said, "yes Luigi can make a dinner last longer than expected. He was looking at both of their faces. She realized that her cheeks and chin were red from rubbing against Harry's whiskers.

She turned to Harry and said, "thank you for a wonderful evening and I l look forward to seeing you soon"

"I also, he replied and good night." Harry nodded to Dr. Blackwell and walked back to the carriage.

Elsa walked into the hallway and took off her coat. She felt like she was floating. Dr. Blackwell was standing there watching her, so after hanging up her coat in the closet, She said. That was one of the most delicious meals I have ever had."

"Good, he replied, "you can tell me all about it in the morning." He then started turning off lights and Elsa headed upstairs to her room. Still feeling Harry's kisses on her lips. In fact, her lips might have been a little swollen from the force they were putting on each other.

Saturday was looking to be an overcast day.

Saturday morning, Elsa was at the hospital attending to a patient with burns over 60% of his body. She had been studying the writings of the French surgeon "Boyer and the thesis by Earle written By Earle J. titled "Lessening the Effects of Burns on the Human Body." The man had been too close to a kerosene container when a fire ignited it and half his body was covered in flame. Half his face was burned and the eyebrow on the left side was gone, He was lying on the examination table with a sheet covering half his body on the right side. No hair was left on the left side and thankfully he was not circumcised because the foreskin protected the head of his penis, obviously not Jewish, she reflected. The burns were red and blistered but the puss coming out was mostly clear and only a little bit of yellow puss could be seen.

She had bathed him with sterile water and covered him with a light clean sheet. They had made him as comfortable as possible, but it was obvious that he was in a great deal of pain.

Dr Blackwell entered the room and walked directly over to her. She was thinking he was going to give me some instructions for tending to the patient, but his look was more of concern and penetrating than a normal patient discussion.

"I'll take over for you here and you should go to your Uncles' house immediately." I'm sorry, but he has taken a turn for the worse and I don't think he has long to live" . His stare was intent on her face and there was caring in his eyes.

She ran from the room and down the hallway to the entrance. Her heart was beating loudly and she wasn't really seeing people as she went past. Tears were starting and the pain was growing in her heart. She went out the front door and hailed a carriage by waving. She realized she had stopped breathing and gasp for breath. She shouted at the driver the address and jumped in, not letting him help. "Please hurry."

They rushed through the streets and as the carriage pulled up, Elsa jumped out handed the driver some money without looking and ran into the house. Ruth and Thomas were there and she ran up the steps to the bedroom without speaking. The Captain was lying in the bed with covers up to his chest. His pale and drawn face were visible with glassy watery eyes looking grey and blank. The eyes moved and he saw her as she crossed the room. Kneeling at the bedside she took his hand, which was cold and clammy to the touch. He appeared to try and smile and lightly squeezed her hand, as if to say I'm glad to see you. There was a slight gurgle in his throat and the eyes turned to the ceiling and he was gone.

His regular doctor came in and picked up his wrist. He reached up and closed the Captain's eye lids and pulled the sheet up over his face. She slumped on the floor and started crying. The man had meant so much to her. He had saved her life and protected her from the evils in the world. She had known terror and loss but nothing like this. She reached up and held the cold lifeless hand as if to keep a part of him with her for a little while longer.

Thomas and Ruth entered the room followed by Letisha, who was crying as much as she was. Tears streaming down her cheeks and sobbing continually. The Doctor turned and said, "He has passed."

There was a quietness in the room and only Letisha's and Elsa's sobs could be heard. Elsa stood and hugged Ruth and Thomas and then Letisha.

"I Will call to get the ambulance to get the body" The Doctor said solemnly and left the room. We all took one last look and Thomas put his arm around Elsa's and Letisha's shoulders and ushered them out of the room and down the stairs to the living room. Still crying, Elsa had started to catch her breath. Thomas had taken Letisha to a chair and had her sit down.

Thomas was looking with concern down at Letisha and said, "Letisha, if you would like, you can come stay with us and help Mary around the house. He looked up at Ruth, who gave him a nod of approval. He continued, "we have plenty of room and I know Mary would love it."

Letisha lifted her head and stopped crying for a moment. "That very nice of you suh, but I would like to go back to dah Island" "I been thinkin daht I been missen my family." "I just don't know how to get down there."

Thomas smiled slightly and rested his hand on her shoulder and said, "that will not be a problem." You see I was executor for the Captain's will and he left you a sum of money to help with your life." "Ruth and I can arrange for your passage and other details to get you home." "It is not the best time of year, but I'm sure that within a month we can find a ship heading down." It will take that long to get the rest of the affairs in order and if it is OK with you, we can arrange everything?" The Captain's adopted son Paul Williams can be there when you arrive." I will send a message to him immediately."

Letisha's face took on a more relaxed look but there was a questioning expression in her eyes. Mister Thomas, I don't know nuthin about money, and what you do with it." "What does sum mean?"

Thomas now grinned and realized numbers would mean nothing to Letisha." "Let me just say, that if you wanted to buy a house and lots of new clothes, it would not be a problem." He continued," the Captain also left a sum to you Elsa." "I will work out the details after we sell the house, but he left half to his son and a quarter to each of you."

This was unknown to Elsa and her first reaction was to turn it down. But then she thought maybe I can do some good with it.

Letisha's head popped up and she said with a start, "I done almost forgot." Dah Captain left this letter to you Elsa" "He said to give it to you, when he was gone." She pulled a letter from a pocket in her dress and handed it to Elsa. "He said you was one of the best things that come into his Life"

Elsa took the letter and Ruth handed her a cloth to wipe her eyes. Elsa opened the letter and started to read it out loud.

Dear Elsa:
If Letisha has given you this letter, then I have gone on to be with Greta. She will tell me about all the things I'm doing wrong, but some things never change. The

important part of this letter is to relay to you some more information about your family.

First your family was buried up on a hill overlooking the harbor. A place your father dearly loved. It is a small cemetery next to a white church with a steeple. There are gravestones covering the four graves. You may want to pay your respects sometime. But there still may be a threat to you there, so be very cautious.

The next is about your father's will. An attorney in the harbour by the name of Grisham had it. He would not let me see it and refused to give me any information about it at the instructions of your father's brother. I felt there was something suspicious about the affair, but having no legal right to the information, I could do nothing. There still may be a copy of the will on record, but I have no idea.

You have made my life much happier and I thank the good Lord, that you were brought to Greta and I.

Wishing you every happiness and with much fondness,

Captain J Williams

Tears filled her eyes again. She had mixed emotions about the island and didn't want to put her life in danger after all these years. The thought crossed her mind to go back with Letisha, but that would only take me away from Harry and Dr. Blackwell. No, going to the island would have to wait. She realized she was crying again.

It has been 2 weeks since the Captain's funeral and Elsa was to hear today from the hospital board, if she was to be accepted as a practicing doctor. Elsa couldn't keep her emotions under control and knew her nerves were on end. Harry was waiting in the hallway outside the offices and he was looking very professional in his white coat and had a white shirt with a particularly colourful blue bow tie. His expression gave her no idea what was going to happen.

As Elsa approached, he said, "this is it." You either go back to being an assistant or get to practice on your own."
"How do you feel?"
"Excited, scared, crazy and a lot more."
He said, "remember it is not the end of the world." "I'll wait for you out here, unless I get called away."

She stepped to the brown oak door and grasp the knob. She noticed that her hand was shaking, and said to herself, get a grip, this is not a firing squad. She turned the knob, took a deep breath and stepped in. She was wearing a light grey blouse buttoned at the neck and sleeves buttoned at the wrists. Her skirt was charcoal grey wool and came to the top of her shoes.

There were six men in the room including Dr Blackwell. All were dressed in white coats with suits on underneath. They were mostly in their late 50's or older. Some were clean shaven and others had neatly trimmed beards. All the expressions were very serious with not a hint of humour. There was a long walnut table in the room with matching chairs. There was a single chair set in front of the table and she was waved to it by a Dr Abernathy, head of the hospital board. He had almost totally white hair and beard. He always had a serious look on his face but his eyes were kindly and he was not prone to silliness. I did detect a very small twinkle of happiness in Dr. Blackwell's eyes and a very small upturn to the corners of his mouth as he sat down.

Dr Abernathy began, "Ms Vanderbeck you have been assisting Dr Blackwell for some 6 1/2 months at the hospital. Your demeanour has been professional and your practices have been observed by all members of this board. Your education in the medical sciences are just beginning and you have proven a conscientious effort to learning the practices of medicine and the preparation and application of medicines needed to benefit mankind, We have noted that you tend to become too emotionally attached to some patients, which can become a lack in good judgement in your practice.

I was trying not to show any reaction or emotion to what was being said. But my mind was racing. My god, how could caring too much be a bad thing. This guy should really try caring a little bit more about his patients, She was thinking.

He was continuing, "this being said, it is the opinion of this esteemed board, that you be honored with a certificate to practice medicine in the State of Massachusetts. We congratulate you on your work and efforts and have the Certificate signed by myself at the request of the board as Chairman.

He stood up and offered his hand in congratulations. She took a deep breath and stood on trembling legs and shook his hand. "This meeting is adjourned", he proclaimed. They all stood and each came around and congratulated her. Dr Blackwell waited to be last. His dark brown eyes were lit with happiness and a proud smile was on his face. "Well done Elsa", he said. "You have made me very proud with all your hard work and dedication."

"I could have not done it without your help and guidance." "The certificate is as much your efforts as mine." "I am deeply indebted to you as a mentor and teacher."

He asked, "What are your plans now?"

"I haven't given it much thought, because of Captain Williams passing." I also want to have a discussion with Harry about his plans." Her face was still radiant with a smile.

"I completely understand, but I want you back at the house for a celebratory dinner tonight." This was more of a command than a request from Dr Blackwell. He continued, "I have invited Thomas and Ruth to join us and Olivia, of course." "Shall we say 6:30?"

"Would it be alright, if I invited Dr Levine to join us." He will be waiting to hear and I want him to share the evening, if that is alright with you?"

"Certainly", he responded and then paused," Have Thomas and Ruth met Dr. Levine before?" He was watching Elsa's face carefully for any sign of embarrassment or coyness.

"I had introduced them 2 months ago at a symphony we all attended." She replied. But there was a little shyness in the tone of the reply and Dr Blackwell knew that Thomas and Ruth didn't know that she had been seeing Dr. Levine regularly.

He excused himself and she followed him out the door. Dr Levine was nowhere in sight, so she headed down the hall to the examination rooms. He was just backing out of the second room and his whole face lit up, when he saw her. The sun was shining through the windows and the white walls, which normally seemed dull took on a glow of radiance. She wanted to jump into his arms, but they had decided that it would be best to be discreet around the hospital. She almost started running but held back knowing others would be watching as several nurses and doctors walked up and down the hall. It was only a distance of 30 feet but it seemed like it took forever to get to him.

"Dr. Vanderbeck, I presume." He said with kidding tone in his voice. "Congratulations." Several of the staff had already told him. They knew something had been going on between them and had given them sly smiles at times.

So much for being discreet, she thought. "Thank you", she said. She wanted him to hold him right then, but it would not have been appropriate.

Harry continued, we haven't discussed plans for tonight, but I would love to take you out." This was more in the form of a question, than anything else.

She grinned and said," that would be wonderful, but." At that point she saw his face go into a slight frown and worry come to his eyes. "Dr Blackwell wants to have a celebration dinner and you are invited."

His expression changed immediately. "I would be most honored to attend a dinner in your honor", he replied.

She realized she better tell him, who the other guests were. 'My adopted parents will also be there. She blurted.

Still smiling he said, "all the better." I think they should get to know me better, and this will give us a chance to really get acquainted." If he had concerns, it didn't show.

She had some reservations about how Thomas and Ruth would handle the fact that she was dating a person that was not First Christian Reform, but there was no better time to brooch the subject. His religious heritage was Jewish, but he didn't practice religion. His scientific education had led him into not practicing any organized religion. Which fit in with Elsa's own beliefs and although they had lightly discussed the subject, they had not had any serious discussions. Their relationship had moved on to a higher level and she knew he was serious about her and she was about him, but it only had been a few months. She questioned why she was really concerned and whether there was more to her thoughts. Was she really committed to this man? She really loved the person he was. Did she have a problem with commitment or the fact her life would be tied to his for the rest of her life.

She smiled up at him and said, "good I will see you tonight." His name was being called from inside the room and she knew he had to go. She really wanted to kiss him, but discretion kept the impulse inside and she just said, "you better go."

He disappeared into the room and went behind a curtain.

Later at Dr Blackwell's House:

Standing in the living room with Thomas, Ruth and Dr. Blackwell, Elsa wondered where the day had gone. She had been busy assisting Dr Blackwell with a patient with a bad case of the influenza and another patient, whose foot was crushed under a wagon wheel. She was nervous about the meeting of Harry and her stepparents, but it was too late to do anything about it. There was a knock at the front door and Dr. Blackwell went to answer it. She could hear Dr. Blackwell say," Harry, please come in." "Let me take your coat."

Harry and Dr. Blackwell then walked into the living room just as Olivia entered from the dining room carrying a silver tray with a bottle of champagne and six glasses. Harry shook Thomas's hand and nodded to Ruth. He smiled at Elsa with those beautiful eyes that were lit up with happiness. Olivia set the tray on a coffee table and Dr. Blackwell moved over and started to uncork the bottle of champagne. Harry looked at Thomas and said "How have you been?"

Thomas had a suspicious look on his face, but said, "We have been fine and are so proud of Elsa and what she's done." "You must see her at the hospital, quite a bit." It was obvious that Thomas was fishing for information.

"Not that often, since we are both so busy."

Just then, Dr Blackwell showed up handing Harry and Elsa champagne flutes filled with a golden liquid with small bubbles rising to the surface. He then handed a glass to Ruth and Thomas. He took the last glass from the tray for himself and raised it to make a toast. "To Elsa, who has persevered and accomplished so much in these last few months. She has succeeded in becoming a doctor and impressed the Board at the hospital and everyone else she met." "We wish her all the best in the future." They all took a sip of champagne and Elsa was blushing from the attention. Olivia said, "I have some canapes to go with the bubbly." She spun around and headed back to the kitchen.

"What are you plans now?' Thomas asked.

Elsa was thinking, she didn't like all this attention, with Harry beaming at her, Thomas with a suspicious look and Ruth's expression was quizzical as she looked from Harry to Elsa. The only one not trying to extract information was Dr. Blackwell and that's because she had talked to him about her plans and what to do next. Taking a deep breath and looking into their faces she said, "I would like to continue working with Dr. Blackwell, but specialize in children's' medicine. There is so much we do not know about the diseases that attack infants " She glanced up at Harry to see his reaction. He was just beaming back at her. She knew he would support her and anything she wanted to do. She could feel her face flushing and was trying to think of something to change the subject, but her mind was to spinning with happiness to come up with a change.

Harry raised his glass and said, "to Dr Vanderbeck." The rest chimed in, "Dr Vanderbeck. "

Olivia then came in carrying a tray of cheeses and olives and little sandwiches.

8

FOLLOWING YOUR HEART: - 2017

Wednesday at 8:45, Lacey was up and heading to the door of her studio. She had a blue and white striped bag with a towel, suntan lotion, dive mask and snorkel and a pair of fins she found in the villa. She had on a white t-shirt and olive-green khaki shorts with blue flip flops. Sunglasses with brown frames, not the wire aviator sunglasses given her by the FBI. She was ready for a day of fun and relaxation in or on the water. She touched the chain around her neck and the feeling of warmth and serenity came over her. The voice from inside said, "enjoy the water and feel the love that surrounds you." Lacey had gotten used to hearing the voice and was sure she wasn't going crazy. She looked back across the room and out the patio windows at the tree. It made her feel peaceful. She went out the door and locked it. Then bounded up the steps, She had grabbed her dark blue ball cap with "FBI" on the front. They were now being sold in all sorts of sundry shops, so nobody took them seriously.

The truck was at the top of the stairs and Daniel was standing by the passenger door waiting for her. He was grinning and said, "your taxi awaits." She immediately jumped in and listened to Willie Nelson sing "On the Road again." He got in the driver's side and put the truck in gear.

"OK," he said, "first we will go to one of the most beautiful beaches in the world." It does not have great snorkelling, but we can get a bite of breakfast. After that we will head along the Northwest side of the island and around to the marina where, I have my boat. Then we will cruise over to another little island and snorkel for a while we'll make it back by sundown. Sound good to you?"

"That sounds wonderful," while watching the twisting and turning road in front of her. They had just come to a full stop at a stop sign with a totally blind uphill curve on her right. He honked and then turned right. There was no stop sign for cars coming from the other direction and the danger was apparent on these narrow roads. They went up and down some dips in the road and then past a magnificent Flamboyant tree with bright reddish orange flowers covering all the branches. It was so brilliant in the sunlight that one could be mesmerized by the colour. Just past the tree was an overlook out to the ocean and other islands. The sun was glaring and small puffy white clouds floated in the light blue sky over a deep blue ocean. Now John Denver was singing "Annie's Song" on the radio and her world was at peace right now. He turned left at a Y which had a stop sign that was hidden behind a bush. She thought thank heavens they can't drive very fast on these curvy roads.

A little further, Daniel said, "we are just about there." He then pulled through a gate and up to a little ticket shack made of that blue black stone and said to the person inside, "Morning, we are going to breakfast.

"OK" came from inside, but the glare on the glass window hid the person's features.

They pulled forward and to the left into a parking area and parked. Walked across the parking lot as a mongoose ran across their path and ducked into the trees and shrubs.

"Mongoose: "Daniel said, seeing the inquisitive look in Lacey's' eyes. "You'll see them all the time here." He kept walking and headed for a brown framed open building with a long bar, and a takeout counter on the other side. The cement gave way to sand with short large leafed trees on the sand. On one of the limbs an iguana was staring down at them. It was sprawled on a limb with all 4 legs hanging over the sides They approached the counter and looked overhead at the white menu board showing omelettes, pancakes, eggs with bacon or sausage and home fried potatoes.

"Try the omelettes," he suggested. "They are not bad."

The person behind the counter looked to be in her fifties, with a surly expression on her face. It appeared she was not happy having to wait on people and would rather be anyplace else than where she was.

"I'll have a ham and cheese omelette and an orange juice," Lacey said. The woman wrote it down on an order pad and stared at Daniel.

"I'll have the same," Daniel said. "That will make it easy." She wrote it down and tore of the sheet from the order pad and passed through to a man about 65 through an opening over the back counter.

The waitress turned to her right and opened a cooler and took out two bottles of orange juice and set them on the counter in front of Daniel. She still hadn't said a word and had the 'ho hum' expression on her face. Daniel picked them up and carried them to a white plastic table on a deck facing the bay.

Lacey had been staring at the white sandy beach about sixty feet wide and the glistening bay just beyond. Small waves were washing up to the shore and the water was crystalline for about fifteen feet out from shore. The white sandy bottom reflected the sunlight making the water appear clear except for the sand kicked up from the bottom by the surf. Beyond the shimmering clear area, the water looked bright emerald green out to a line of white buoys bobbing on the surface. There the water turned a shade of blue and was a patchwork of light blue where the sand was on the bottom and dark green where the seagrass covered the bottom. She saw a small dark knob on the surface for a few seconds and then disappear.

Daniel watching her gaze said, a turtle just came up for air." "They feed on the seagrass and come up for air every few minutes. The sea is always full of life." The shallows are always full of little fish and you'll see the pelicans fly over looking for a snack."

He saw the waitress put two paper plates on the counter, he had already paid. He picked the plates up, walking over to the table and setting them down. Lacey sat down and noticed a sign on the wall, "Don't feed the iguanas." She then noticed 2 rather large iguanas eyeing their food from the roof. They were staring at them with hungry eyes. "You don't get privacy when you eat here." Lacey said with a hint of sarcasm.

After eating, they noticed the beach was starting to fill up with people from the cruise ships trying to take advantage of the mile long beach and tropical sun. They threw their paper plates and plastic ware into a trash can and started back to the truck. She could see the overweight Americans getting beers in the morning and the Europeans in speedos with stomachs hanging over. Not a pretty site.

As they walked across the parking lot another mongoose ran across and into the dense green vegetation.

Daniel held her door. "How did you like the beach"? He asked.

The beach is spectacular, but why do all the people stay near the entrance"?

"Cruise ship people get off the ships and get a taxi here." They huddle around the bar and restaurant and then get back in the taxis back to the ship." "If you are coming from the cold, I guess you want as much sunshine as you can get with all the creature comforts available. The locals stay at the other end of the beach and away from the tourists."

They drove to the other side of the Island and down a road to a marina with small boats tied up to mooring balls dotting the harbor.

Daniel opened his door and said, "I will be right back." He then went into the little white building. She got out and walked around to the tailgate of the truck. It was a warm sunlit day and the water did not show a ripple from the wind on the surface.

Daniel and another black fellow came out from the building. and walked over. They were smiling and laughing about something.

As they approached Daniel said, "Lacey this is David. His father knew my father and his grandfather knew my grandfather."

She reached out to shake hands and said "Nice to meet you." She was looking up into dark brown eyes with a twinkle in them like he knew something she didn't.

David said, "a pleasure to meet you." "You are prettier than Daniel described you" He spoke with a slightly British accent, Lacey guessed that it was from his education. He didn't have the lost syllables of the islands.

She said, "You'll have to tell me how Daniel describes me."

David smiled and said, "that will have to wait, until we have a lot more time. Now I have to take you out to Daniel's little fishing boat." Make sure you wear a life jacket, just in case the rust bucket sinks." David had a sarcastic look on his face and was chuckling to himself.

Daniel gave David a frown and said, "I hope the dink motor can make it that far" They were teasing each other that was obvious, and Lacey was thinking boys will be boys.

They walked down the pier, Daniel climbed down a ladder stepping into a grey RIB with a hard plastic floor. The boat had a center console with a seat behind it and hard white plastic storage in front to sit on. It was powered by a Yamaha outboard.

Daniel said, "Pass me down your bag and then I'll help you down. She handed down the bag climbing down the stairs and into the boat before Daniel could turn around from putting the bag down. He just grinned,. David untied the line holding the boat from the cleat on the dock and came down the ladder. while Daniel held the dinghy to the dock. David went over to the console and turned the key and the engine immediately came to life. He turned the helm and pushed gently on the throttle. They slowly came away from the dock. and Lacey was waiting for him to add more speed, but they only travelled maybe fifty feet pulling alongside a 36 foot dark blue hauled fishing boat. It had a hard Bimini covering the aft deck and twin 240 HP engines on the stern. There were several fenders hanging on the side as David eased the dingy up to the boat. Daniel immediately tied a line from the dingy to a cleat on the boat. David quickly stepped from the dinghy's tube to a swim step at the stern. Daniel handed Lacey's bag to David and offered a hand to help her from the dingy to the swim step. He was beaming at her as she took his hand and stepped on the boat.

"This is what you call a rust bucket", she said to David.

"Well it only looks good, because I take care of it." By the way don't let him tell you, he has run out of gas." This has two full tanks and only runs off of one at a time."

Daniel said, "Thanks buddy, now you've ruined my plans." Daniel was trying to look angry when he said it, but you knew it was all in fun.

David stepped down on to the swim step and back onto the dingy. The engine had been idling, Daniel through the line into the dingy saying, "You can go bother someone else now." David just waived and pushed the throttle forward, heading back to the dock.

Daniel turned to Lacey and said, "let me show you below." He opened a hatchway and walked down a short ladder into the salon. She followed. Inside was a small galley on the right with even a microwave oven. There was a sink on the forward bulkhead and small stove next to it. Along the side was a dark blue fabric couch or bench with cushions and a table in front that looked like it collapsed against the far wall. There were several portholes above the bench back cushions with little curtains to cover them. Across from the table on the other bulkhead was a shelf with lots of electronic instruments and a navigational table. Forward of the salon was a door leading into a V berth. On the side of the door was another door that opened into a bathroom. Daniel had said "Here is the bathroom or head, if you use boat talk."

"This is all great", she exclaimed. "I could live here", She said and realized how forward that sounded. Lacey tried to recover by saying, "I was not looking for an invitation."

He had that little smirk on his face and said, "I hadn't taken that the wrong way, but I am glad to hear you like her. "Let's get underway, we are wasting daylight." They headed back up the ladder. He went to the console and started checking things and turning switches. When he was satisfied, he turned on the engines and a deep throated rumbling sound started from the two large engines.

"What can I do" . She could feel a slight breeze in her hair and wanted to do more than just sit there like a lump.

"Pull in the fenders and stow them under the seat on port side."

"Got it," She had learned a little about boats when she was a child, her mother and father took her to San Diego, where they had gone out for the day on a chartered boat. She felt comfortable on a boat and the vastness of the ocean made her relaxed and excited all at the same time. She pulled up the three fenders one at a time and untied them from the cleats they were attached to. She shoved them under the rear seat. She came forward to the helm and stood beside Daniel. She wanted to hug him but held back taking in the view of the harbour.

Daniel went forward, and untied the mooring line, walked back to the helm and pushed the gear shift forward as the boat started slowly to move. He turned the wheel to starboard and the boat pivoted to the right. She could see the harbor clearly and the moorings on the far side. As they moved out of the harbor. She saw with the sun reflecting off the white haul and there was grey smoke coming from one of the huge stacks of a cruise ship. It had red and black painted stripes on the stacks and what looked like a "mickey mouse" face and ears. Daniel said, "that's the Disney line, she'll play "A Pirates Life for Me", when she leaves."

Daniel pushed the throttles a little farther forward, they had picked up a little speed, the water was still calm and the ride was smooth. She looked over the side, she could see the sandy bottom through the crystalline water. They were passing by the little island and the white house with the red tile roof. She could see from the villa. The locket on her chest was warm, she was filled with a sensation of pure bliss. It was overwhelming. She began to feel limp with euphoria. There was something about that house, because at the same time, her whole body went taught and she wanted to scream in fear. She became dizzy and held on to the door frame in front of her. The voice inside said, "It's alright you are safe now." The house was in a little alcove that could hold maybe three boats, protecting them from the open sea. She thought maybe I am going crazy, the locket had seemed to get brighter when she passed the house and now looked its normal self. The warmth was gone and she wasn't dizzy anymore.

Daniel was staring at her and asked, "are you alright."

"I'm fine, must have been something from breakfast. Where are we headed Captain Williams?"

He flushed, "that is what I was told they called my great grandfather." He was just beaming with happiness. A big smile on his face and eyes were as bright as starlight. We were heading out between these two little islands, where we can anchor and snorkel, usually without other company. With the seas the way they are today, it should be perfect." Daniel pushed the throttles a little farther forward as they passed the end of the little island and the nose of the boat came up. The swells were a little bit bigger now, still the sea was calm and there was only the wind from the boat moving forward. There was spray coming up the sides of the boat but not reaching into the cockpit. They would bounce off a wave every once in a while, it was exhilarating feeling the fresh air and warm breeze on her face.

They came to a passage between two small islands and Daniel slowed the boat down coming to a little inlet. He put the engines in idle, stepped up onto the deck and went forward to drop an anchor. He dropped the anchor over the side hand feeding the chain until it went slack. He fed out some more chain putting the chain through a notch on the bow. He came back to the cockpit and climbed down. As the boat drifted backwards and the chain became taught. The anchor was set.

Lacey walked back to the stern and looked into fifteen to twenty feet of, what looked like, an aquarium tank. she could see the bottom, rose colored fan coral and reddish orange staghorn coral. A black reef shark swam along the bottom. It was about 3 feet long. Its tail swaying left and right and appeared in no hurry. Then a sting ray swam by. This was unbelievable.

Daniel looked over, down and said, "time to get in the water. This is a perfect day to get your feet wet and enjoy all nature has to offer." "you can go below and get into your bathing suit."

"No need, she had it on under my shorts." She slipped her shorts off and pulled her t-shirt off over her head. The bikini was teal green which was cut high on the hip. The top matched in color and had a cross twisted fabric between the cups with a tie that went up to the back of her neck.

Just like a guy, Daniel was staring. He managed to say, "have you got plenty of sunscreen on?"

"Plenty but you can put some on my back." He stepped behind her and rubbed lotion all over her back. She looked right and there was a black cloud in the water about 30 feet long and about 15 feet wide. What's that"? Pointing to the cloud in the water. It appeared the cloud was moving and changing shape.

He looked and said, 'you're in for a real treat. Have you ever seen the pictures on Nat Geo TV of the schools of bait fish?"

She recalled watching large schools of fish get herded into a ball by dolphins and sharks off of Africa. The pictures were amazing. She said, "yes I think so."

"Well now, you are going to be up close and personal." He handed her fins and said, sit on the swim step and put them on." She did and he handed her the mask and snorkel. She slid into the warm clear water and was not sure if she should be looking where the shark was.

Daniel slipped in next to her and took her hand, squeezed it gently for reassurance. He gave a little tug and started swimming using just his fins toward the bait fish. She followed using the same motion leaving her arms at her sides. She felt relaxed as she got use to breathing thru her mouth. As they approached what first looked like a billion silver flecks dancing in the water, she realized there were hundreds or thousands of silver iridescent fish ranging from 4 inches long to maybe 6 or 8 inches. The water magnifies everything, so she wasn't sure. The fish moved together in one great mass and darted in mass in one direction or another. On the edge of the school a fish would miss a turn and suddenly panic and swim back into the mass. She swam right into the middle and visibility dropped to about 2 feet. She was engulfed in the cloud, as sunlight bounced of the shiny little bodies like a handful of silver crystals. The cloud turned and suddenly she was on the outside of the mass at the tail end. Looking to her left she could see the reef shark with a black tip on its dorsal fin. There was another large fish, all silver bodied with dark grey along the back. It had large black eyes and a mouth that appeared to be the size of her foot. Gleaming large pointed white teeth filled the mouth. she recognized the barracuda, which kept swimming back and forth behind the bait cloud. He wasn't charging in, so he must have had a good meal already. Below and to the right of the barracuda were two large fish with large silver scales like armour plating. They had mouths that curved upward like a mouth on a bulldog. They had to be 3 or 4 feet long. They paid no attention to her. Daniel was at her side looking like a clown in his mask with a grin on his face. She was fascinated and frozen in place just watching what was going on. We swam back toward the silver cloud just as the 2 armour coated fish came closer to the silver cloud. It swirled just like on television and formed a circle like water swirling down a drain but had a bulge at the center and tapered at the bottom and top. She got so excited and peed in her bathing suit. Realizing that few people had experienced the panorama of life acting out. Daggers of sunlight came down through the water and danced off the fish. Then the whole school expanded and stretched out again as if dancing to some unheard tune.

 Daniel touched her arm and waived for her to follow him closer to the island and some rock outcroppings. He pointed at a black hole that had 2 long sticks of red and black poking out of it. The sticks were tapered and grew in diameter as they entered the hole. He wiggled his first and little fingers at Lacey. I gave him a look like I didn't understand. He did it again. I got it, lobster. He must think I'm a moron. He guided Lacey a little further along the rocks. There was a head of something sticking out of a hole. It had a pink purple mouth and the rest of the body was filled with a design of brown and gold spots. It had a head similar to a snake. A yellow and black striped tropical fish swam buy and looked like it was trying to annoy the purple mouth thing.

Daniel took a knife out of a leg sheath he was wearing and used the blade to cut open a black spiney sea urchin. The tropical fish and the purple mouth thing came out and went for the cloud of meat that rose from the center of the sea urchin. The purple mouth thing looked like a snake as it slithered through the water. A big black and white fish with the worst overbite you have ever seen came in for the food. It had black tail with a wide white band around the middle and then a black head. The black and white fish dove in and the little fish and the purple mouth thing backed away. The black and white fish and the purple mouth thing started to eye each other as if a fight was going to start. The purple mouth thing then turned and went back to its hole. Stare down won by the black and white fish, which made me think of a police car paint job. Daniel motioned to Lacey to head back to the boat. She had lost all track of time and couldn't tell how long She had been in the water. She swam to the step ladder and raised her head out of the water, so she could hear.

Daniel was on the other side of the ladder and pulled the snorkel and mask higher up on his head. "Take your fins off first and put them on the swim step. Then climb up the ladder."

He was right, it would be very difficult to get up the ladder with fins on. She pulled them off with her right hand and dumped them on the swim step. Then it was easy to walk up the ladder and stand on the swim step. Daniel did the same thing and came on board.

Lacey grabbed a blue and white stripped towel that was lying on a bench cushion and started drying her hair. She blurted, "wow that was amazing. "It was surreal being in the middle of all those fish and not being able to see anything but them moving like little silver panicked pieces of glass. "What were the 2 big fish that looked like they were in armour plates? What was that snake like thing with the rose purplish mouth? "And what was that black and white fish with the big overbite?"

Daniel held up his hand to stop her from saying anything else. "First the 2 big fish were Tarpon. Next the snake thing was a purple mouthed Moray Eel." And last, the black and white was a Sheepshead. They use their teeth to scrape barnacles and food off rocks."

He was grinning from ear to ear letting his happiness show how he liked that Lacy had enjoyed herself. He was wiping some of the water off him too. "It is rare that you can swim in a bait ball in calm waters and even better, when you can get close up." There aren't a lot of people, who have had that experience. We were lucky." "Why don't you go up on deck and get some sun, while I get the anchor up." Would you like a beer to take with you?"

She said, "sure" and ran the towel down her legs to get water off. He lifted up one of the cushions on the bench, there was a cooler underneath. He opened the top, took out two beers, unscrewed the top off one and handed it to her. He unscrewed the top of the other and took a gulp. "Nothing like a cold beer after you've been in the ocean."

Lacey took a drink and thought he was right. It takes away the saltwater taste in your mouth. She took her towel and climbed up holding onto the rail and went to the bow. Daniel was busy getting the equipment stored and getting the boat ready to get underway. He had a strong tanned sculpted body. She was enjoying her eye candy. His bathing suit was surfer styled in light blue with a flower pattern on it. He stepped on a silver rimmed black button on the deck and the anchor chain rose up and went through a hole in the fore deck. It rattled as the chain came up and the boat moved forward, until it stopped. Daniel went to the cockpit and she heard the engines rumble to life. He gave a little forward nudge to the throttle shifted to neutral. He came back to the foredeck reached down and lifted some chain straight up. She assumed the anchor was free of the bottom and he pushed down on the black button again with his foot. The chain clanked as it went into the hole again and soon, he lifted the anchor under the tail and fastened it onto the deck. He turned and said, "just relax and enjoy while I get us under way."

Lacey just smiled at him and feeling the sun all over her body closed her eyes. She was thinking this might be what heaven was like, if there was a heaven. She could hear the engines a little louder and felt the boat moving forward. She turned her head to watch the cloud of bait fish pass by as the boat headed out the little alcove and into open water. She looked straight up through her sunglasses and there were only little white cotton balls for clouds and pale blue sky over head. Somewhere far off a gull shrieked. As they went past the end of the 2 islands, She could feel the boat bounce as it rode over the little swells.

She felt a little to hot from the sun. She grabbed hold of the hand rail, steadying herself, she got up and walked back to the cockpit. She stepped down onto a cushion and then the deck.

She was getting her sea legs, she thought. She stood beside Daniel and put her arm around his waist. This was now really heaven. If you care about someone, it should show, she thought. He put his arm around her shoulders and gave a little squeeze. They could make out the outline of an island in the distance. "Where to now Captain."

He beamed. "Well matey, it looks like we better head for port and find us some rum." "We'll head back to the marina and get cleaned up." Which will put us just about to sundown, and then I'm going to treat you to the best Roti on the island and as many Dark and Stormys, as you want." "How does that sound?"

"It sounds great, if I knew what a Roti is and I never had a Dark and Stormy." "Which I am assuming is a rum drink."

Daniel smirked and said, "We will stick to the code." She assumed it was the pirate's code from the Johnny Depp movies.

"You are saying, every person for themselves." The wind was starting to pick up a little and swells grew a little higher. The sun was sliding to the horizon and the water was now all dark blue except for a little white foam every few moments that bubbled from a wave. No ominous clouds about, only well-rounded cumulus clouds in the sky. Wind was pushing his hair back and his faced showed the sun he had gotten today.

She looked at her shoulder and the skin were pinker than this morning, even though she had put on sunscreen. It didn't look like it would hurt later. "Time will tell", as they say. Whoever they are.

She was watching a person that was in his element. He loved being on the water. She was starting to feel that itchy feeling from having salt on your skin. "Are we going to get a place to shower and change?"

Daniel didn't take his eyes of the horizon, which now showed an island growing out of the water. "There are showers and places to change at the marina" "I have a fresh water hose here on the boat, but it is more comfortable at the marina." Plus, I don't know if I could trust myself, if you were showering here."

He was being honest. After another half hour, They came into an inlet and we were approaching the marina from a different direction. The little island was on our right, but we did not go through the harbour to get there. Daniel had picked up a hand held microphone and called to David to meet us at the mooring ball. David was standing in his dingy with the mooring ball bobbing next him. Daniel eased the boat up to David and stopped it, as if he had done it a dozen times.

Which he probably had. David reached up and took hold of the bow rail as Daniel moved up on deck and handed a line to David. They were secured in seconds and Daniel came back and shut down the engines. He picked up the trash and beer bottles, while Lacey got her bag and said, "Hi David."

David was wearing burnt orange shorts that hung from his hips. He was smiling like a Cheshire cat. "Did he behave himself and did you have a good time?"

"First,. He was a perfect gentleman after I told him, 'don't hand me no lines and keep your hands to yourself" David raised an eyebrow at Daniel. Who merely shrugged?

David said, "sounds like he is losing his touch, must be age."

Daniel mocked a frown and said, I don't know why I hang out with perverts like you." Meaning David. You two have enough time to kid me later, let's go get a shower."

They got in the dingy and headed over to the marina dock. Daniel helped me up on the Dock and said the lady's showers are on the left side." He handed me my bag, that David had handed up to him. As she walked down the dock the sun was still 15 degrees above the horizon. She could hear Daniel telling David about the bait ball and the purple mouth eel. She was feeling wonderful from head to toe, except for the salt itch, which needed to get off her body and get out of the bathing suit which seemed dry now. She found the shower room door and went in. There were 3 shower stalls with curtains on one side. The whole place was white tile and had sinks and two toilet stall on the other side. There was a light green bench on the front side with hooks above it to hang things. She set down her bag on the bench and took out her towel and hung it on the hook above. She stepped in the first stall and turned the knob for water. The water was not heated but it felt great and she stripped off her bikini. Wrung it out, what there was to wring out and flipped it onto the bench. The fresh water was refreshing and she could feel her skin respond to the soothing massage. There was no shampoo but a container with body soap. She let the water cascade through her hair and down her body as she held her eyes shut. She was remembering all the sites today, when the door burst open. An elderly woman ran in. Grey hair, round face and even more rounded body. She headed straight to a toilet stall and rushed into it. From behind the door Lacey heard her say "when you gotta pee, you gotta pee." The whole scene made Lacey chuckle that truer words were never spoken. She turned off the water and walked over and got the towel. She dried herself and slipped on a pair of black thong nylon panties. She wrapped the towel around her and took a brush from the bag.

The woman came out of the toilet and started to apologize. Lacey said, "not a problem, we've all had to go at some time."

Lacey detected the woman's Canadian accent when she said, "when, I was your age I had better control." She checked herself in a mirror and made sure the knee length turquoise shift hung over her shorts down to her knees and dashed out the door.

Lacey finished dressing and went out front near the dock. Daniel was standing with David discussing something about the boat. They looked relaxed and enjoying the discussion. You could see in their faces that they loved the ocean. They both turned as Lacey walked up.

"Looks like somebody got some sun today" David said. Try some aloe tonight, so you don't hurt, and don't fall for the old line, "I'll just rub it on your back."

Daniel hit him on the shoulder and said, someday he'll learn to keep his opinions to himself." "You look wonderful."

"A shower brings out my best qualities." " It helps if you wash sand and salt out of your hair." She could feel the heat from the suntan raising in her face and shoulders.

Daniel picked up her bag and turned to David. "See you in a couple of days and thanks for taking care of the boat."

David said, "Later and nice meeting you Lacey." "Daniel think about going fishing next week."

Daniel just nodded. Lacey said, "it was nice meeting you too, David and I will heed your advice." Daniel just smiled and opened the truck's door for her to get in. He put the bag behind the seat. Closed the door and went around to the driver's side. The door opened with the usual creaks and groans of an old truck. He started it up and drove out of the marina.

"We're heading to Latitudes", he said "and I hope you enjoy it."

She was hungry from all the snorkelling and in need of something to quench the thirst you get from being on the ocean. The sun was just resting on the horizon but the sky was still bright with the sunrays beaming up from the water. They turned onto a dirt road with huge potholes. The truck bounced and groaned as they went down a very rutted road. The road had not been scraped or levelled for a very long time. They came to the end where the beach started. On the left was a marina and a tiki bar restaurant with a sign that said "Latitude" in blue letters. There was a deck with wooden tables and plastic chairs. They were facing out on an inlet crowded with boats at anchor bobbing on gentle swells. She felt a chill but it was from all the sun that day. There was a slight breeze and you could look about a quarter of a mile to the open sea toward the island off in the distance. The edges of some clouds were turning pink and crimson from the setting sun and felt she was looking at a travel brochure for any of the tropical islands around the world saying, "come visit." They sat at a table near the water. The waitress came asking "can I take your drink order?" as she handed them menus.

Daniel looked at me for approval and said, "Two Dark and Stormys, please."

What is in a "Dark and Stormy"?

"It is dark rum, ginger beer and a lime wedge." They go down very easily and if the bar has it, it should be Gosling

Dark Seal rum and Gosling Ginger Beet." "You tell me after you try one?"

Roti's can be vegetarian, chicken, beef or conch." He continued, "What do you prefer and they come with a salad?

She thought for a second and said, "I'll go for the conch, why not?" He smiled and said "Me too."

The waitress came with the drinks and David ordered. Lacey tasted the drink and it was a strong ginger ale with the flavour of rum and lime. It went down easy and she could tell that you could gulp these and before you knew it you were loaded. She remembered he said go easy, but the drink was very satisfying. Thinking, she really did not have a busy schedule tomorrow, she should relax and just enjoy herself. Sitting here with this handsome man, who I noticed the waitress gave a long look. He wasn't paying any attention, and was really just watching her. "So, this is what leisure time is like for you down here?" Lacey asked.

"More or less", he said. "Usually, I go fishing or diving." "We work some crazy hours depending on the cruise ship schedules and days can run 10 or 12 hours." We work 3 on and 1 off for 4 weeks and then get 2 weeks off." But pretty much you can be on call 24/7 when you're on duty." We've talked about this before, so let's just relax.""

Lacey could tell he didn't like talking about himself and he was gazing at her eyes with calm steady intent as if he wanted to be a good listener. All right, let's keep it light and easy, she thought.

The waitress arrived with 2 plates with salad and Rotis, which looked like a burrito with no toppings. Cutting into it there was a dark brown gravy with potatoes, conch and vegetables. The aroma was rich and dark like a beef stew. "This is way more than I can eat", she said.

"Eat what you can and don't worry they can wrap the rest." Would you like another drink"? Daniel asked. She hadn't noticed but she had drained her glass. "Sure, why not?" They do go down easy, so she thought and better to cool it after one more. They both dug into the food and Lacy noticed a day on the water can give you an appetite.

The dinner was over and the sun was gone leaving a beautiful night with few clouds a soft breeze and stars high overhead. She looked at the sailboats in the bay and they had anchor lights on at the top of their masts. That rocked gently on the invisible little swells seeming to dance. She thought of Jimmy Buffet song, who called "it stars upon the water." The night felt magical as she watched.

Daniel paid the bill and took her hand as they walked back to the truck. She hadn't felt this calm and relaxed in a very long time. Life can't always be this good, the curve balls will come and the ugly side of society will show up. But as my mother would say, "what are you going to do." She wondered why she was being cynical after such a beautiful day. Daniel was watching her face in puzzlement as he opened the door.

Sensing Lacey's mood, he asked, "is it something I said?"

"No", "It is just the brain bringing up history that should be left alone." She got in the truck. He went around and opened his door with the creaks and groans coming from the metal hinges. He started it up and they backed out of the parking place and turned onto the dirt road with all the potholes and started bouncing and swaying with the uneven road.

They talked about nothing important on the way home, just small talk, but she could feel a little tension building inside. He wasn't pushing and seemed to be trying to keep the conversation light. She could sense a little nervousness in him. We are not teenagers, so we should be past this by now or maybe you never get over it. He stopped at the top of her stairs and came around to open the door.

More squeaks and groans from the old truck.

She knew what she wanted and took his hand, walked down the steps and fumbled with her keys opening the door. Once inside, the urgency of their love making was brought on by a heady need to satisfy passion brought on by sun, salty water and alcohol. Their bodies greedily demanding each other and eagerly giving. Tenderness came later in a winding down of kisses, while exploring each other's body.

She could feel the places where she had gotten too much sun as the raw skin hurt a little as it rubbed against the roughness of the comforter. We had not even pulled down the covers to get in bed. Daniel was lying on his left side with his arm across her shoulder as she curled into his chest.

The hallway light was still on" He said, I can feel the heat coming off your skin from the sun, let me get some aloe and put it on your burns." She was so dreamy from the sex and the comfort of the moment that she didn't want him to move.

"Wait a moment, "I don't want to move just yet" She could smell his skin and the mild fragrance of whatever soap he had used to shower with. He had a few small hairs on his chest, but not enough to even tickle. Her hand was resting on his rib cage and she could feel the bones and sinew beneath the skin. It was a dreamy state that she did not want to disturb. Lacey raised her head and they gently kissed. She raised herself so he could slide off the bed and went to the bathroom. He was back in a moment with the plastic bottle of the green lotion with little air bubbles suspended in it. He squeezed some on her shoulder, which felt cold and she flinched.

He said,"sorry." He started to softly spread the lotion over her shoulders and back. He put some on the back of her legs and she flinched again from the cold substance. She swung her legs over the edge of the bed and stood up pressing herself next to him. He hugged her tenderly trying not to touch the sunburned areas. She reached back and pulled the comforter down and then lifted the top sheet. She slipped between the sheets and they cuddled again. She was asleep in seconds in his arms, totally satisfied and spent.

9

FIRST TRANSFERENCE – 1800'S

Elsa was lying in a bed in a room with windows on two sides, bright sunlight came through while lace curtains hung on brass rods across the top. Fifty years had passed in the blink of an eye and her skin had wrinkles, around her eyes, across her forehead, and on her hands. Her hair was now all silver and much thinner. Her eyes had dimmed with age but still radiated the love she had for life.

Thinking over the years after she had married Harry and moved to Chicago. He had been given a residency at a hospital in Chicago and she was happy then to stay at home and raise their two daughters, Ethel and Sarah. She loved then both. Sarah was born 2 years before Ethel. They had grown up in Chicago and gone to the University of Illinois. Ethel knew she wanted to teach mathematics and loved the straight forward approach to solving complex problems. She added a teaching credential and went to teaching higher mathematics to high school students. It was never add and subtract to her.

Sarah leaned more to the philosophical and artistic side. Sarah looked at the world more whimsically and believed everyone was good. This frustrated her mother, because she knew that evil lurked in some peoples souls and the world was not all milk and honey. She loved them both and they had brought both immense joy and more than enough stress to her life.

The voice now weak after the lungs had started getting less air to the body. "Sarah, I want to give you something, but it comes with a need of a promise that you can never break."

Sarah immediately started to refuse whatever gift it was, but Elsa held up a finger and said, "let me continue." Elsa took shallow breaths and seemed to have a hard time getting to the point. "I want you to have the locket that I have worn around my neck since I was a little girl. It was given to me by your grandfather and he made me promise never to take it off. I want the same promise from you." "This is very important to me and is a link to your ancestors."

Sarah's mouth started to quiver and tears were forming in her eyes. She inhaled deeply and said, "I can see that this means a lot to you mom, but you should continue wearing it. There will be plenty of time to give me the locket."

Elsa's old fire came into her eyes and she shook her head. She spoke in a more authoritative tone, "no Sarah this is important and I want your promise. I don't want to chance what might happen without my control." I've seen death and pain and know that people do not always have things go the way they plan. So, I want your promise here and now and along with it at some time in your future to pass this locket and chain on to an heir of your choosing. "

Tears were now running down both of Sarah's cheeks and she took a hanky "I promise to do as you request, but what makes this locket so special?" You have never talked about your parents before."

Elsa's eyes became deep pools of memory taking her back all those years as she spoke. "A long time ago on an island in the Caribbean something terrible happened. My Father and

Mother and my sister and brother were killed. I was saved by a native girl name Letisha. Who brought me to a family named Williams? From there they sent me away to the Vanderbeck's. Who adopted me and raised me as their own. I have never told anyone. I felt it was my secret." But now, I think you and Ethel should know the history of our family. I don't think there is any threat after all this time." So, undo the clasp and put it around your neck, so I can see." You'll be carrying the family close to your heart."

"Mom, why now after all these years?" Sarah said softly with affection gleaming from her eyes. You could have told us earlier." She didn't sound scolding, but with a desire to share her mother's emotions.

Elsa took a frail wrinkled hand from the bed and touched Sarah's cheek. Warmth and affection flowed from the touch. "There were much more worthwhile things to discuss or talk about through the years. So much life to embrace and no need to bring more of the evil in mankind into our world."

Sarah reached out and undid the clasp that was holding the chain and locket from around her mother's neck. She placed it around her neck and closed the clasp. "I will never take it off, until I pass it on to the next person, who will wear it. Sarah was wearing a high neck mauve blouse that was the style in the late 1800's. Her blonde hair was in a bun up on her head. She reached down and undid the two top buttons on the blouse, so the locket could rest underneath. As she did there was a feeling of warmth from the locket and a warm wind seem to pass through her chest. She felt her cheeks flush and although it was not particularly warm in the room a slight sheen appeared on her brow. She looked down at Elsa's face seeing a thin smile at the corners of her mouth and the pale skin started to take on a glow.

Elsa said, "you should let me rest now, I feel a little sleepy." Her face did have the expression of having a great burden relieved from her. It was the expression that whatever pain she was in from ailments, things would work out.

Sarah stood and left the room quietly and closed the door. She reached the head of the stairs, when she saw Ethel come in the front door. She quickly walked down the carpeted hallway and down the staircase to meet her sister. "Have I got something to tell you", Sarah blurted. She had never been a person to keep a secret.

Ethel had the more serious temperament. Her deep blue eyes focused on her sister and the expression was more of, what now, that I can't wait to hear. Ethel said flatly, "what are you talking about?"

Sarah took Ethel's hand and let her into the living room for privacy. She sat on the fabric couch with an embroidered print of flowers on it. The room had large windows on two sides. The windows had brown wood frames around them and curtains that were tied back to open a view on the street and yard. All of a sudden Sarah was more subdued. She had lost the excitement of the little girl with gossip to tell. She started to think before blurting things out. It was as if her whole personality has changed. She touched her chest wear the locket was resting underneath her blouse and she cleared her throat.

"Well', said Ethel. What is it?"

Sarah looked up and in a soft but serious voice said, "our grandparents on Mom's side were not really our Grandparents.

"Don't be silly, Thomas and Ruth were our Grandparents."

"No, 'Sarah said. "Mom just told me that she was adopted by them and was sent to them by some person to protect her from being killed. Her maiden name was Gufsterson. "Sarah reached out and took Ethel's hand and held it gently. "I don't think she is doing well and wanted us to know."

Sarah's gold flecked hazel eyes became distant and sad. I think you should go up and see her. Unlike the previous

Sarah, this person was thinking of others and their feelings.

Ethel was not one to accept information from anyone without checking it out. She stood and said, "I'm going up now to hear it for myself. "

Sarah nodded but softly said "be gentle with her."

Ethel had on a full skirt and a white long sleeve blouse buttoned at the collar. She marched more than walked to the stairs and went up and down the hall to Elsa's door. She turned the white porcelain knob slowly and peeked in. The room was still and the ashen face on the pillow had its eyes closed. Grey hair matted to one side and the lips had a grey paler to them. Ethel approached the bed slowly and took hold lightly of the withered hand that was resting on the sheet. The hand was cold and there was no sign of breathing. Ethel shouted "Sarah."

Sarah was standing in the doorway with a sad and knowing expression on her face. Ethel started to cry and moaned "Momma", both were crying now letting the pain take its toll. Hearts were so easily torn apart when someone you love isn't there anymore. The pain is immense and leaves a hole that may never be filled with all the loving memories the brain holds.

Sarah came over and rested her hand on Ethel's shoulder which was shaking with sobs. Ethel turned and hugged her sister. A hug can relieve some of the pain at the time as your world is being spun out of control. They stood hugging for several moments. Time loses value at moments like these.

Sarah spoke first, "let's go down to the kitchen and call the doctor. He will know what to do now." Ethel simply nodded and leaned herself against Sarah as they left the room.

Two weeks later after the funeral, Sarah was sitting in the living room in the early morning light. A cup of tea set on the wood framed glass coffee table with lazy steam slowly rising from the cup and moving with the hidden wind current that crept about the room. She was no longer happy with philosophy and art as her majors and thought about political science and law as a more fitting career. By accident she had run in to a young attorney by the name of Clarence Darrow. He had spoken of civil liberties and human rights. It had stirred her in to looking into law, but she knew it was dominated by men at the time. Still she felt compelled to give it a shot. She would head out to the University this afternoon and look into her options. There was a feeling that she was doing the right thing and the world for her was at peace. The locket felt warm against her chest and seemed to be humming next to her skin. She touched it lightly, it seemed as if she could hear Elsa's voice coming to her.

 She stood up and headed to the stairs to go change her clothes and get ready for whatever challenges were out there.

10

LIKE SAND THROUGH AN HOUR GLASS - 2017

Lacey blinked and opened eyes laden with sleep. She had dreamily seen Daniel get up and get dressed, then dozed back into the warm comfortable world of the dream. . She rolled over to take a look at the digital clock sitting on a night table next to the bed. Better get up and see what the day will hold. She had planned to do some cleaning of the upstairs bedrooms and patios, then go down to the harbour for some grocery shopping. Daniel kissed her lightly on the forehead before he left but had not said anything.

Her cell phone chimed and she looked at the caller. It was Daniel. She pressed the answer key and said, "miss me already?"

"Yes, but don't make too much of it." It's only because, I left my watch on your dresser."

"They say that people leave things, just so they can have an excuse to come back."

I don't need and excuse, I have a desire." His voice was light and she could tell he was enjoying the stupid banter.

"Men, they think with their smaller heads, all the time.'

Changing the subject, he said. "What are you doing Friday night?"

She said, "I will have to check with my social secretary, but I might be available" What did you have in mind, or let me rephrase that, what is going on?"

"You know you have a dirty mind, but I like it." My cousin wants me or us to come for dinner. Would you like to come with me?"

"You're not telling me something, what's the catch?"

"The catch is, she has two kids that at times can be a bit much. They are three and five, they have been known to be a real brats, at times. So, if you want to pass, it's OK with me, but I did want you to meet part of the family."

She thought for a moment, because she didn't know if he did or didn't like kids. They haven't even come close to having those types of discussions, but she could tell when he talked about his daughter, that there was real love and devotion in his voice. She hadn't pried into his past that much, but there was plenty of time for that. "I would love to go and be your backup for the evening." Do I need to bring body armour?" She could hear him chuckle.

"No, body armour not needed, however, I would wear something that was somewhat stain resistant or cleanable. There have been several accidents concerning milk spills and other things of that nature."

"You sound like the voice of experience." Don't worry, I have been around kids before, and have survived." She could feel the anticipation from him through the phone and knew she was making him happy. She reflected on why that meant so much to her and how far she was willing to let the relationship go.

"Then I will pick you up about six, because my cousin doesn't like to eat late with the kids. I can fill in any other details then. Got to go, bye."

The phone screen went blank and she stared at it for a moment. They hadn't had a real discussion about the future and it was too early for that. She thought, way too early for that, so just relax and enjoy the time together. You can always be serious. She went to brush her teeth.

Friday night at 5:55 she locked the door to the apartment and walked up the stairs. It was a typical night on the island with a cooling breeze, grey clouds and a bright moon. Shadows were cast from the palm trees, which were black against the sky. She could hear the throaty rumble of the old truck engine and the squeak of the truck springs as it came down the driveway. As usual right on time. The truck brakes screeched as it stopped, Daniel jumped out to get her door. As she moved around to get in, he took her shoulders and kissed her tenderly on the lips.

Looking down, he said. "Missed you."

She kissed him back and said, "ditto." She climbed in and smiled inwardly to herself. Just enjoy for now and see what else happens, she thought.

He jumped into the driver's seat and fastened his seat belt. "Where do they live," she asked.

In the harbour, 2 streets back from the main street. The house originally belonged to my great grandfather and has gone through a lot of renovation new wiring, new plumbing and some remodelling. It was built in the early 1700's, so you can guess everything that needed to be done. My Dad and his sister each owned half and my cousin and I now own half. My cousin's name is Jane and her husband is Jeffrey. The kids are Elizabeth, who we call Lizzy and her brother is Phillip."

They had driven downhill to the harbor and turned onto the main street. They went about 5 blocks and turned right to go back into the residential area. The main street ran along the harbor. She could see the water in the harbor inconstant motion with little waves coming to a halt against the seawall.

They turned right again and went up a slight rise and parked next to the curb. It was a narrow cobblestone street. The sidewalk on the other side was very narrow. The houses were built into the hill with steps leading down to the street. After parking, he waited by the front of the truck as she got out and he took her hand to cross the street. There was traffic noise from the main street 2 blocks away. Sounds were very clear because they came off the water. They walked across the street and up some white steps that led to a small landing in front of a dark brown door. There was a brass knocker in the middle of the door and Daniel used it to knock twice. Lacey could hear running footsteps of little feet from inside and someone with a strong male voice said wait. The door opened and a tall, thick man with brown hair and deep brown eyes with bushy eyebrows looked at Daniel and smiled. He moved the door farther open and 2 sets of impish staring eyes were looking at them. Something between a screech and a yell came the words, "Uncle Daniel." The kids obviously were happy to see him and threw their arms around his legs and hips.

    Daniel was smiling from ear to ear and bent down and scooped both of them up. The boy, who was the younger of the two had grabbed a handful of Daniel's hair, while the little girl had a chokehold around his neck as they stepped into the house.

    The man who opened the door held out his hand and said, "Hi, I'm Jeffrey Logan." This is normal when Daniel comes over."

    Hi, Lacey Lockhart and a pleasure to meet you."

    Daniel was moving into a dining room on the left with the two kids still poking and prodding him. Daniel was pretending to bite at their necks and growling. A woman came out from a door on the other side of the dining room. The dining room had a long table covered with a white tablecloth and six place settings. A brass and crystal chandelier hung from the ceiling with bright lights that sparkled off the hanging crystals. It looked antique and gave the room a feeling of old-time charm. The woman was about 5ft 10 inches tall with long black hair tied back in a ponytail. She had the dazzling blue eyes that seem to run in the family and the face of refinement. She gave the two kids a stern look, which you knew was a bluff and proceeded to give Daniel a peck on the cheek.

"Hi, I'm Jane and my dufus cousin has the manners of a tablecloth."

Daniel blushed and said, "I was just getting to the introductions."

"Lacey and it does look like he has his hands full." Trying to give Daniel the benefit of the doubt.

The giggling, growling and prodding was still going on from the kids and Daniel was continuing to play with them. He finally put them down and they went and stood on either side of their mother. "These two are Elizabeth and Phillip. Phillip had a firm grip on his mother's jeans, but the girl stood a little apart and had a serious expression on her face and was giving Lacey the stare. That only kids can give. Like who are you and what are you doing with my Uncle. Lacey could tell that winning them over was going to be a task.

Jeffrey, who was calmly watching the scene finally spoke up. "What can I get you two to drink? We have wine, beer, assorted beverages both hard and soft."

"Beer sounds good to me", Daniel said.

Lacey was still being observed, said a beer for me too."

Just then a black woman came out of the door Jane had come through.

It struck Lacey that she knew the kitchen was on the other side and a feeling of Déjà vu came over her. She had been here before and the room changed before her eyes. It looked like a much older room and the chairs had different cushions on the seats. There was a large man in a naval type clothes with bushy eyebrows and mutton chop side burns. Next to him was an older woman with black hair and a calming smile. Then there was a large black woman and a little black girl with braided hair and soulful eyes. They seem to be apparitions as their appearances floated behind everyone else. A voice was saying, "Lacey are you alright?"

She shook her head to clear the visions as her hand came up to the locket, she was wearing. I'm fine," She said. She remembered Daniel saying, that this home was owned by his Great Grandfather. A voice inside her head kept saying "it's OK."

Jane turned to the black woman and said, "this is Sayia and she lives here on the island." Sayia, why don't you get Lacey a glass of water. "

"Oh, I'm OK, the beer will be great." Lacey felt horrible, everyone was staring at her including the apparitions. Daniel had come to her side with a serious expression of concern on his face. The apparitions were actually smiling, except for the Captain, who had a kind face but one that didn't smile that much. Sayia had gone back through the door and was back with two bottles of Red Stripe beer and she set the beer on the table with a couple of glasses. She poured one beer into a glass and handed to Lacey.

Then handed one to Daniel. She had beautiful deep brown eyes and straight black shiny hair that hung down to her shoulders. She had a full figure but wasn't fat. Well rounded breasts that fit well with her. She was staring at Lacey and Lacey felt like there was some connection between them, but she wasn't sure what it was. She could feel the locket throbbing next to her skin.

Jeffrey broke the silence by saying, "let's all go into the living room and sit down."

Sayia spoke for the first time, "I'll bring in the hors de oeuvres. She had a soothing voice, that sounded well educated. It was as if she was a person Lacey could bond with.

They all went into the living room. Daniel and Lacey went to sit on the couch. As they sat down Lizzy climbed on Daniels lap, keeping her eyes on Lacey. Obviously, she was the unwanted competition for her Uncles affections.

Lizzy blurted out, while looking at Lacey, "are you his girlfriend?"

Jane said, "Lizzy" somewhat exasperated and consciously embarrassed.

Lacey smiled and said, 'we are very good friends, if that's what you mean." She knew she was definitely stepping into Lizzy's territory.

Daniel added, "Lizzy, you will always be my very special girl."

Lacey was not sure it mollified her, but it helped. This room seemed to be familiar also and the 4 apparitions were standing in the corner watching her. It appeared that nobody else saw them, but it was giving her the shivers. She decided to change the topic, so Lacey said to Jeffrey, "what do you do for a living?"

"I'm an attorney, he replied. I have an office just a few blocks away."

"What kind of law do you practice?" Lacey asked. Phillip had crawled into Jeffrey's lap and was making himself comfortable. Sayia brought in a tray with a drink on it for Jeffrey and a glass of wine for Jane. Sayia also brought in a plate of round crackers with cheese, olives and some kind of spread. There was a little wooden handled spreading knife on the tray also.

"I practice mostly civil cases and some business." He answered. "The real business person in the family is Jane with a linen shop."

Jane just smiled and said, "it's just a little place, but come in sometime, and I'll show you around." She looked at both Daniel and Lacey, "Would you like another beer?"

"I'll switch to wine, if you don't mind?"

Daniel chimed in, 'I'll have the same."

Sayia, who had been standing there observing, turned and headed into the dining room. She was back in a second with two glasses of red wine and handed them to Daniel and Lacey, "thank you," they both said in unison.

Lizzy had staked a claim on Daniel's lap and was still giving Lacey the evil eye. This little girl was not going to be mollified easily.

Jane said "the wine is just an ordinary French called, "Haut Bicou" but I like it plus it's inexpensive."

"I like it too, said Jeffrey so we pick up a case every so often."

Lacey took a sip and found it easy to swallow with a hint of pepper and the flavour of a Bordeaux.

The 4 ghosts were now moving about the room to the other wall. Lacy was more than just distracted. This was creepy, in a non-threatening way. She wondered if anyone else was having the same problem. They didn't seem to be aware of them. Daniel had slipped his hand into hers without letting Lizzy notice and he gave her hand a little squeeze, probably trying to show support. Lacey could see Sayia putting dishes on the table and Jane jumped up saying she needed to help with dinner.

Lacey asked, "if she could help?' thinking that Lizzy would be happy to have her Uncle all to herself.

Jane said, "sure." As if knowing that was my intention all the time or did, she want to get me alone.

Lacey followed Jane through the dining room and into the kitchen.

The kitchen was a gleaming place with stainless steel oversized appliances and a very old wooden table in the middle. Jane said, "we had the whole kitchen redone but for some reason, we could not get rid of this table."

The 4 ghosts were there and they were watching from a corner. Sayia was busy with some food and a serving platter but she kept looking up at Lacey. Sayia spoke while looking at her, "I don't know what it is, but I feel we have met before." It is almost as if we've known each other a long time." The two black ghosts were starting to fidget excitedly and the little girl was jumping up and down.

Lacey felt the warmth on her chest again from the locket and unknowingly her hand came up and touched it through her blouse. She said "I have the same feeling, do you know about your heritage?"

A little, Sayia said, my Grandmother and Great Grandmother were born here, but my Great Grandmother spent a few years in, I believe Boston then came back.

That is strange Lacey said, because my Great Grandmother was born here but she grew up in Boston.

Jane who was boiling water and putting some form of pasta in the pot said, "that really is a coincidence." Daniel's and my Great Grandfather lived here and spent the last years of his life in Boston. We all have pasts that cross. I know that Sayia's mother and Grandmother worked in this house." Maybe there is a connection." Jane then tested the pasta to make sure it was done and took it off the stove. "Looks like dinner is ready." Hope you don't mind but the kids go for rigatoni stuffed with cheese and a marinara sauce." Not the greatest but filling."

Sayia was setting salad plates and silverware on the table.

Jane poured the steaming contents of the pot in a colander at the sink and ran cold water from the tap over the contents. Then she poured the pasta into a large bowl and took it into the dining room.

Sayia followed with the sauce and big bowl with salad in it. Lacey picked up a basket with rolls, and a dish with a cheese grinder on it with a chunk of parmesan cheese in it.

"Thank you," Jane said, taking the rolls and cheese plate from Lacey. "You and Daniel sit on the far side out of harm and dirty fingers way" She had a smirk on her face and seemed to have been in this circumstance before.

Daniel and Jeffrey came in followed by Elizabeth and Phillip. Jeffrey and Daniel were carrying the wine glasses from the other room, which were all empty. Sayia took them and Lacey noticed there were clean wine and water glasses next to our plates. The smell of the marinara sauce was making her hungry and for the moment the ghosts were not in the room. Lacey went over to where Jane had shown her to sit and Daniel started to head around next to her. Elizabeth made a beeline to cut Lacey off.

"Lizzy" Jane said in an authoritative tone. "You sit next to me tonight and Jeffrey will sit on my other side."

Lizzy pouted and said, "I want to sit next to Uncle Daniel." Her head was tilted a little down and her eyes were looking up in defiance. Lacey expected her to cross her arms and stomp her foot for effect.

Jane simply smiled and said still in the authoritative tone, "not tonight. Tonight, though you can sit right next to Daddy."

That obviously mollified her a little and Jeffrey patted the chair next to him and gave her a smile that said you are daddy's girl. Lacey thought, she is going to be a handful when she gets to be a teenager. Lacey asked if Sayia was going to join us, but had noticed there wasn't a place setting set.

Jane said, 'normally she would but Sayia said she had some people she wanted to go see."

Lacey unconsciously pulled the locket out from under her blouse and fondled it for a second. Lizzy's eyes opened wide and she said." that pretty." And in a childish manner trying to win favour continued," and you're pretty too." Can I see it?"

"After dinner, I'll show it to you." Is that OK?" Lacey knew that she had just scored with a 7-year-old and some of the rivalry was dissipated. She thought how free that children were with their emotions, and how open and honest they were. Dinner was just chit chat after that. Lacey kept having the feeling that there was a connection between the Williams and my ancestors. I also noticed that the locket seemed to become brighter and the gold seemed to be glowing. Jane got up and started clearing dishes and Lacey got up and started doing the same thing. Jane backed into the kitchen and Lacey followed after her.

Inside the kitchen, Jane said, "just stack them on the table and Sayia will get them in a little while." She is really part of the family and I couldn't get along without her." Jane headed back out to the dining room to get more dishes and Lacy was right behind her.

We cleared the table and Jeffrey; Daniel and the kids were in the living room and the Winter Olympics were on the TV. Jeffrey and Daniel were discussing how political the games had become and why couldn't they return them to an amateur event. Both agreed that they didn't think that this was going to happen. Reasoning being that to many countries with too much ego invested. Sort of win at all cost and ethics and morals be dammed.

Jane and Lacey walked in and Jane said, "OK Kids time to get ready for bed."   "

"Can I help?" Lacey asked.

"Sure', Jane replied. Just then Lizzy was at Lacey's side and took her hand.

Lizzy said, "I want Lacey to put me to bed with an award-winning beautiful smile looking up at her.

Lacey now knew what angels looked like.

Daniel smirked and winked at Lacey and said, "You seem to have won the favour of someone's heart." And once attached, they never leave."

Lacey smiled back and said, "I wouldn't want them too." Looking down she said, "why don't you show me where your room is." Lizzy started taking Lacey to the stairs, never letting go of my hand. Lacey followed along as they went up the stairs to the second-floor hallway. There was a long-carpeted hallway and a short way to the left was another set of stairs which led up to a door. The hallway was carpeted with a heavy dark maroon rug and as we walked, she noticed the footsteps were muffled by the carpeting. Lizzy continued to the left past the second stairway and was at a door which Lizzy opened and flicked on a light switch.

The room had 3 pink walls and one wall covered in a pink wallpaper with white small unicorns, stars and white clouds. There was a four posted bed with a white canopy and matching nightstands with lamps on either side. Across the room was a white desk and chair. The hardwood floor was covered with a mauve area rug that took up most of the room. There was what looked like a very old chandelier that somebody had hung different colored stars from with what looked like thread. There was an overstuffed chair in one corner with an autumn. There were windows on the far wall facing the harbor and had white curtains with pink balloons on them. Lizzy bounced onto the bed, kicked off her shoes and Lizzy sat down and motioned for Lacey to sit next to her. Lizzy's little hand came up and touched Lacey's locket. Her eyes were wide with curiosity and she leaned her head onto Lacey's shoulder. She knew how to work someone that was for sure, but there wasn't any guile with it.

"Does it open up?' she asked.

"Yes," I answered.

Just then, Jane and Phillip entered. Phillip had "Spiderman" pajamas on and looked washed. His cheeks were pink from being washed and his hair was still damp. Those gleaming blue eyes sparkled and he said, "night Lacey'. He came forward and Lacey leaned down and he gave her cheek a kiss,

Lacey said, sleep tight Phillip!" Lacey knew her heart was again stolen. Lacey was again thinking this kid was going to be a heartbreaker. They were going to have to beat the girls away. He raced from the room and was gone. Jane followed him out, but stopped at the door, looked back and said, "I will be back, so Lizzy get your nightgown on."

Lizzy jumped off the bed and went to a white dresser against the wall next to the door and opened the 3rd drawer.

She took out a pink night shirt and dropped it on the bed. She then started pulling off her clothes and slipping the night shirt over her head.

"I bet your favourite color is pink?" Lacey said.

She just squeaked like a little mouse. And ran for the door way. I got up and followed. There was a bathroom across the hall and Jane was coming out of a door down from Lizzy's room. Lacey made the assumption that was Phillip's room and Jane held up one finger in front of her lips for quiet.

Jane followed Lizzy into the bathroom as Lacey hung back in the doorway. The bathroom had been updated and had a little stool in front of the sink, so Lizzy could get up and reach her toothbrush.

She put the toothpaste on toothbrush, which you could tell was very important to her and brushed her teeth. Jane had picked up a washcloth off a towel rack and ran it under the faucet as Lizzy brushed.

Jane rubbed a little soap on the cloth from a bar on the sink. Lizzy had stopped brushing and put the tooth brush back in a glass on the sink. Jane washed Lizzy's face and neck. Lizzy jumped down from the stool and grabbed a towel off the rack and rubbed her face dry.

Just then Jeffrey and Daniel came up the stairs and walked to the bathroom door.

Lizzy face brightened at the site of her Daddy and asked loudly, "will you read to me tonight, daddy?"

"That's why I'm here pumpkin," Jeffrey replied.

Lacey could see, Lizzy really was Daddy's girl. Lizzy was beaming and giggling and Jeffrey had a smile from ear to ear. Lizzy dashed across the floor and ploughed into Jeffrey's legs. He just lifted her up and held her in the crook of his arm. Her arm was around his neck. He kissed her cheek and blew on her neck, causing her to giggle.

As Jeffrey and Lizzy went into Lizzy's bedroom, Lacey asked Jane, "if she could see the rest of the house.

"Sure" Jane said." Just let me throw these towels in the hamper." She had picked up a towel off the bathroom floor and lifted the lid on a blue grey wicker hamper which was against a wall in the bathroom. Jane turned on a nightlight next to sink. She looked a little tired and Lacey thought two young kids can wear a person out.

Daniel was still standing behind Lacey, and he backed up and Lacy backed out so Jane could come out.

Jane said, "you'll have to wait on Phillip's room." With any luck he is sound asleep by now.

Lacey noticed that the walls were real cement and plaster. Sound would not permeate walls like these and it would be good insulation against the heat of the sun. Jane started back down the hall toward the stairs and a voice in my head said look in the attic.

As we came to the flight of stairs that went up, Lacey asked, 'is it alright to look at the attic?"

Jane stopped at the foot of the stairs. "Haven't been up there in a long time, but Daniel for you it's been ages." "There may be an old scrapbook up there with baby pictures of Daniel in it."

Daniel rolled his eyes and said, "oh great, now she'll see me naked on a rug, with my butt in the air."

Lacey was enjoying this and said, "But what a cute little butt. Jane's eyebrows went up and Lacey realized she had just admitted to having seen Daniel's butt.

Jane said, "I hope they didn't take a picture with him rolled over."

Both Daniel and Lacey were blushing. Lacey could feel her ears turn pink and then red.

He mumbled, "no big thing."

They all laughed and started up the stairs. At the top Jane reached up and undid a dead bolt and the door opened. She then reached around the side to a light switch. The interior lit up and it was a long attic with exposed untreated beams, cross beams and plywood roofing above. It was night but it was still warm in the attic even though there were vents at the end with a slow turning fan in front.

Daniel walked along the floor and commented. "I use to be afraid to come up here because there were spiders. You have really cleaned the place up Jane. "

Lacey was looking down the length of the space and on the right side was an old chest with leather straps, brass buckles and a brass lock on the front. She asked Jane, "What is that, it looks very old." Daniel and Jane looked at the chest.

Daniel said, "that has been in the family for years and my Dad told me when I got curious not to touch it." It goes back to my Great Grandfather, Captain Williams." There was a slight layer of dust on the top of the chest and it looked as if it had not been disturbed for years.

Lacey said or blurted, "Can we look inside?"

Daniel smiled and said, "Sure."

Lacey reached up and touched the locket, which felt warmer and glowing again.

Hanging on a nail on one of the beams was an old key and Daniel took it down and inserted into the lock and twisted the key. The lock popped open. He then undid the two straps from the buckles and opened the top. Inside was an old officers' uniform and a two-pointed hat with gold braid. Daniel held up the coat and it looked enormous next to him. They all laughed.

There was a wooden box underneath the clothes and it had a simple brass latch on it. Daniel picked it up and the two women gathered around.

The locket on Lacey's chest seemed to be humming now. Lacey put her hand on it to see if it was vibrating. It was and wasn't, but Lacey felt excitement run through her whole body and was getting an adrenalin charge.

Daniel opened the box and took out a very old piece of paper or parchment, that was folded in thirds. He unfolded the paper and read to himself. Written in pen and large letters, "Last Will and Testament of Heinrick Gufsterson."

Lacey now saw a ghost in the attic, watching over them. It was a man with long hair and a bushy moustache and beard. He wasn't dressed in a uniform, but woollen trousers and a heavy linen shirt. He was smiling at Lacey with an affectionate grin and he had a very strong face with round cheeks. But his eyes reminded her of her mother.

Daniel was thinking, who is this and why do my relatives have his will? Jane was thinking the same thing. Daniel finally spoke, "I don't know anyone named Gufsterson and then he looked at Lacey. Are you alright?" he said.

Her eyes were transfixed on the corner of the attic and she had a blank expression on her face. Daniel touched her arm and she looked up.

He said again, "are you alright?" You look like you just saw a ghost."

"I did, I think."

"Do you know someone named Heinrick Gufsterson? he said for the third time.

Looking at both of them Lacey continued," I think that was a distant relative." Maybe my Great Great Grandfather." I told you I thought that I had a connection to the island and my Great Grandmother was born here." Another apparition appeared in the corner. It was a little girl in a nightdress with blonde hair and smiling face. The little girl looked excited and curiously she had the locket around her neck. Lacey instinctively reached up and touched the locket she wore. The little girl did the same thing. The girl's eyes were the same as the man's. Lacey heard a sound and realized Jane was talking.

"Let's take this downstairs and show it to Jeffrey." Being an attorney, he might be able to give us a little help."

Daniel closed the chest but kept the box with the will inside. They all went to the steps and Jane flicked off the lights. She closed the door behind them and they headed down the stairs. Jane said, "we'll continue the tour later."

Lacey was sure that she had been in the house before and knew what all the rooms looked like. She was a little disoriented from seeing the apparitions but from deep inside her, she knew that this was the right thing to do. How would she know that and why was she so sure, she thought?

They entered the living room and Jeffrey was sitting in a chair reading some papers. There was an open leather briefcase setting next to the chair and he had his legs crossed in front of him. He looked up and said, "Lizzy is sound asleep. I guess even angels have to rest sometime." He had a relaxed smile on his face, but when he saw Jane's expression the smile disappeared. "What's up?" he said. He looked at Daniel carrying the box and said, "You haven't brought me a dead iguana in there? he kidded.

"Not so lucky big boy, we have a document we want you to look at." Jane replied.

Lacey noticed how relaxed they were with each other and there was no tension in their voices when they spoke.

Daniel handed the box to Jeffrey. Who opened it and took out the paper, as they watched.

He studied the document for a minute or so. Reading and rereading the words and looking at the bottom closely. He looked up and said, "looks like you have found a very old will and it appears authentic from the stamps and seals at the bottom." It was signed by both the attorney, the person and someone who was the Governor of the Island at the date of May 7th, 1775. The property listed at the time was a house, furniture and an island, a boat, some goats, a bank account and a business repairing ships." Looks pretty legal to me and everything is left to his nearest remaining relative and he lists his family." Why is this important?"

Daniel spoke first, "Lacey believes that she is the Great Great Granddaughter of this person's daughter."

"So, he lists the nuclear family, Wife Dorta, Son Lutwig and two daughters Katherine and Elsa." There is probably nothing of the estate left after all these years." Jeffrey said.

Lacey spoke for the first time as this was going on. "There was a family story that was documented in a letter that the family was murdered in the 1700's and the only survivor was the daughter Elsa." Elsa was adopted by Thomas and Ruth Vanderbeck after she was sent to the United States by a Captain Williams. "

Daniel said "that would be my great Grandfather, who adopted a son by the name of Stephen Williams, my Grandfather.

Jeffrey thought for a moment and said, "there is a Harry Gufsterson, who owns and lives on the little island in the harbour. "If this is authentic, you could be looking to actually own the island and most of what's on it, including the house." But to prove you are the rightful heir and get title will take a lot of legal work and searching."

Lacey was going to say something, but Jane cut her off. Can't you give the family discount to her since she may be a distant relative through adoption?"

Jeffrey rolled his eyes realizing that Jane volunteered him for lots of things without asking him first. He just smiled and spoke after a moment, "in order to have peace in the family and a foot rub at least monthly, I can go with the family discount."

Lacey now spoke, I have some extra time now and then I'd be willing to do whatever you want to help." "I still have some contacts at the FBI that can get things done.

Jane and Jeffrey's mouths dropped and they looked at Daniel together.

Daniel now with a sheepish look on his face said, "I might have missed telling you that Lacey was once in the FBI." "It must have slipped my mind."

Jane hit Daniel in the ribs with her elbow jokingly and said. "What there is of it. She then turned to Lacey and said, 'hi Cuz, welcome to the family."

11

SARAH AND THE LOCKET – 1900'S

It had been many years since she found a law school and was accepted and met Joel Binski at a law review board meeting and fell in love. Sarah had fought against prohibition, fought even harder for the women's right to vote and civil rights. She had the spirit of her ancestry and the steel blue eyes of her mother. The years had been good to her and Joel. They lived just on the edge of Chicago, which had grown and grown due to the Swift's and Armour's meat businesses. Chicago was the hub of meat packing and distribution to the country. It was a main spoke in the railway system.

They had a daughter late in life named Valerie. She had grown up in her mother's image and had the spirit and fire of her mother. She also had the desire to be an attorney like her parents. She wanted to right the world and make it a better place for future generations.

Valerie had the grades and extracurricular activities to get into Yale. It helped that her family had some wealth behind them. The strike against her of course was her gender and having a Jewish father.

Valerie had made it to her last year of Law school and had come home for the Christmas break. The weather in Chicago was cold and there was ice on the roads. Typical for this time of year with the winds coming off the lake. The wind could cut you like a knife and it was not good to stay outside very long. She had gotten a call from her father that Sarah wasn't feeling well and wanted to see her. She was picked up at the train station by Joel.

Joel was about 5 foot 6 inches with a barrel chest and dark hair that had turned grey, now thinned out leaving a bald spot on the back of his head. His features were fairly plain and he was the type that always had a 5 o'clock shadow even though he just shaved. His disposition was generally happy and seeing his daughter brought a huge smile that lit his face with joy.

They hugged at the station and hurried to the car. He took her suitcase and threw it on the back seat.

The car was fairly modern with four doors and roll up windows. It was black of course. Henry Ford said "You can have any color you want as long as it's black." They got in and Joel started the car, before Valarie asked, "how is mother?"

"She is feeling better, but at our ages you have aches and pains all the time. What are you going to do?" It wasn't a question, just an expression he used.

Valerie was looking at the grey overcast sky and the bleakness of the black grey slush that built up on the sides of the streets at this time of year. Pollution from the traffic was ugly, she hoped it would snow and cover the grime. Driving was slow because of ice on the roads as any moment you could hit an ice patch and spin out.

Valerie was wearing a heavy maroon wool coat, light grey cashmere scarf and grey gloves that matched. She had on black boots to keep the cold out. She was a pretty woman with dazzling steel blue eyes and bright blonde hair. Her nose was not petite, fit her face and went along with her medium mouth with full lips. She had not gone unnoticed at school but other than casual flirtation and even to the extent of heavy petting, nothing was serious. She had a boyfriend in high school, when hormones were flaring and she had gone as far as letting him put his fingers inside her and rub her vagina, and she stroked him, but that was it.

Her full firm figure attracted stares. . Her breasts stood out but were not out of proportion to her shoulders and long waist. She was 5 foot 8 and her legs were firm from running and tennis. She had tried basketball in high school but didn't really like it. She liked competition but stopped when it became violent. She had a small waist which gave her curves in all the right places.

They pulled into the driveway of a grey stone three story house and Valerie could see several lamps lit inside. There was a wide covered front porch across the front with stone steps leading up a porch. Marching stone pillars stood on either side of the steps at the corners of the porch. The driveway was shovelled by the caretaker and the path to the door had been cleared. Joel got out and opened the back door to get her suitcase. She jumped from the car dashing to the front door, which was already open with Sarah standing in it. She was beaming at her daughter. She stepped back a little to let Valerie inside. Once Valerie was inside, they threw their arms around each other. "Let me see you", Sarah said after they stopped hugging.

"Mom let me take off my coat first."

Joel came through the door with the suitcase and set it down in the hallway. He went back out and said, "I'm going to put the car in the garage before it starts snowing again." He went out the door and closed it behind him.

Valerie took off her coat, scarf, gloves and little grey beret. She put everything in a hall closet and turned to look at her mother again. Under her coat she was wearing a grey wool skirt, white long sleeve blouse and royal blue knit waist length jacket with an emblem on the left breast.

Sarah was wearing a full-length brown dress with a beige knit sweater over the dress. She had put on make up to give her face some color and deep red lipstick. Her eyes still sparkled and the joy never left her face. They hugged again. The sound of Joel coming in the back door and stamping his feet echoed through the house. Sarah had the locket on the outside of her dress as the sweater was only buttoned at the bottom.

Valerie stared at the locket and realized; she had never seen her mother without it. It had never occurred to her to ask, why her mother always wore it. They walked arm in arm into the living room. The room was spacious with a large window looking out to the front yard. There was a row of bushes on the outside of the porch which were barren this time of year. Valerie could see the brown branches against the snow on the ground. It looked dreary thinking more snow would come shortly. There was a fire going in the fireplace and above the mantle hung a portrait of Sarah done 15 years earlier.

The portrait was Joel's idea. As Valerie looked at it, she noticed the locket again. She asked Sarah as they sat down on the red velvet couch, "Why do you never take off the locket"? It came across as merely curiosity and nothing else.

Sarah smiled and said, I made a promise to my mother that I would never take it off." She made me promise at the very end of her life and I wanted to honor the promise and her memory." "I have never had the desire to take it off."

Just then Joel came into the room carrying a tray with a bottle of Champagne and three crystal champagne flutes. He was very careful setting the tray down on a side table. Both women smiled at him trying to give an imitation of a waiter. He said, "We need to celebrate you being here and all being together at the holidays." There was a menorah on the coffee table with 2 candles in it, signifying the start of Hanukkah.

The family had never been very religious, but followed some traditions from Joel's past. There were presents stacked on the left side of the fireplace. Joel unwrapped the foil and uncorked the bottle with a loud pop. Valerie said, "you would think I had been gone for ages." It really was only a few months, she had been away.

Joel was pouring the Champagne. The women were waiting for him to over pour and the wine run down on the tray. It did, but that was what the tray was for. He handed a glass to Sarah and Valerie and took one for himself. He raised the glass and said, 'here's to the beautiful women in my life." They all took a sip.

"Where is Mildred"? Valerie asked. Mildred had been with the family as housekeeper and maid for eons. Since Sarah had practiced law with Joel, Mildred had practically raised Valerie.

"She's in the kitchen, Joel said. She is making your favourite soufflé and turkey stuffing." ."

Valerie jumped up and ran into the kitchen and was immediately overwhelmed by the aroma of roasted turkey, onions, seasoning and cinnamon. Mildred a well rounded women with grey hair, bright brown eyes. As Valerie burst in, she threw down the large wooden serving spoon in her hand on the counter hugging Valerie in her short pudgy arms. She squeezed so hard Valerie felt like she would crush her lungs. Letting go and stepping back, she gave Valerie the all over look appraising her. Mildred said, "You are too skinny. They don't feed you at that school."

"Yes, they feed me at school, but not as good as you do." Mildred just smiled with the flattery and her plump cheeked, rosy face crinkled with a huge smile.

Mildred spun around and over her shoulder said, "go kibbitz with your parents, I have a dinner to finish, then will talk."

Valerie said, "can I help?"

As Mildred took the roasting pan out of the oven, she said, "no." Now go!.."

Valerie left walking back into the living room. Joel and Sarah were sitting on the couch talking about something.

They looked up as she entered and the conversation stopped. Whatever the conversation was, it appeared serious to Valerie.

Joel smiled and said, "Mildred said, you are too skinny, right?"

Valerie smirked and said, "How did you guess?" They all laughed as Valerie realized somethings never change.

Joel and Sarah stood up. "Let's finish the champagne in the dining room," Joel said. He picked up the bottle and followed Valerie and Sarah into the hall to the dining room. It was a short hall with an archway that opened into a formal dining room. There was a door on the far side that also entered the kitchen and Mildred came through carrying a large carving tray with a perfectly cooked turkey on it. Turkey legs were sticking up with white paper cuffs on the ends. The smell was mouth-watering and the aromas coming from the kitchen were permeating all the senses causing the stomach to grumble. The table was already set and Mildred placed the turkey on the corner next to the head. A large fork and carving knife were set next to the carving plate. There was a bowl of mashed potatoes with a golden glaze over the top. One of Mildred's tricks to grate gruyere cheese over the top and then put the bowl back in the oven till the cheese melts. The smell of the cheese was mixing with all the other smells in the room. Mildred came back out with a green bean casserole with "Frenches" fried onions on top. Then scurried back in the kitchen for a basket of warm croissants.

There were 4 place settings at the table, as was custom. Mildred ate with them at dinner. Joel handed Mildred a champagne flute already filled and said, "to the cook." They all looked at Mildred and sipped the wine.

Mildred smiled and said, 'something I just through together." They all laughed.

Joel started carving the turkey and Mildred, who was sitting next to Valerie on her left, took Valerie's plate and started putting mashed potatoes and green bean casserole on Valerie's plate.

Valerie knew she could never eat that much, but said thank you and smiled. Joel then put a slice of turkey on. There was rich brown gravy in a little tureen on the table and Valerie poured a little on top of the turkey.

Mildred started chatting as she filled her plate. "So, what is going on at school? Are there any cute boys? Did you meet someone? How are your classes and are you enjoying it?"

Valerie took a croissant from the basket and broke a piece off. "Let's see, that is about five questions. First, football season just ended and Yale did very well in the Ivy league. Next, there are lots of cute boys. No, I haven't met anyone particular. Classes are going well. And yes, I find school enjoyable and stimulating."

Sarah, who had been sitting watching the banter, said. Have you chosen any particular field of law to specialize in?" That caught Joel's attention too."

"Well, I've ruled out corporate. I find it the most boring and to become another grey suit on Wall Street doesn't interest me. Criminal law is interesting but defending people is really interesting but again, it is almost always a man's practice. Civil Law and human rights are something that intrigue me and I think there is going to be major changes in the structure of our country over the next few years."

"I agree with you", said Joel. "We are rapidly moving into a whole new world and it seems to be getting smaller or closer together all the time." Next thing you know we will have people in outer space or walking on the moon." He continued, "technology is advancing faster and faster and I don't know if it is all good for mankind. We have just finished the Second World War and unleashed the most destructive weapon known to man. We have won the Korean War and persisted into a Cold War with Russia. We may kill all ourselves one day."

Sarah spoke, "this is supposed to be a happy family diner, so cut the doomsday nonsense." She was irritated with Joel for preaching and it showed. Creases forming around her eyes and mouth a pallor rising from her neck to her face.

Joel said, "Sorry, I do get carried away." He reached over and patted Sarah's hand and she gazed at him and smiled.

Mildred piped in, "OK, on that cheery note I have your favourite desert. Apple crumble with ice cream."

"You are spoiling me," Valerie said. "I will go back to school the size of a blimp."

Mildred had already stood and started clearing dishes from the table, and heading for the kitchen. Valerie stood also and started to help clearing dishes. She noticed that a little color had come back to Sarah's face, but she still appeared pale to Valerie.

After desert with the dishes were all cleared; Joel, Sarah and Valerie headed back to the living room. Valerie could see the dark of night out the window and some snow flurries swirling around being pushed by the wind. The fire in the fireplace was blazing as Joel put another log on stirring the burning logs around a little. Valerie walked over and warmed her hands, then walked over and sat down in the armed chair next to the couch Sarah and Joel were sitting on. She had a feeling that they were hesitant to talk to her. It was like they were trying to pick the time to tell her something. The fire crackled and she could hear plates being stacked and pots being put away in the kitchen.

Joel stood up and said, "I'm going in the den to watch TV." Ed Sullivan should be coming on."

Valerie sat with her mother as Joel walked out of the room. "What is up? You are not telling me something."

Sarah looked in Valerie's eyes and took both of her hands. There was a tremble on Sarah's lips as she sighed and spoke. "I've been to the doctor," "He believes I have breast cancer. He is going to send me to a specialist next week." Sarah's voice was barely audible.

Valerie was shocked by the news. Her mind seemed to stop working and she searched for the right thing to say. Emotion overwhelmed her and tears filled her eyes. "Oh Mom,' was all that came out and she leaned forward hugging her mother. A sob escaped her lips and she tried to control herself. "I'm sure it's an error, she blurted and I'm going with you next week."

Sarah s putting up a good front, said, "you are probably right. Nothing is definite."

The next week, sitting in the Doctor's office waiting room, which like most waiting rooms, had cushioned chairs with padded backs and no arm rests. The walls were light grey with a few pictures of landscapes. There was a table in the corner with brochures and magazines on it. Mostly "Ladies Home Journals" and 'Time." The brochures were on breast self examination techniques. On the interior wall was a door, next to the door was a counter with a sliding window that the nurse or receptionist on the other side could open and talk to people.

Sarah was sitting in the middle between Joel and Valerie. Valerie was holding Sarah's hand and making idle chatter about school. Valerie was attempting to keep Sarah occupied and not thinking about the appointment. Joel was just staring into space as if in a trance. There were two other ladies in the room waiting on their appointments.

The door opened and women in all white uniform said, "Mrs. Binski" Sarah nodded and stood up. Valerie and Joel stood up also, but the nurse said, Only Mrs Binski at this time." You can come back after the examination." "It won't be long." She was a brunette with dark eyebrows, high cheekbones and a full mouth.

Sarah went through the door being held by the nurse and turned to the left.

Valerie turned and looked at Joel. He was almost in tears, the quiet man of few words, looked as though he was in pain.

Valerie could feel the fear in his heart and the the pain in her own. She decided on trying to distract him, while they both sat down.

"What about the plans to get a place in Florida and get out of the winters, up here?'

Joel looked at Valerie and smiled. She could tell he knew what she was trying to do. After a moment he said, 'We looked at some brochures for Sarasota and Venice, we've talked to several real estate agents." We also have looked into a place called Sanibel Island. We have been considering going down and looking around in another month. These winters are getting to the both of us, being able to get outdoors in sunshine would be great. We are not getting any younger and I'm ready for us to leave the firm and retire."

"That sounds great Dad, have you got anybody interested in the firm?" Valerie asked.

Joel answered," Benny has been with us for 15 years and so has Saul. Both have been doing the major work for the last 5 years and want a chance to own the practice. We have a good solid client base and Chicago is still growing. So, with a little help from us, they should be able to buy us out and takeover."

Valerie asked, "How many people in the office now?"

"Total of eleven, not counting Sarah and I." He responded.

The door opened and they both looked up. The nurse looked at them and said, "You can come back now"

They went through the door and turned left down a hallway to a moderate office with windows looking out toward the lake. There were bookshelves against the wall with built in cabinets below. They were all dark wood either oak or mahogany. In front was a matching desk, which was cluttered with papers, files and a gold "Cross" dual pen set in the front. The papers were on top of a green desk pad with black leather sides. There was a brown leather desk chair behind the desk and two chairs of the same color leather in front of the desk. There was a small wall on the side of the windows, which had a series of three diplomas hanging in a row.

Sarah walked in carrying the coat she had been wearing. Behind her was a tall man with reddish blonde hair cut medium and a square face. He wore glasses and his manner was a bit brisk or no nonsense.

Joel moved a chair that was in a corner closer to the desk as all sat down. Valerie was studying her mother's face and she seemed to have brightened up a bit. In fact there was visibly some relief on it.

"Hi, I'm doctor Sherman, "I assume you are Joel. Looking at Joel. And you are Valerie, looking at her. "Well," he said not wasting any time. "The good news is I don't think the lump is cancerous, but we cannot tell definitely until we take a sample." This is a simple procedure and we can do it here in the office on Monday. We will send it to the lab, they will test it to see if it is malignant." This normally takes two days." If the test is negative, we can remove the lump, probably a fibroid cyst and be done with it or leave it and you just go on with your lives." "However, if it turns out to be malignant, we will immediately have to talk about options." He was looking from one to the other to see our reactions.

Joel spoke up first. "How long does this procedure take on Monday and are there any side effects?"

Doctor Sherman calmly looked at Joel and said, "The procedure takes about a half hour, start to finish and if we use a local anaesthetic the side effects are a little minor discomfort."

Valerie was next and said, "Will there be any scarring?"

These were expected questions, "none normally, said the doctor, that are that noticeable."

That seemed to end the conversation for a moment and Sarah said, "Schedule it." She didn't wait to ask anyone else's opinion and seemed to be anxious to get out of the office.

"Alright "said Doctor Sherman and stood up. Let's go up to the reception desk and they will have all the forms and information you need,"

They all followed him up to the reception desk, which was really a counter with a young women behind it. Dr Sherman looked at the young women and said, "Ellen please schedule Mrs. Binski for a right mammary biopsy test on Monday. The woman looked about eighteen with plain features and mousey brown hair.

On the way home, Joel said, 'let's go out to dinner tonight. A little Italian food sounds good to me."

Sarah spirits seemed brighter and Valerie felt that some of the strain had been lifted.

A few hours later, Sarah and Valerie were sitting on the couch in the living room as Joel was in the den watching TV. Sarah was looking better Valerie decided, she was happy that she had come home from school. Sarah said, "do you want something to drink?"

Valerie just shook her head no. "I'll be here next week for you," she said.

Sarah was looking intently at her and said, "Don't you have to get back for classes?"

"No," Valerie replied, classes won't start till the end of next week after the holidays. I wouldn't go anyway, with you going in for the surgery."

Sarah frowned, "it's not much of a surgery, Joel will be with me. He can be a nuisance sometime, but he is very sweet. He'll be so tense; you could play him like a violin."

Valerie giggled, and said "He can get emotional at times."

Sarah was still smiling and gazing at her daughter. The corners of her mouth curled up as she said, "So tell me about the boys at school and your social life?" She added, "you know I'm not getting any younger.

Valerie could see the thought of grandchildren made her Mother happy. "She told Sarah, she would be the first to know when she had found the right man, and was ready for children." But you have to stick around to bug me about getting married and making you and Joel Grandparents."

Valerie could see Sarah's eyes twinkle and her mouth widen to a grin. Valerie thought now she is going to pry into my social life. I know it is coming.

Valerie wasn't sure she wanted to think about that. Having children is a big responsibility to those who really care and are ready to take on the burden. She didn't want to think about that yet. She wanted to get her law degree and make the world a better place.

Valerie knew she was being kidded and loved this time with her Mother not being serious. "Well most of the boys at school are self-indulgent, spoiled, narcissistic with small penises." They are either looking for some girl to get in the sack or reading playboy and masturbating."

Sarah, who knew when she was being toyed with simply said, "how do you know they have small penises?"

Valerie laughed and said good point counsellor. "Since I'm guessing, I will have to do further research and verify the assumption."

Mildred came into the room just then and with a funny look on her face said, "what about small penises?"

Sarah and Valerie were first startled and then laughed. Sarah said, "don't worry Mildred we were simply discussing the legal issues of male egos."

Mildred relaxed and said, I should have come in earlier to get more information."

They all laughed.

12

LACEY'S HERITAGE – 2017

A gazillion thoughts were going through Lacey's mind as she walked down the steps from the house. The night was dark without a light from the moon. Street lights were far apart and were not the strong halogen bulbs found in big cities in the US. Daniel had taken her hand as they walked down the steps and gazing down at her. Jeffrey had walked them to the door and said, "think about all of this, it is a big undertaking that might not be possible to prove."

Daniel broke the silence when he said, "He is right, you should give it some thought before heading into what might be impossible to prove."

"I'll give it some thought , Lacey said." They continued to walk across the street. They got to the front of the truck. The night was still, deep shadows were cast by infrequent street lights at the corners, with dim yellowish light coming from the bulbs.

As Lacey reached the passenger side front corner of the truck, two men came racing around the corner 30 yards away. They were both looking back over their shoulders and definitely running from something. They had on dark slacks and dark t-shirts. It was too dark to make out if there was any color to the material. They appeared afraid and didn't notice Lacey directly in front of them. The fellow on Lacey's right was carrying a gym bag with the" Nike" swoosh on it.

Lacey's training kicked in and all the time spent with the instructors was not wasted. She held up her hands and said "halt" The fellow next to the building on her left, dropped his hand reaching for his jacket pocket. . Lacey didn't wait to see what he was reaching for and launched a kick off her left leg and kicked him squarely in the balls. He gasped and went to his knees. Lacey was still moving, as her right leg dropped to the ground, she spun and put her left foot in the other fellow's solar plexus.

This sent him backwards and falling his head hit the heavy metal rear bumper of the truck. His head cracked and he was not going to wake up for a long time.

Lacey still in motion spun again and brought her elbow on the bridge of the nose of the fellow she had kicked in the balls. You could hear the cartilage in the nose crack and the man went face down on the sidewalk. About six inches from his right hand was a revolver. An inexpensive 38 short barrel which was good up close but no accuracy at any distance more than 10 feet. Lacey turned to Daniel and said, "call the police." The whole thing took place in seconds. Daniel was on the front side of the truck for all it, without a moment to react.

Daniel pulled his cell phone from his pocket and called. As he did this, two more men came running around the corner with what looked like a gun in one of their hands.

Again, Lacey reacted and grabbed the .38, dropped to one knee holding the gun in front of her. The fellows running saw her, stopped and one raised his arm with a gun in his hand.

Lacey fired a shot over their heads in warning. They both froze in their tracks, spun around and ran for the corner. This didn't last more than a minute and a half.

Jeffrey coming out the front door was shouting "what's going on?" Panic written all over his face as he jumped down the steps.

Daniel held up his hand to tell Joel to stay away. He shouted, "stay back over there for now" Daniel looked around the truck where Lacey was slowly rising and keeping a watchful eye on the corner.

Lacey stood and said to Daniel, "snatch and run drug deal gone bad." Don't touch anything, the police might get prints off something." They could hear sirens and blue flashing lights now as cop cars came around the corner on both sides. They boxed Daniel's truck in and came out. Lacey had put the gun on the sidewalk away from where the one man was laying. She and Daniel kept their hands up in the air to give notice they were empty. Jeffery was coming down the steps and crossing the street.

The doors of the cop cars opened and four officers got out Three of the officers had their guns drawn, but one walked over to Lacey and Daniel. Jeffrey stepped back a step to let the officer confront Daniel and lacey.

The officer was tall about 6' 2" with slightly greying hair and a cautious expression on his face. He had plain features that showed the years served and tension from seeing too much violence. His name tag read Fowler. He spoke articulately with an island accent" Someone explain what happened and why two men are lying on the sidewalk injured?"

Lacey gave him a quick explanation of what occurred and about the two other men that ran off. The other officers were standing over the men on the sidewalk.

The Sargent grabbed a handheld radio from his belt. Pressing the mic key, he said, "Fowler at Staneslaw Gade in need of ambulance." He released the key.

A voice came over the radio and said, "ambulance in route, about 5 minutes.

Fowler turned and looked at the 3 officers and said, "you had better cuff the two on the ground and put gloves on." The officers started putting on latex gloves and cuffing the two men, who were coming around and moaning in pain. The man, who had hit his head on the trucks rear bumper had stopped bleeding but the other with the busted nose still had blood running down his face. They could hear the ambulance siren as it approached.

Fowler turned and looked at Lacy and said, so you fired this gun, pointing to the revolver on the ground into the air to scare two other men that came around the corner?"

Lacey knew what was coming and got ready for the lecture about discharging firearms in a public place. "That is correct," she said. The adrenaline had dissipated and she was calm and relaxed and spoke in a calm manner.

Fowler still concentrating on her face said, "did you look in the bag?'

Lacey said, "no, we did not want to contaminate the evidence."

Fowler's expression changed and a wary look came into his eyes. "You sound like you have dealt with crime scenes and criminals before." It was a question disguised as a statement and he was now studying her reactions carefully.

"Ex FBI, and yes to answer your question, I have." Lacey replied.

Fowler's eyes now had a look of thought so he started looking at Jeffrey, who he obviously recognized and then at Daniel. Then his eyes shifted to the duffel bag still sitting on the side walk.

In the meantime, the paramedics had come over from the ambulance that arrived and were examining the two men on the ground cuffed. They had put cotton in the man's nose and had him sitting up. His hands were cuffed in front and he was holding his groin.

The other fellow was being place on a gurney and they were taking him to the ambulance.

Fowler put on latex gloves and said, "Let's take a look in the bag." They were all expecting drugs, probably marijuana, or cocaine.

Fowler with two fingers picked up the bag and rested it on the hood of the truck. He carefully opened the zipper wide enough to see inside. It was full of little plastic bags of powder that appeared dark inside the bags. You could see little crystals inside the plastic bags inside the duffel that sparkled as light hit them. Fowler took out one little bag and opened it and touched the crystals with his index finger tip. He smelled the fingertip and then touched it with his tongue.

Daniel, who was watching said, cocaine?"

Nope said Fowler. "Probably heroin, would be my guess." After being in the service for many years, his guess was probably correct. He zipped the bag and motioned for the other police officers to come over and said, "put this in the trunk of my car along with the revolver, which had been placed in an evidence bag. He handed the bag to the fellow with only two fingers holding the strap and the other officer followed the example in carrying the duffel bag.

Fowler then turned to Jeffrey and said, "you have been quiet this evening counsellor."

Jeffrey nodded and with a smile said, "just observing our finest doing their work."

Lacey thought these two had known each other for some time. Both were actually enjoying themselves and some kind of court room casual animosity going.

Fowler's expression changed back to business as he spoke, "did you witness any of what was going on and do you have anything to add to the description of the events?"

"I was in the house for most of it and only came out after hearing the gunshot." "I can vouch for the fact that Daniel is my wife's cousin and this is his friend Lacey Lockhart."

Fowler then turned and faced Daniel and Lacey. Daniel was now standing with his arm around Lacey's shoulder. She thought it was a protective measure and liked the feeling that someone was trying to be protective.

Fowler continued, "you'll both have to come down to the station and give statements." "Since, Jeffrey here knows you,

I'll let you either follow us back to the station or ride in the back of our cars and then bring you back." Which would you prefer?"

Daniel said quickly, "we'll follow you over. It's getting late."

Jeffrey turned and saw Jane and the kids standing on the porch. They were all gawking at the goings on. He waived at them turned back to Daniel and said, "I will talk to you tomorrow." Then turned to Lacey smiled and said, "thanks for a fun evening, if you need any help Daniel has my cell number."

Lacey smiled back and said, "anything to provide a little excitement in our lives."

Daniel went around the truck and opened the passenger door for her. She got in and he closed it before heading to the driver's side. He opened the door and got in. Sargent Fowler got into his car and started the engine and turned off the overhead flashing lights. He pulled forward and Daniel pulled out to follow him. The other police car stayed where it was as the other two officers waited for the Crime Scene Investigation unit.

Trying to break the silence Daniel said, "remind me never to let you get really angry with me."

Lacey was deep in thought about what might happen at the police station. She turned her head as he spoke and said, 'just don't break the law and you'll be fine or do anything to piss me off, of course." She smiled. Her mind had flashed back to the night she had shot the boy and the guilt was still there and probably would never go away.

The Sargent's police car turned left into a parking lot and parked in the first row. Daniel found a spot in the next row back that wasn't marked for police vehicles and parked. They got out and looked at a cement and glass eight story building, with the ocean fifty yards away with a street in between.

The Sargent was waiting next to his car as the deputy got the duffel bag and evidence bag with the gun out of the trunk. Fowler turned to the deputy and said, "take those down to the crime lab and have them confirm what is in the little bags."

Lacey, Daniel, and Sargent Fowler all walked across the parking lot and Fowler opened a large glass tinted silver door for them to enter the lobby. The Lobby had a reception desk with a metal detector archway on the right side. There was a deputy, who straightened up when he saw Fowler and another Deputy inside the archway. They both had come to attention when they spotted Fowler. Lacey sensed that Fowler ran a tight ship, but the deputies did not appear afraid meaning they thought he was a fair man.

Fowler smiled at the thirty something fellow behind the desk and said, How is the baby, George?"

George relaxed a little and said, "doin fine." Fowler stood at the desk as Lacey and Daniel signed in. They then went to one side of the chained barrier and the other guard came over and pulled the metal stand aside.

Fowler just said, "they're with me and they all walked through. Marble floors and a bank of two elevators were in front of them. It was quiet at this time of night. No one standing in the halls. Fowler walked over and pushed the up button. The door slid open and they stepped into a stainless steel box with a handrail halfway up from the floor around the sides. Fowler then pushed the five button and stood waiting while the elevator went up with a bell dinging with every floor passed with a lit panel above the door signifying the floor number as they passed.

The doors opened into a room with linoleum floors and fluorescent overhead lights. There was a counter to the right with a woman in uniform behind it. She was short and large with only the slightest indication where her neck stopped and her face began. She had short black hair that looked dyed. She had small squinting eyes and when she saw Fowler, you could tell there was no love lost. They almost showed open hostility over a wide nose and mouth. Fowler just nodded and kept walking with Lacey and Daniel following.

The room seemed to be like every other police station room with rows of desks on the left, mostly empty. Two desks had people who were working keyboards on desktop computers. They were in street clothes and Lacey thought they may be detectives. The scene was right out of every police detective movie on TV. On the right were three glassed in offices with names on the doors. First door said "Conference", second said, "Sargent", and the third which was larger said Captain. There was a grey haired man sitting inside studying papers on his desk. He looked in his fifties and wore glasses with dark frames. He had a squarish face with a pinched nose and small mouth.

Fowler stopped about halfway back in the center aisle and said, "wait here." He then weaved through the desks and went to the "Captain's office and knocked, then entered.

Lacey and Daniel could see him talking to the Captain however could not hear the conversation. . They saw Fowler answer his cell phone and converse briefly with someone on the other end. He then went back to talking with the Captain. Fowlers face stayed neutral but at times the Captain got animated. Another cell phone conversation by Fowler and more discussion with the Captain. Lacey was thinking they probably were going to give her trouble for firing a gun and lecturer her on safety. She just wanted to leave, and think about the fact that her Great Grandmother lived here and what it really meant.

Finally, the Captain stood and both Fowler and the Captain came out the door. Lacey was trying to read facial expressions as they came over. Flower introduced Captain Stimson to both of them and they shook hands.

Captain Stimson had a smile on his face at the introduction, which relieved some of the doubt that Lacey had been feeling. Her shoulders relaxed a little and she said, "nice to meet you Captain."

Fowler commented, "I was right it was heroin in the bags." The two men you stopped had records and were known low level drug dealers. It will be good to have them off the streets." We will need you to write out a short statement of what happened and then you'll be free to go. You can use any of the empty desks and I'll bring over the forms."

Captain Stimson looked directly into Lacey's eyes and said, "Before you go, please stop by my office to say goodbye."

Lacey and Daniel both said "We will" almost simultaneously. Lacey thought she saw a little lechery in the Captains' eyes. She thought, no big deal just another dirty old man.

Fowler led them over to two empty desks and they sat down. Fowler then brought over some blank forms and pens. He paused for a moment and said, "details are good but don't overstate or embellish. Attorney's will try and read something into this when they are at the trial. You will probably be called as witnesses, if they don't cut a deal. "I'll be over in my office, so just come over when you are done." "And thank you again for all your help."

Lacey thought about this evening and felt tired from all that happened. She glanced at Daniel and he read her expression and said, "let's get this done and get some rest." We are both beat."

Lacey smiled at him and said, "good plan."

They finished quickly and went over to Fowler's office. Daniel rapped lightly on the door and opened it without waiting. Fowler was at his desk typing on a computer key board. He looked up and smiled. They handed him the statements.

He said, 'thanks again." They were tired and just nodded and backed out the door.

Lacey turned and walked to the Captain's door. She knocked lightly and stuck her head in. "We are about ready to leave."

The Captain looked up from what he was doing when she knocked. He said, "I know it's late and you have got to be tired, but if you have some time in the next few days, I would love to talk to you about your future." I know we could have a place for someone like you and want to discuss possibilities." "Here is my card, give me a call, when you get a chance."

Lacey took the card, saying, 'thank you and I will call in the next few days." She backed out the door and turned and started walking toward Daniel, who was waiting in the aisle.

As she approached Daniel said, 'what was that about?"

Lacey now felt bone weary and just said, 'job offer," as they walked out the door and across to the elevators. They rode down the elevator in silence, with her just leaning against him. It was now after two in the morning. She thought in the novels the heroes could go three days with no sleep, be fresh and ready to go. That was not her. They both dragged across the parking lot to the truck, Daniel opened the door for her.

She got in and watched as he came around and got in. He started the truck and they headed up the hill to the Villa.

The next morning when she woke, she remembered falling asleep on his chest and that was it.

There was a note on the bed as usual, "Have to work and you look like an angel when you are sleeping. Love D"

She glanced at the clock; it was 8:15AM. She got up and went to the bathroom to get ready for the day. Her elbow was a little sore from breaking the guys nose last night.

She showered and got dressed. Shorts and t-shirt were good for today. She had to open the villa and make sure it was ready for guests that were to arrive in two days.

About noon she thought about the will and decided to give her pal Tony Marconi a call. He worked in the lab for the FBI doing DNA analyzation. She looked up the number in the contacts of her cell phone tapping the call icon.

"Marconi," a man's voice said.

"Is this the bureau for fractured intelligence?' Lacey joked.

"Well I'll be", Tony said. "Lacey, how the hell are you and are you enjoying retirement?"

"Tony, I'm fine and not retired yet." She responded. It was good to hear his cheerful banter and the kidding that went along with it. She pictured the dark complexion and dancing brown eyes with a bushy moustache, that went along with the personality. Actually, Tony was a well-respected lab rat that had matched the DNA of some very dangerous criminals. "So how are the wife and kids?"

"They are a pain in the ass, as usual but they are staying out of jail for now." This was the typical response when Lacey asked about his family, although he was a devoted family man. "Did you call because you wanted to have that affair with me?" Tony asked

"No, I haven't sunk that low yet, but if I do, I'll let you know."

"You know flattery will get you almost anything, so why did you call?"

"Got a couple of questions for you about your favourite subject." And no, it's not about sex." Have you got a moment?" I can call back at a better time if your busy."

"I'm fine right now, what's up?"

"Well, if you had a DNA sample from a person from about 250 years ago, could you link it to someone living today?" And without waiting for a reply she continued, "and how accurate would it be?"

He didn't even pause to respond, "first, we could definitely tie the two persons together." As to accuracy it would depend on the samples that we would have to deal with." Bone samples and hair follicles would be really needed or skin even better. But after 250 years, skin is usually hard to come by." Who are you planning on digging up?"

He was joking again, but Lacey felt a presence inside her that said, "learn more." "Ton, it's my Great Great Grandfather, I think and it's a long story, but if I got you the samples and I gave you mine, could you match them up?"

"You are going to owe me big time, but if you got the samples up here, I could see what they say." He liked to talk as if he were speaking to the DNA itself. But give me the short story now, just in case, I have to explain the sampling to someone."

Lacey paused and said, it has to do with a will my great great grandfather left after some nasty business about who should have title to some property"

"Whoa, you gonna be rich?"

"No, she replied, but if I become rich, you'll be on my Christmas list."

"Fair enough," he said, "and I gotta go. Send it to me and I'll give it a shot."

"Thanks Ton, you're a dear." She heard the line disconnect. She thought, even if I can prove I'm his Great Great, Grand Daughter. I would also have to prove that Elsa was his daughter and she was my Great Grandmother and down the whole line. This is going to take more than just one test. She was thinking Tony was going to have a fit. She really did over simplify the fact to him. But first I have to find the graves. She was excited and felt that something inside her was pushing her. . The locket got warm again. She had a feeling in her heart that all was as it should be. I'll call Jeffrey and get some more advice. This is not a straightforward thing that you could just prove with one test. I better call Daniel and see what would be a good time to call Jeffrey. The day was warm and there were only little white wisps of clouds up high. She was standing on the deck next to the pool and could see the little island down below. She felt a chill all of sudden and the voice from inside said, "you have to fight for what is right." Goosebumps rose on her arms and she looked around to see if anyone was there. Not seeing anyone she pushed it aside and went back to getting everything in order for the guests.

13

ONE MORE EXCHANGE – 1900'S

Valerie had finished exams and only had to finish a bar review course before sitting for the Bar. She was eager and felt confident that this was going to happen. She would be a lawyer and would go to work for the ACLU. Although they had not offered her a position yet, but a Professor at school said he knew some of the administration with them and could put in a good word.

She had signed up for a law review course in Chicago, so she could be at home and see her parents before everything moved on. She had just enough time to finish packing, say some goodbyes and get to the airport. There was a spring in her step and she felt like the world was her oyster. Sort of Barbara Streisand in "Funny Girl" nobody is going to rain on her parade. She leapt up two steps at a time to her 2nd floor apartment opened the door and bounced in. Her luggage was on the bed, she threw in a few last items and pushed the suitcase shut. There were two black bags with fabric sides and a carry on satchel in red and black. She put a hairbrush from on top of her dresser into the carryon and called a cab. She got one suitcase out the bedroom door and through the living room to the front door and went back for the rest. It was spring and her mother didn't have cancer and all was rosy. She lugged the next suitcase to the front door and grabbed the carryon and her black leather purse looked around and left. She never got attached to the apartment but it had served its purpose while in law school.

She saw a cab pull up in front and honk. Grabbing one suitcase and the carry on went down the stairs to the front door and opened it. She set down the suitcase on the landing with her carryon and waited as the cab driver got out to open the trunk. He was an older fellow with white hair and about a day's growth of white stubble on his chin. He walked with a slight limp. He moved fairly quickly as came up, picked up the suitcase and carryon. Valerie said, I'll be back in a second with another bag."

She spun around, ran up the steps to the other suitcase picking it up. Took one last look at her apartment door and thought about the next chapter in her life. She turned around, went down the stairs and handed the suitcase to the cabby. He took the suitcase by the handle, carried it over and put it in the trunk.

She walked over, opened the rear door of the cab and got in. Valerie thought, he must be a shy man because he had not looked her in the eye. He came around to the driver's side and got in. He looked into the rear view mirror and said, "Where to Miss?"

She noticed the tired eyes and bland expression of someone who had been ground down by life. "The train station, please." She thought, he must have driven students to the train station over the years. Just passing the time until the end.

He put his flicker on, checked the outside rear view mirror, pulled onto the street and headed for the corner.

He said, "You must have just finished classes and heading for home." "Where is home?" He was trying to make polite conversation, not really caring.

"Chicago", she replied. "And yes, classes are all over and I've graduated." She was watching the trees outside, not really seeing anything.

Ain't you going to the Commencement ceremony? "He asked.

"No, the speaker Manning is a socialist, I would rather be with friends in Chicago," she replied. "My parents are a little disappointed, but it really isn't that big of a deal to them. She had a half hour before the train took her to the Boston Airport to catch the flight to Chicago. She had plenty of time to think about the future on the flight. She would have about an hour and half before boarding at the airport and plenty of time to grab a meal.

Later, she was standing at the luggage conveyor at O'Hare when her father walked up. He was grinning ear to ear and his eyes were joyful at seeing her. "How is my new lawyer?" He said as he put his arms around her and kissed her cheek.

"Doing just fine, now that I am seeing you." She thought his hair was getting thinner and there were bags forming below his eyes. The wrinkles at the corners of his eyes and mouth had increased. But his bright spirit always showed through and his half full personality never wilted. He at times could be stern with her, but never angry.

The luggage was coming down the conveyor belt and she stepped forward to lift the first one off. A pushy man tried to nudge her out of the way to get his bag and she pushed back and said, "excuse me." The fellow gave her a dirty look and she thought the ugly Americans are all around. He turned his back to her after grunting and said something in a foreign language to a stocky woman standing a few feet back. Valerie ignored him, lifted her suitcase off the conveyor, over the rubber and metal edge. Joel came up on the other side taking it from her.

"What have you got in here bricks?" He joked.

"No," she said. "Just some law books." He rolled his eyes.

The next suitcase came and she reached out grabbing the handle. This one was just as heavy, so she took two hands setting it next to the other. "You should get a cart; we don't want to lug these to the parking lot."

Joel just signaled to a valet, the man brought over a two wheeler and folded down the front platform.

"Just these two and the carryon." Joel said. The man just nodded and stacked the two suitcases on the carrier putting the carryon on top. They started heading to a bank of elevators that would take them to the parking level. The valet was right behind them.

Joel pushed the down button and the doors immediately opened with a bunch of people inside all waiting to exit. They waited as the group exited the elevator. You could tell the ones with manners as they held back and didn't try to push their way out first. Just as the last person was trying to exit a heavy set woman went in front of the older man trying to get off and bumped him aside to get on. She didn't apologize or even look at him. Great to be back in a big city Valerie thought. They let the fellow off and held the door so the valet with the luggage could get on first and then Valerie and Joel entered. Three other people got on and it was crowded inside. Valerie was crammed next to the fat woman and could smell the sweet perfume and sweat coming off the women's body. The doors closed and Valerie tried to hold her breath till they reached the parking garage level. Thank heaven it was the first stop and Joel held the door as the valet and Valerie got off. Valerie let out her breath and breathed in.

They followed Joel as he walked past the rows of cars and white numbered parking stalls. Joel was now driving a new Ford Bronco which was dark blue with a white roof and outside step to help people get in. Joel opened the rear window and pulled down the tailgate. The valet put the luggage in and Joel paid him the valet said, "thank you" and turned and left.

Joel closed the tailgate and closed the rear window. He came around and unlocked the passenger door with a key. She looked at him and said, "so this is your car now?"

Joel smiled as he answered, "Boys and their toys." He walked around and got in the driver's seat. "I wanted something less sophisticated, when we are down in Florida."

Well you found it; she was thinking. She had to use the sidestep to get up to the seat, because it was so far off the ground. This didn't fit, because Joel would never be accused of being a redneck or an outdoors man. "What does mother think about the car?"

"At first, she was a little skeptical, but now she rather likes sitting up higher and getting out on the lake." "Ask her yourself when we get home."

This was all news to Valerie, who grew up with a mother that likes to shop in downtown Chicago and out to dinner in fine restaurants. She didn't go camping and Valerie had never seen her in anything but high heeled shoes and nice clothes. She didn't think her mother owned a pair of jeans. She was wondering if this is some sort of late life crises for both her parents. They pulled into the driveway, Sarah was waiting on the porch, wearing grey slacks, a white cotton blouse with an aqua crew neck sweater over the blouse. She was wearing a pair of dark blue pumps with three inch heels. Valerie thought, yeh right, going out on the lake. She jumped out of the car and ran around and hugged her mother.

Sarah grabbed Valerie by the shoulders and said, "I'm so proud of you? Tell me all about graduation? "

Valerie looked at the grey haired lady in front of her thinking she was looking older. Deeper wrinkles seemed to be creasing her face. Time takes its toll on everyone. "Skipped all the parties and hoopla. A few friends went out to dinner and it was sad, because we were all heading different directions. I do have some news for you and Dad, but it can wait."

"Let me get the luggage into the house and get freshened up." "Then you can tell me all about your new lifestyle."

Sarah still smiling said, "So you like the new car." It was a statement not a question.

Mildred was coming down the steps now, with arms extended wide and Valerie turned to take the bear hug. She was nearly knocked off her feet. She was squished between large arms and big round breasts. Mildred's round face had a broad smile but tears were running down her cheeks from joy. Mildred squealed, "oh it's so good to have you back."

Valerie had to catch her breath from the hug and said, "it's good to be home."

Meanwhile, Joel had already gotten the luggage to the front porch and was putting one bag inside in the hall.

The three ladies with arms intertwined walked up the stairs to the porch and some shade. Mildred grabbed the last suitcase and carryon as Joel held the door for her. Mildred seemed not to have to struggle with them. She was used to moving heavy things around.

They all went in the house and the screen door closed behind them. It was now about 5:00 in the afternoon and Valerie noticed that the dining room table was set for 8 people. "Somebody coming for dinner?" She asked.

Sarah said, "Well, we thought it would be nice to have Sybil and Anna over." They have been calling and wanted to see you as soon as you got home." You'll have a couple of hours to get ready."

Sybil and Anna had been Valerie's best friends growing up and through high school. They had gone to college in Illinois and stuck close to home. Sybil wanted to be a writer and was hoping for a job with a newspaper, Anna had her mind set to go into business with her father in real estate. They had been wonderful friends but did not have her passion or better yet obsession with civil rights. Sybil had a passion for the opposite sex, which she didn't mind flaunting at times.

Mildred said, "let me help get these up to your room" and lifted both suitcases as if they were light and headed up stairs.

Valerie picked up the carryon and followed her up. She said over her shoulder, "I'll be back down in about an hour." "Then we can talk." Joel and Sarah stood at the base of the stairs and watched as their daughter went up to her room

Joel turned to Sarah and said, "do you want to tell her before dinner or after?

Sarah was still.

Sarah looked into Joel's face and tried to interpret his thoughts. His eyes as usual were bright and showed that he was trying to think of the plans needed not to cause stress to their daughter. With Sybil and Anna coming over they might know from their parents and blurt it out without knowing or thinking Valerie already knew. We should probably tell her before they get here.

"I agree," said Joel. "After she comes down, we can sit in the living room and talk." I'm going to take Sasha for a walk. She is bored in the backyard and it will give me time to think."

Sasha was a 40 lb brindle golden retriever about seven years old. She was a slight female with the forever golden smile and the little dome of knowledge at the top of her head. They kept her coat trimmed down in the summer to keep her cooler, but she shed on everything anyway. She loved to chase squirrels and they loved to run up a fence or tree and taunt her.

Joel went into the kitchen to get the retractable leash and open the backdoor for the dog. You could hear the prancing of paws on the tile floor and the excitement being exuded from every muscle available. Joel clipped on the leash and took a firm grip on the plastic leash holder with his thumb pressed firmly on the lock position. His slacks already had dog hairs on them from her brushing against him. He walked her to the front door and said, "Sasha sit." The voice was firm but not loud and the dog, who adored him sat looking up waiting. He opened the screen door with his left hand and said, "OK"

The dog immediately walked out the door knowing she would have to wait before Joel would release the lock on the leash. "Good girl" he said with pride at her behaviour. They walked down the stone steps across to the driveway and down to the sidewalk. The sun was out and there was only a slight breeze. He released the lock on the leash handle, immediately Sasha started sniffing at the base of the trees that lined the street, checking for messages of who or what's been there.

It was about 4:30 when Valerie came down the stairs, wearing jeans, white tennis shoes, no socks and a light blue button-down cotton shirt not tucked in. Her dark hair was pulled back in a ponytail and with a little eye makeup and lipstick. She looked young and vibrant and full of life.

"Joel had come back from the walk. "We are in here," Sarah said from the living room. Mildred was in the kitchen getting dinner prepared.

"Would you like some wine" Joel asked.

"No thanks, but a coke sounds good." Valerie responded. Let me go get one and I'll be right back." She went through the dining room to the kitchen.

Joel and Sarah were sitting on the couch with the picture window behind them. Joel had a drink in a short tumbler with ice and a dark brown liquid, probably scotch on the coffee table in front of him. Sarah had a glass of white wine in front of her on the coffee table.

Valerie burst through the kitchen door and came through the dining room and plopped down in a stuffed chair on the side of the couch. She had a glass with ice and coke with a can containing the remainder of the "Coke." "So, what's up?" She asked. She could tell that by their expressions they had news for her. She knew them so well, that she could tell they were going to give her some news. She also could tell that because they did not have serious distraught looks in their eyes, the news was not bad.

Sarah spoke first, "your father and I are moving to Florida."

"Great," Valerie exclaimed. When and where, are you keeping the house here and is Mildred going with you, what about Sasha?" "Wait, you're throwing me out."

"Of course not Joel said, we will always have a room for you." "Don't be silly." Both Joel and Sarah were smiling, because they thought Valerie would be upset losing the home, she grew up in.

Valerie continued, "You've been talking about this for some time, getting out of the cold and slush, sounds like a great plan."

Joel spoke up, "last time we were down in Florida we found a place we really liked on the Gulf side called Tarpon Springs." It's just above St Petersburg It has a subdivision called Pointe Alexis with tennis courts, swimming pool and club house. It is out on a peninsula and quiet. There are bike paths, walking trails and the place we found looks out to the Gulf of Mexico with spectacular sunsets." "There is the Anclote River nearby, where we could keep a boat and a golf course.

"Whoa, again," Valerie said. When did this thing with boats get started?."

Sarah spoke up, "We have been taking sailing lessons for the last month and a half." We found we really love the freedom of the water." Although after the lessons, we feel we our leaning more to power boating." We could have a small boat on a trailer or have a slip right there in Tarpon Springs. You'll love it. It's like a little Greek Village."

Valerie's brain was churning. "Sounds great, what is the timing of all of this?"

"Well, Joel said. We have an offer on the house in Florida, contingent on us selling this house." We have an offer on this house and the real estate agent is making sure the buyers will qualify, before we accept. "We thought about you sitting for the bar and didn't want to disrupt your review class. So, we told the buyers that we will not close for three months after you sit for the bar. Then if everything goes well, we will move down in the end of September." There are a lot of ifs in there." "What do you think?"

"What I think is go for it." The whole plan sounds wonderful, you have worked so hard your whole lives, why not enjoy." The place sounds great and "thank you for not throwing me out until I pass the bar." "Assuming I pass the bar."

Sarah shook her head and said," You will dear."

Mothers always take a positive approach to good things happening, Valerie thought. She could tell they were both relieved that they had shared the information. They had not wanted to disturb her during finals and not really shared a lot with her. "Well", she said. "I have news to share with you too." "And, coincidently it ties right into your plans." After sitting for the bar, I have been accepted into an internship program with the ACLU to become a staff attorney in Washington, D.C." This will be great; you can move to Florida and I can move to Washington D.C." She was watching their faces and Sarah's was lit up, while Joel's was not happy and she knew why. She knew this discussion was coming and was prepared for it. In 1978 the ACLU took a very controversial stand for free speech by defending a Nazi group that wanted to March through the Chicago suburb of Skokie, where many Holocaust survivors lived. Although, Joel was Jewish by heritage and was a strong Zionist, they never really practiced the religion. They had gone to Seders at her Grandparent's home and every once in a while, had attended Bar or Bat Mitzvahs, but they didn't practice the religion. They had many discussions about religion growing up and her parents were more concerned that she learns the philosophy behind the religions. But Joel had dislike for anything dealing with Nazi's as he had an Uncle who was a survivor of Auschwitz.

"Why the ACLU?" He asked. There are so many other organizations that promote and defend our civil rights and social justice. Why them?

"It is because they appear to have an unwavering commitment to principle even though it goes against our strongest dislikes of human behaviour. You're the one who says, "I might not agree with what you're saying, but I will fight for your right to say it." She was throwing his own words back at him.

Sometimes, when others are being hurt even by words, it is necessary to set principles aside and respect the feelings of all. They were tramping on the emotions and feelings of people, who had suffered so much. Allowing this march was an insult to every fibre of my being and to fight for the principles of these vermin, this is where you have to draw the line. You also heard me quote, "the only way for evil to prosper is for good men to do nothing."

Valerie quickly saw that no one was going to win this battle and Sarah was starting to get agitated. Valerie changed tactics by saying, they do a lot more than just freedom of speech. They fought for women's rights and upholding Roe Vs Wade. They continue to fight for the woman's right to decide for herself. You believe that women should have the right to privacy. She knew he was a strong believer in women's rights and even a stronger fighter for equality of genders.

Sarah finally spoke, "enough you both have good points, but in the end, we want Valerie to do what she feels is right." We will discuss logistics later and now we can celebrate her graduation."

Joel smiled and said, "I agree, I can see she got the fire and brains from her mother, and of course the good looks from me."

They all laughed and each raised their glasses and clinked them together. At that point, there was talking outside and Sybil and Anna were at the screen door. Squeals of "Val" coming from their mouths. Joel just shook his head and took a long drink. Valerie ran for the door. Sarah sat back grinning.

It was now September and Sarah was finishing the packing for Florida as Valerie was finishing the packing for Washington. Sarah wondered how they had accumulated all this stuff half of which they never used. She had given a small truck load of things to Goodwill and still had five cartons left to go. They made the deal with two of the Attorney's in their practice to buy them out. The closing on the house in Chicago was a matter of just signing forms and shaking hands. She looked around and thought she would miss this place. They had an attorney represent them at the closing in Florida and that was completed. Joel would be back in a half hour from getting the car prepared for the trip. He stopped by AAA to get a 'Trip Tick" that had detailed maps of their route, books with accommodations and restaurants along the way. There was a blue highlighted line on the maps, so you would not miss the roads and detailed driving instructions all in a little booklet that you only needed to flip the pages that were in order to follow the entire trip. Standing in the now barren living room, she heard Valerie coming down the stairs lugging what must have been a very heavy suitcase that was bulging from being over packed.

Mildred was in the kitchen doing something. She had elected not to move to Florida She was going to stay near her relatives and grandkids. She had bought a little apartment with the severance gift Joel and Sarah gave her. After all these years, she was more like family than anything else. There were promises that she would visit Florida often.

Valerie dropped the suitcase on floor in the halll with a loud thud. "Moving is the pits," she said to Sarah. "Where is Dad?" she asked.

"He is out finishing getting the car ready and running errands." He will be back in a little while." Sarah replied. The movers had worked all morning loading a semi truck full of furniture they were taking to the house in Florida. It had taken them about two hours to complete. They would meet Joel and Sarah in Tarpon Springs in three days at their new home.

Sitting at the curb in front of the house was an almost new 1979 shiny red Mustang GT convertible. It had a white roof with a black interior and 5.0 liter v-8 engine. It was the newer style with the angled hood and 4 rectangle headlights. It was Valerie's present for graduating and passing the Bar. She loved it and new this was her first real step to being independent. She was about to pick up the suitcase beginning the struggle getting down the steps to the car, when Sarah said, "leave it there for a moment and come talk to me."

Valerie walked into the living room and looked in her Mother's sombre face. She knew they would not be seeing each other for several months, but she wasn't moving out of the country. She had promised both Joel and Sarah that as soon as she got her first break from the internship, she would fly down to Florida and spend a few days. From her mother's expression, she could see that she was trying to construct what she wanted to say. All Valerie could think of to say was, "Mom, I love you. "

Sarah shifted her shoulders back and said "I love you too." There is something I want to give you but it comes with a commitment from you." You have got to give me a promise and keep it."

Valerie tried to lighten the moment by saying, if this is about grandchildren and you're not getting any younger, I'm not making any promises." She had a smirk on her face.

Sarah smiled, no it's not about grandchildren." But now that you brought it up." Sarah was chuckling now. Valerie kept the smirk, because she got her mother to laugh. Sarah was wearing jeans and a violet silk blouse with an open collar and mother of pearl buttons down the front. She had a long slim neck that started to show some sagging that comes with age. On her chest was the gold locket that Valerie could never remember her without.

Valerie said, "So, what is this all about?"

Sarah face turned sombre again, "I'm going to pass on to you something that has been in the family since your Great Grandmother. It's this locket. But with it you have to promise me that, you will always wear it and never lose it." "Also, you will pass it along to your next heir." "I made this promise to my mother when she gave it to me, she said, "It contains the souls of our family."

Valerie's face was no longer smiling. She could see that her mother was serious and that it meant a great deal to her. The room had taken on a strange feeling, a slight chill came over her and the hair on her arms seemed to be moving. All she could think of to say was, "I promise." She could feel how important this was to her mother and felt the weight of a lifetime responsibility being passed on.

Sarah turned her back to Valerie and over her shoulder said, "unclasp the chain and I'll help you put it on."

Valerie reached up and unclasped the chain and lifted the locket over Sarah's head. Then she handed it to Sarah and turned around.

Sarah placed the chain and locket over Valerie's head and reattached the clasp. Valerie thought a moment earlier to make a smart remark like, "is there now a secret handshake. But she could feel something running through her body and the air in the room stood very still. Goosebumps ran up her arms and her mind had gone blank. As if in a trance, she turned and faced Sarah. "I'll keep my promise," she said solemnly and kissed her mother's cheek.

Sarah just smiled and hugged Valerie.

Joel came leaping up the steps and opened the screen door. He was a new man, with a rakish smile and bounce in his step. He had a white plastic bag with the AAA logo on it. He said, "this is for you and it details your trip to Washington." Your first stop is in Cleveland, stay with my cousin Michael." Next you can drive down the turnpike to Mechanicsburg, PA and stay with Arnie. Then the next day, you'll have an easy drive to Alexandria, VA to your apartment ." "This way you get to see the relatives and never have to stay by yourself."

Dad, I'm not a little girl and I have had my own apartment for two years," Valerie said.

"I know," he replied. "But it makes me feel better." "You can never be to careful" "Now let me put your bag in the car, so you can get going and not drive in the dark." He had spun around and was already heading to the suitcase in the hall. He grabbed the handle and lifted it very slowly."

Sarah said, "Don't hurt your back."

Valerie said, "leave it I'll get it."

His face was a little red, he was now lifting with two hands and heading for the screen door. In a huffing sort of voice, he said, "no problem I'll be right back." As he leaned to one side and pushed the screen door open with his shoulder. He stepped on the porch and struggled with the suitcase one step at a time. He was now huffing and puffing from the exertion and hobbled across the lawn to the car. He set the suitcase down and caught his breath and then with two hands and a heave, he got the suitcase resting on the trunk deck letting the suitcase flop into the trunk. He rested by leaning on the cars fender getting his breath back.

14

GETTING THE FACTS - 2017

Lacey scheduled a meeting with Jeffrey and wanted Daniel to be there at 6 o'clock.

Daniel had to finish work as a cruise ship was leaving at 4:00 PM. She had gotten the guests situated in the Villa and given the introductory tour, even though they had been there before. They were a group of 8 that were from the Midwest and appeared to just want to lounge around the pool.

She dressed in nice khaki shorts, aqua pullover blouse and sandals. As usual she d made a pitcher of pina coladas for their arrival and set out some assorted munchies.

She told them that she would be gone for a couple hours and they could reach her by phone, if they needed anything. She grabbed the car keys and went up to the driveway. It was a little tricky getting out. She had to back up to where their rental car was sitting and then swing up the rest of the drive to the street. After doing it several times, it was not a problem. She drove down to Jeffrey's office and parked in a lot on the corner. She walked back entering the building on the second floor. She went in the door marked in white block letters "Jeffrey Logan and Associates LLC, Attorneys at Law." The reception area had a desk over to one side with a receptionist. There was a window on the right side wall which lit the whole room. There were padded armchairs around the rest of the walls, a coffee table in the corner with magazines on it.

She walked over to the receptionist sitting behind the desk. A woman in her 40's with mousey brown hair and a protruding lower lip, she had been organizing some papers and looked up as Lacey spoke. "Lacey Lockhart to see Jeffrey Logan."

The receptionist said, "one moment please, picked up the handset and buzzed someone. She held the phone to her ear and said, "a Ms. Lockhart for you." She hung up the phone and looked up at Lacey. "It is the office at the end of the hall, just go through that door." She pointed to the door on her left.

Lacey said, "thank you," she crossed the room and opened the door. Inside was a hallway painted light grey with offices on both sides, further down an opened door revealed a conference room with a mahogany table and ten chairs all matching mahogany. There was a matching bookshelf at the far end with a center shelf holding a TV screen about 50 inches and some recording equipment with a phone below. There was a speaker phone unit in the center of the table.

Lacey continued down the hall to a mahogany door which she opened with a large brass handle. Sitting behind a large oak executive desk was Jeffrey. Blue shirt, red and black tie, horned rimmed glasses perched on his nose. There were two matching oak armchairs in front of his desk, which was covered with folders, papers and a wooden two story file basket on one side. There was an onyx dual pen set on the front edge with two Montblanc pens in gold holders and a plate in the middle that said Jeffrey Logan in script.

"Hi Lacey," Jeffrey said, with a genuine smile, he stood to shake her hand. Behind Jeffrey was a window looking southeast. The view was blocked by a building and a hill with more buildings. On either side of the window were shelves and credenzas. The shelves were filled with law books and pictures. Most of the pictures were Jane and the kids.

She shook his hand and said, "Hi Jeffrey, thanks for seeing me."

"No problem. But Daniel called and said he would be a few minutes late." He also grumbled about "cruise boat assholes." "So, what are your thoughts and what do you want to do?"

Lacey thought for a moment and then said," I've spoken to friends in the FBI and they can run the DNA tests needed." They believe that if we can give them proper samples that they can show proof up to 99.9% that I am a direct descendent of my Great, Great Grandfather. However, I was thinking, that might not be adequate to have the property titled to me. If contested, the current owner may say that I have no link to being his closest living heir and the only way to do that is to link me to my Great Grandmother, Elsa" "His daughter."

At that moment the door opened and Daniel walked in looking harried. He was slightly out of breath and his hair was windblown. He was wearing what looked like a uniform with dark blue pants, light blue shirt with epaulets and a name tag over the left pocket. He was wearing black shoes with rubber soles. He smiled when he saw Lacey and said, "what did I miss."

"Not much, Jeffrey replied. "Sit down, can I get either of you something?"

Lacey said, "Water would be great."

Daniel plopped in the other chair in front of the desk and said, "a beer would be great but I will settle for a Coke.

Jeffrey reached for the phone and picked up the receiver and held it to his ear. He hit a button. "Cindy", he said "can you bring us a glass of ice water and two Cokes?" Thank you." He hung up.

Daniel was now calming down and relaxed in the chair. Lacey continued, I believe I can get a DNA sample from my Great Grandmother and that should tie back to the closest living relative.

Jeffrey said, "does this mean you are going to exhume your Great Great Grandfather's body?"

There was a light rap on the door and Cindy entered with a wooden tray with two cans of Coke and a glass of ice water. She set the tray on the side of Jeffrey's desk and headed back to the door without a word. Jeffrey said, "thanks Cin" and she left.

"I don't see any other way to get the sample. My Great Grandmother donated her organs to medicine and there may be tissue samples at the hospital in Chicago. "Lacey replied.

Jeffrey put his two index fingers on his lower lip and said, "this still may not be enough to convince a Judge. I just want you to understand that you may be going to a lot of expense without a positive outcome monetarily.

Lacey immediately replied," this isn't about the money. It has to do with putting a family back together, that has a missing piece torn from its history." For some reason, which I do not fully understand, putting this property back with the rightful owners is important."

"Well then, I would use your influence with the police and get the body exhumed and the samples needed." Then have them tested and get back to me." I'll look into the necessary legal petition to have the court award the title of the property to you." "Also dig up anything you may have in your family especially documents that link you back to your Great Grandmother."

He paused as if going through his mind to see if he missed something. "Oh!", Jane had wanted both of you to come over on Saturday night to celebrate Lizzy's graduation from first grade with honors. She even got a citation, which we'll have to put in a picture frame and hang in her room.

He had the look of a proud father on his face, even though he was trying unsuccessfully to hide it, Lacey thought. Daniel looked at Lacey to see if there was an indication, if she would accept or reject the offer. She smiled and said, "that sounds wonderful, if Daniel doesn't mind risking his life again."

Daniel smiled and said," I will get a hold of full body armor and an AK-47 by then and warn the police we are in the vicinity. "You better warn the neighbors that they should stay away from their windows, too."

Lacey was smiling also and replied, "that's what I like a big strong man to protect me. "

"Alright you two," Jeffrey cut in. "Save the cute remarks till when you're alone." "I've got work to do and I don't see any billable hours coming out of this."

Daniel said, "Do you know when it is really cold around an attorney?"

Jeffrey blurted, "you two out, I don't want to hear any bad attorney jokes or I will start billing you both."

Daniel and Lacey stood and Lacey said, "Thank you, Jeffrey."

Daniel said, "see you Saturday night." Then they both turned and walked to the door and opened it. Lacey looked back and Jeffrey was already studying some documents on his desk. He had been jotting notes as they were talking and now pushed the legal notepad aside.

Once outside Daniel closed the door and said, "Sorry for being late."

"Not a problem, we were just getting started." She was thinking about the meeting and who to approach about exhuming the body. Would she need a court order? Who should be contacted to start the process? Bingo, she thought time to talk to the police Captain, Who seemed to want to get on Lacey's good side.

Daniel's voice cut into her thoughts. "Want to grab a beer and pizza?"

"That sounds great." "I'll follow you." They entered the reception room and smiled and thanked Cindy for the drinks again. She just smiled.

Daniel took her hand as they walked down the hall to the stairs. Daniel held the door open for her as she exited. Where are you parked?" She asked.

"Down in the lot." How about you?" He asked.

"Same," she said. The sun was below the horizon and the colors of sundown near the ocean were an amazing multitude of blues, greys, pinks, oranges, purples and a touch of white on the corners of clouds. The air smelled of the sea and salt. A breeze was coming from behind them and taking the heat of the day off of the buildings and sidewalks.

(Later on Saturday night)

Saturday night and they had parked the truck in the exact same spot as they had the last time. Daniel got out and came around to open Lacey's door, but she had already opened it and was getting out. She was looking up and down the street from force of habit.

Daniel closed the door which made the creaking sound of metal rubbing against metal.

He said, "looks like the coast is clear ."

She smiled and said, "you're safe till the door opens and then you'll be attacked," She was anticipating seeing the kids again. They crossed the street and went up the steps. Daniel pressed the buzzer and waited for the attack. They could hear footsteps running across the hallway floor with a heavier footstep walking behind. Jane opened the door and four arms and two, giggling heads smacked into Daniel's legs and waist. There was a simultaneous loud screech "Daniel."

Jane was smiling and looked down at Lacey. "Nice to see you Lacey," Jane said. "I see you're still hanging around with my brother."

"Hi," Lacey said. "He has some good points to him." She was laughing with Jane as Daniel gave a phoney disapproval.

"Do you treat all guests this badly?' Daniel said

"Oh no, Jane replied. "Only brothers with big ears and funny faces."

Lacey carried a box wrapped with bright silver paper and a purple bow. There was a smaller package with silver wrapping and a little stick-on bow in blue on top of the box she was holding. "What's that?' Lizzy inquired.

"It's a present for someone, who did very well in school. Lacey answered.

Lizzy's eyes grew wide and gleamed. A big smile spread across her face and she reached for the box.

Jane's hand quickly caught Lizzy's shoulder before she lunged for the box. "We will wait till after dinner to open presents." Jane said.

Lizzy lowered her arms but was still staring at the box. However, Phillip had a hurt expression on his face feeling like he was left out.

Lacey noticed the look of a five-year-old, who was clearly not happy about the situation. The other item is a little something for Phillip, because I know he has been a very good boy."

Jane said, "very diplomatic." She looked at Daniel, who was smiling approvingly at Lacey. At least one of you had the forethought to bring presents."

"These are from both of us," Lacey said. "Daniel helped pick them out." She was covering up for him again, he just didn't hang around kids that much, she thought. However, he seemed to enjoy playing with them.

"Right," Jane said looking directly at Daniel. He was just beaming with a huge grin on his face. Jane continued, "your lucky someone has your back, dweeb."

Daniel gave his sister a snarky grin. Phillip was now punching Daniel in the stomach and pulling on him. "Ok, let's go into the living room," Jane said. Jeff will be down in a minute. He is just cleaning up after having a hard day at the golf course."

Sayia was in the dining room getting everything set for diner. Lacey again felt that there was something very familiar about her and was aware that the locket had a warm glow about it. Lacey just couldn't get over that feeling everytime

Sayia was around. Jeffrey came down the stairs smiling. "you made it on time again. I guess we have Lacey to thank for that."

Daniel looked up and said, "what is this, pick on Daniel night?"

Jeffrey gave Jane a quick look. She was smirking. "My wife has been picking on you again" "Sorry, I will stay out of the rivalry."

"No problem," Jane said. Daniel is such an easy target." They all moved into the living room with Phillip now in Daniel's arms and Lizzy pulling at his shirt.

After dinner, they all went into the living room and Lizzy got to open her presents. She tore into the silver wrapping paper of Lacey's and Daniel's present and opened the box. There were three colouring books a huge package of washable crayons in every color and a little note that said. "Congratulations for graduating First grade. Love Daniel and Lacey." Lizzy was squealing with delight.

Jane immediately said, "what do you say?'

Lizzy ran over to Lacey, who was sitting on the couch, and said, "thank you." She gave Lacey a hug and a kiss.

Lacey felt the unconditional love that comes from a child and was glad she got the crayons. She said, "thank you, but they are from your Uncle also. "

Lizzy's eyes shifted to Daniel and her faced brightened even further and actually looked like she was flirting. "Thank you," she said, with a coquettish grin and fluttering her eyelashes.

Phillip had opened his toy Spiderman figure and was busy playing with it.

Lacey was feeling the effects of two glasses of wine with dinner and felt totally relaxed. She was looking at Sayia and had the strange feeling she wanted to hug her. This is getting weird she thought. Maybe I'm drunker than I thought.

Daniel and Jeffrey were sitting in the chairs enjoying a Balvenie 12-year-old, double barrelled, single malt scotch. Neat, of course, in crystal glasses. Daniel watched Phillip pretend Spiderman was swinging behind Jeffrey's chair, when he noticed the stack of leather bound log books which his Great Grandfather, the Captain, always kept. He was feeling the buzz from the scotch, but stood up and said to Jane. "Aren't those Great Grandpa's old log books?"

"Yes, they are." Why?" She asked.

"Because there might be something in them about Lacey's Great Grandmother and what happened to her." He walked over to the shelf they were all stacked on. There were at least ten. All leather bound with a leather strap through the front to keep them closed. He opened the first one and looked at the date and closed it. He looked at the dates in the one six down and closed it. He picked up the ninth one and started thumbing through the pages. About midway through he stopped and started reading.

> *"When I came down for my morning meal, I was confronted by a small girl and a servant not much older. They relayed a story of the young girls' parents being murdered the night before and only due to the other girls' efforts did she escape to our servant Tina's home. They had come to our house on the following morning for refuge and seeking shelter. I went to the Governor's House and found that indeed the young girl's family had all been murdered in the night and there was no evidence, who had done it. The little girl's name was Elsa Gufsterson and I was acquainted with her father, Heinrick Gufsterson. The servant girl was named Letisha and her aunt Tina was our housekeeper.*
>
> *Not wanting to put the girl in any form of danger, I did not mention that she was at our home to anyone except my wife, Dorta. As of this day in the year of our Lord January 7, 1779.*

Daniel looked up and said to everyone, "this details how your Great Grandmother disappeared after the murders."

Jeffrey spoke, "that could definitely be used as a key piece of evidence."

Sayia spoke up, "there were stories in my family, that my Great Grandmother had rescued a little girl and that is why, your great Grandfather, the Captain, gave my Great Grandmother Letisha such a large sum in his will. There is a commemorative brass plate at the restaurant in his honor."

"Wait," Daniel said. "Your Great Grandmother is the person who started Letisha's Latitudes?"

"Yes," was Sayia's only reply.

Jeffrey said, "Well I think we should get a family discount. They all looked at him and started laughing. Anyway, we are certainly building evidence for Lacey's case." How long before they can go after the body?"

"It was not easy, but Captain Stimson pulled some strings and spoke to the judge that it may have reference to a criminal case." So, it should happen next Thursday at about three in the afternoon." Lacey said. Then it will take another 2 weeks to get the samples to the lab and the results back."

Daniel spoke, he was still reading the Log book. "This even has when your Great Grandmother was put on a boat to go live with the Vanderbeck's in Charles Town, South Carolina."

"You mean Charleston, don't you" Jeffrey interrupted.

Nope back then the War for Independence was still going on and it was called Charles Town."

Jane looked at Lacey and said, "This is getting really exciting." A real murder mystery." "Time for two little ones to go to bed"

"I'll help," Jeffrey said.

Lacey had moved over to Daniel and was looking at the Log with him, along with Sayia. They were all engrossed in the pages. Lacey put her arm around Sayia's waist. She could feel the locket glowing again and the warm breeze was blowing in a still room. Lacey raised her eyes and could see apparitions that looked like her murdered family and Letisha and

Aunt Tina standing there with the little girl standing in front, all grinning. She closed her eyes and took a deep breath. She felt stirrings of emotions with an intense desire to be able to hold and hug them. It was almost blissful. Was she really being able to get in touch with another world apart from reality? Was this real or was she just imagining. She shuddered and said to herself, this is not a dream.

15

WASHINGTON, DC – 1900'S

Valerie was sitting at her desk at the Trone Center for Justice and Equality. She was working with four others all crowded around. Each reading a draft of the challenge to an Arkansas statute requiring that the biblical story of creation be taught as a "scientific alternative" to Darwin's theory of evolution. It was 56 years after the Scopes trial, and yet the fight was still being fought.

The year was 1981 and she was feeling upbeat and looking forward to winning in Arkansas. The day had started out dull and grey, but the sun had burned off the fog that came off the Potomac and although the leaves hadn't started on the trees yet, the stark side of winter was subdued by the sunlight. "Let's break for lunch and get back to reviewing in an hour," she said. The rest of the group seemed happy to have a break from the eye strain that came from reading legal text for hours. She was the type of person, who kept to herself most of the time. She had dated a few times in Washington, but nothing that really sparked her interests. She walked over to a little deli and got a hot pastrami with coleslaw and thousand island dressing on rye. They had stacked the pastrami two inches thick, as usual. She had taken the paper cup they had given her to the drink counter and put the cup under the ice slot and pressed down on the silver bar to release ice cubes for just a second. If you hold it too long, you have ice flying all over the place. She then placed the cup under the water tab and pressed the tab down. The cup immediately filled up and she let the tab up. Carrying the sandwich and cup over to a little table next to the window, she sat down. She unwrapped the sandwich from its white paper and picked up half of it to take a bite. Biting down she had the juice from the coleslaw start to run down her chin. She reached over and grabbed a napkin from the metal napkin holder and wiped her chin before the juice could get to her blouse. The blending of flavours was delicious but her cheek was puffed out from the bite like a chipmunk with a mouth full of nuts. She looked out the window and walking in her direction was a Naval officer in a white hat and long dark blue coat. He was talking to another fellow in a grey suit. Both weren't very tall about 5 foot 8 inches. They had reached the door to the Deli and the man in the suit pulled it open, the sailor walked in and headed for the order counter. The deli was typical with about a 3 foot counter top and a long glass case to pick out meats, cheeses, bowls with potato salad, egg salad, three bean salad, and various others. There was a blackboard behind the counter with the menu and prices on it in white chalk and the daily special in orange chalk with various designs around it to show it off. There was a cash register setting on the counter and a heavy-set young girl of about college age with mousey brown hair and tired eyes standing behind it. They both ordered something and she placed two paper cups on the counter. The sailor paid and got his change, handed one cup to the fellow with the grey suit and walked down to wait for their food. In a matter of minutes two white paper wrapped sandwiches were slapped on top of the window case and they each picked one up and walked off to the drink dispenser. All this time Valerie was watching the sailor's movements. He walked with an easy gait that was not arrogant but as if he was sure of himself. She thought he had the Cary Grant look, solid but full of fun. He filled his cup with lemonade, when he looked up and saw her looking at him. She averted her eyes immediately and stared down at her sandwich. How embarrassing to be caught staring at someone, she thought as her cheeks flushed a little. She looked up, they had gotten a table a little further back in the deli and the sailor was sitting with his back to her. He had unbuttoned his coat and taken off his hat. She noticed he had sandy brown hair cut neatly and smoothed on the sides. She hadn't seen the color of his eyes yet but she liked the profile. He was talking to the grey suit, but then turned and looked her way. There were many conversations in the deli, but nobody was paying attention to others talking and eating in the deli. She took a drink from her cup and was aware by the little tingling of what had entered her stomach.

He got up and walked over to her table and looking down with beautiful grey eyes said, "Hi can I be forward and ask, where you're from?"

She was now really turning pink and thought I will be a smartass and get rid of him. Looking into his eyes said, "why heaven of course."

He didn't even pause with his response, "I knew you were an angel"

She thought at least he is quick, but corny." I'll bet you say that to all the girls." Was her reply. She could see he was not fat, had broad shoulders, long fingers, he was not handsome but not unattractive. She was enjoying this and she was assessing his manners and his grey eyes, all seemed to pass her inspection. All the damn pheromones were acting up again, she thought.

"Now that we have that out of the way," my name is Joshua Lockhart, but my friends call me Josh." He said.

"Nice to meet you Josh," She replied. "My name is Valerie Binski and my friends call me Val." "I'm a lawyer at the

ACLU." Why did I add that she thought? He is probably one of those individuals that dislikes lawyers. She was watching his face and did like the smile and the no nonsense approach.

"I don't want to seem forward, but with the slight bit of dressing on the side of your mouth, would you like to have dinner with me sometime?" He said.

Valerie was caught off guard and grabbed her napkin and wiped the sides of her mouth. Slightly flustered, trying to act like it was no big deal, she said. "Well, I suppose I could do that, as long as I can have food on my face."

He chuckled, and said, "I can arrange for the dinner but the food on the face is totally up to you. What day would be good for you?"

His friend had come up behind his shoulder and tugged at his sleeve, then said, "I hate to break this up, but we need to get back to the briefing"

His friend was shifting from foot to foot and either had to go to the bathroom or really wanted to go, she thought. "How about Friday night?" She said. I'll give you my card, give me a call, with the time and place." She was thinking this was all fast, but dinner can't cause any problems and if he turns out to be a real dork, I can always leave. She reached down and from her purse she took out one of her cards and handed it to him.

"Sorry," Josh said. "This is my brother Ben." I will call you later this afternoon," he said over his shoulder as they headed for the door. Ben was already opening the door for Josh and looked like he really was in a hurry. They turned right and walked at a fast pace down the sidewalk.

She glanced at her watch and realized, she had to get back too. It would not look good for the leader to be late. I really find him appealing and interesting she thought. She wrapped the rest of her sandwich in the white paper and carried her cup to the trash container and dropped it in through the hole in the top. She turned and opened the door and felt the cold air and sunshine hit her face. She headed back to the Trone Center with a spring in her step and a smile on her face. This will be fun, she thought and a distraction of worrying about making the world a better place.

Later that afternoon, the meeting had broken up and she had reported to the lead counsel on the case, when her phone rang. She answered "Valerie Binski"

"Hi, it's Josh from the deli." The familiar voice said." "Am I interrupting anything?"

"Nope," she replied. "So, are you fully briefed? " I am fully briefed and debriefed as we speak." Did you save my civil liberties this afternoon?"

"Only the civil ones." She replied. She could hear him laugh. At least he has a sense of humor. He had a strong, but not too deep voice and she was remembering the face and the serious eyes that sparkled when he looked at her. It wasn't leering but she could see how the look could be interpreted as such.

"Would you like to go out to dinner tonight and do you like Mexican food?" Josh asked.

She asked. She paused for an instance and replied, "Yes I like Mexican food." What time did you have in mind?"

"Well, how does 7 sound to you?" He responded.

Valerie was thinking, get to her apartment, shower, change, the traffic around Washington can be bad. "Let's say 7:30 and I will meet you in front of my apartment." That way she didn't have to invite him up, if he turned out to be a total jerk or some kind of crackpot.

"Great," Josh said. "Now all I need is an address?" He asked."1410 Mercer in Georgetown, and I will meet you out front." She said a little too quickly. She realized that she was portraying that she didn't trust him.

"Good," he said. "Play it safe, I may be a serial killer." He was playing with her and she knew it.

"I'll see you at 7:30 and now some of us have to get back to work." "Bye," she hung up. His voice stayed in her memory and she ran over the conversation in her mind to see if any red flags popped up. None that she was aware of. She did realize that she was a little anxious to leave and checked the clock on the wall. Two and half hours and she would see him again. Settle down girl, she thought. You only met him today.

7:30 and she was out in front of her apartment with a dark red coat with large grey buttons and large lapels. The night was chilly to downright cold. She had a white wool scarf around her neck to keep the cold out. She was wearing black short boots with small heels. A slight breeze was making it even chillier. There were a few clouds, the moon was partially covered by them, but she could see some stars twinkling down on her. A dark blue, four door sedan turned the corner, it had "Dept. of the Navy" in white letters painted on the door. It stopped in front of her and Josh jumped out and ran around the front end to open her door. He was right on time, she thought. She liked punctuality. He had the dark blue Navy overcoat on, but no hat this time. He was grinning but it was more like a warm smile, his eyes were bright and clear and he radiated happiness.

"Hi, hope you weren't waiting long." It is cold tonight." He said as he helped her into the car Without waiting for a reply ran back around the front of the car and got in behind the wheel.

"Hi, yourself and where are we off to?" She had looked around the dark interior as she had got in. She thought, government issue and not high up on the car pool chain. He was putting the car in gear and checking the rear view mirror as they pulled out. The heater was on, so the car was warm inside, it had the no nonsense interior of a government car with a VHF radio microphone mounted on the dash.

"I was thinking "Los Amigos Grill" over in Alexandria. It is my favourite Tex-Mex place with killer margaritas. "Does that sound good to you?" He asked.

"Sounds great, "she replied. "So, what do you do in the Navy to get a set of wheels like this?" She was watching his face as he concentrated on the road. He had a good jawline and high cheekbones. Eyes were clear and focused with a glint of mischief coming out in just a small smile at the corners of his mouth. She couldn't see his teeth at the moment, but he had a dazzling smile earlier in the day. She found him more than interesting and realized that she was attracted to him.

"I'm with NCIS and I do investigations for the Navy." He glanced over quickly to see, if there was any reaction on her part. Some people have strange reactions to law enforcement, he thought. She didn't show any reaction at all and was gazing at him as he drove. He thought that she was beautiful and as the street lights flashed on her long neck, face and dark hair, it took his breath away. He went back to focusing on the road ahead with an image imprinted on his mind of her face. He had to keep his mind on the driving, he thought. "I'm basically a cop for the Navy. "

"Well, am I under investigation, right now?" She kidded. Now there was almost a leer on his face.

"No, not at the present time, but you never know about the future." He was smiling with a small laugh now. They turned around a corner and he parked in front of a patio with a short fence around it. There was a red tiled roofed building behind it. Bright lights and busy waiters hustling around. There were 8 tables on the patio with closed umbrellas coming out of the center. There were silver space heaters about seven feet tall with the orange glows coming from the wires inside. Josh put the car in park, turned off the engine and got out to come around and open her door. His movements were quick but balanced and he had a confident stride. He opened her door and held out his hand to help her out. She took his hand as she got out and he closed the door.

She liked the way her hand felt in his. It was a caring feeling without being aggressive. His hand was dry and strong as they walked toward the door to the restaurant. There were three groups of four people sitting at tables with the heaters nearby to take away the cold night.

"Inside or outside?" He said as he reached for the door.

She thought for a moment and said, "inside for me on a night like this." There was a small waiting area and a second set of wood doors with glass panels. There were dark red Spanish tiles on the floor. They approached the reception desk, which was dark wood with painted blue tiles on the top. A young woman was behind the counter with a white low cut no collared blouse with puffy short sleeves at the shoulder. She had large, dark brown eyes and straight black hair. She had large rounded breasts and when she spoke, she had a slight Spanish accent. "May I help you?" She asked and flashed a big smile at Josh.

Valerie immediately thought, she was flirting. She realized he was not even noticing the attempt.

"Could we have a booth for two," he replied.

The hostess picked up two menus and came around the counter. "Please follow me," she said. They headed into the restaurant to a row of booths and the hostess placed the menus on the table. "Your waiter will be with you shortly," she said and left still giving Josh, a come-on smile.

"Thank you," Josh said as they sat down. He was gazing into Valerie's face and asked, "So tell me about your family?"

Valerie was gazing back at him. She thought standard questions for the first date. But he seems genuinely interested. His expression was calm, relaxed, the eyes were deep and thoughtful. Not a person to rush or do rash things. "Not much to tell, both parents were lawyers and had a practice in Chicago. Mostly business litigation and some domestic work." The firm was small with a staff of eleven." They worked side by side for a lot of years."

A waiter showed up and introduced himself as Miguel, and asked, "would you like something to drink?" He was looking at Valerie.

"I heard you have great margaritas, so I'll have one. She replied.

"I'll have one too, and two glasses of water also, thank you" Josh said. He looked down at the menu, which was really a book with 4 or 5 pages with pictures of plates of the food in glossy colors. He closed it almost immediately. He had seen it before and obviously knew what he wanted.

Valerie was studying the menu and asked, "what are you having?"

"My usual, the two-chicken enchilada dinner which comes with refried beans and salad." "I think everything is good here, so you can't go wrong."

Still looking at the menu, she said. "I think I'll have the smothered burrito with pork green chili, guacamole and sour cream." "It looks like a lot of food, but I can take part of it home for lunch." He gave her a warm smile and his eyes lit up. "What?" She said. "Did I say something funny."

"No, he said immediately. "I was happy to hear you are not one of those women, who orders just a salad, to try and impress their date."

Miguel showed up carrying a tray with two margaritas in large glasses and two glasses of ice water. He set them down in front of them and put the tray under his arm and took an order pad from his apron, which had a pen stuck in it. Have you decided what you would like for dinner or would you like more time?" There was no accent when he spoke as he was born and raised in the US.

"I think we are ready," Josh said and looked at Valerie for approval and for her to go ahead. He wanted to let her order herself and not try to order for her.

"I would like the smothered burrito with green chili," She said without hesitation.

"That comes with refried beans and a salad." Miguel said. Confirming she wanted the dinner and not the burrito alone.

"That's fine." She said. Miguel was making notes on the order pad and smiling politely. He turned and looked at Josh.

"I'll have the two-chicken enchilada dinner."

Miguel asked, "Would you like red or green chili?"

Green please." Josh replied. Miguel made some more notes on the pad, spun on his heels and left.

Josh turned back looking at Valerie and said. "So, your parents had a successful law practice and you got a law degree. Why did you go for the ACLU?"

Valerie's expression turned serious and she was calculating her response to give him insight into her beliefs and values. "I believe that the work of defending freedom and civil liberties never ends." She said. My parents fought for victims on an individual basis one at a time. I wanted to expand the fight for many by protecting our citizens from arbitrary government actions." "I may be somewhat of an idealist but I feel strongly about it." She stopped for a second and thought this is getting into a serious note.

Josh had been watching her intently and noticed the sudden change. He tried to lighten the conversation by saying. "I only go after one criminal at a time usually." "I better up my game." He was smiling as he said it.

Valerie took a savouring taste of her margarita and relaxed a little. "I get passionate on some subjects; it all depends on the subject" She said.

He was about to say, I hope I'm one of those subjects, but decided that would seem pushy and thoughtless. He could think it just the same. He was studying her full lips and thinking it would be wonderful to kiss them. He said, "so, what is your favourite hobby?"

Knowing that he was trying to change the subject and keep it light made her smile. He was obviously nervous, but kept that cute smile on his face and boyish twinkle in his eyes. She felt a warm feeling in her chest and for some unfathomable reason, she thought that the locket was humming or vibrating. She had kept her promise to her mother and never lost it and wore it faithfully. She took another drink of her margarita and noticed that she had drained the drink. She was relaxed by the alcohol but not intoxicated. "My parents played golf and I have tried both golf and tennis." "But I don't consider them hobbies." What about you?" She asked as she studied his face.

"Love golf." He said. I can watch it on the TV and play it whenever I can." Would you like to play sometime?"

"Maybe." Was a careful response, because she did not want to embarrass herself on the course.

Josh noticing the concern said. "We can go to a driving range first and see how you do."

Miguel showed up carrying a tray with plates of food and set it on the empty booth next to them. Then he placed the plates in front of them. "Would you like another margarita?" He asked.

Josh looked at Valerie and she nodded a yes. Josh said, "Yes, thank you."

She took a knife and fork and cut into the burrito. Then put a portion in her mouth. The tase of the green pork chili, tortilla and ground beef with spices was delicious. "This is wonderful." She exclaimed, after swallowing what was in her mouth. "You were right about great Mexican food."

Miguel showed up with the two margaritas. "Is there anything else, I can get you?" He said.

Josh looked at Valerie to see if she wanted something. He wiped his mouth with the cloth napkin and said. "Nope, this is great." He took a sip of the new margarita and looked at her.

She was digging into the refried beans and rice. At least, She wasn't a picky eater, who just took little bites and pushed the food around on her plate. He thought this is a woman I could love. He went back to his enchiladas and cut off a piece with his fork

They kept the conversation casual until after the meal with talk about favourite movies and music. Josh paid the check with a credit card and they walked outside. As they reached the car, he opened her door and then suddenly pulled her to him by the shoulders and kissed her tenderly, but with passion. She returned the kiss and they stood together in a warm embrace for several seconds. He finally backed up a little still holding her and in a husky breathless voice said. "I have wanted to do that since I picked you up."

She was holding his waist and looking up into his eyes. She was also trying to catch her breath and could still feel his lips on hers. She pulled him closer and kissed him back and they stayed in the embrace for several more seconds. She could feel his body through his coat and his hands wrapped around her body as her hands held the back of his neck. Their lips pressing against each other and not breathing. A couple came out of the restaurant and the fellow said. "Get a room."

They finally separated and laughed. "It's a good thing you waited till after dinner to do that, or we would have never gotten through the meal." She said. They were both flushed and watching each other, not wanting to move. He took her hand and squeezed it lightly. She slid into the car seat and he closed the door without taking his eyes off of her. Words are not needed to understand the love and passion that was radiating from them both. For love truly is a fire and you have to be careful not to get burned. Her heart was pounding like a jackhammer and she could hear it in her ears.

He was around the driver's side and slid into the driver seat and started the car. "I really dislike using clichés, but your place or mine." Josh said.

"I like a man who gets right to the point" She said. She was grinning from ear to ear and her voice was a little throaty from the previous kissing. "I've got an early meeting tomorrow, so let's go to mine." "You can come up and we can discuss, whatever comes up"

"Sounds great," He replied as he looked at her. He wasn't sure whether or not she had meant all the innuendos, but he thought she was the most beautiful women in the world at this point in time. He looked in the rear view mirror checking traffic and pulled out and was caught up in an over whelming desire to just touch her, but he kept his hands on the wheel.

She reached over and touched the back of his neck. "You seem to be speeding a little, so don't rush the night is young." We don't want to spend it in jail."

"Jail is definitely not the place I want to spend the night." He said smiling. He could feel the eagerness in his voice and he didn't want to come on to strong. Trying to cool the conversation, but not break the moment. Like most men, their rather intimidated and unskilled at the things to say about mutual affection. At least, that's what he thought.

She was watching his flushed face and realized, that he can be cavalier and even debonair at times, right now he was in a whole new ballgame for him. It was more of a turn on than a turn off for her and she enjoyed seeing him working mentally on what to do. She realized that she was falling for this man in a way she never had felt before. There was almost a hunger to stop the car and make love to him right there. They reached her apartment and with luck found a parking spot a couple of cars down from the door. He parked easily backing into the space and pulling slightly forward. He turned off the ignition and turned and kissed her quickly on the lips. Then jumped out and ran around opened her door.

She swung her legs out and stood in front of him and looked up and kissed him deeply. She couldn't tell if it was hot or cold out. She had her arms inside his top coat and pressed against him. She could tell it was having effects on him even through the outer clothes he had on. As he pressed his body into hers, they both moaned slightly. They had to stop and breathe and she looked up and down the sidewalk to see if anybody was watching. It was empty. She took his hand and led him to the front door of the apartment house, while fumbling for her keys with the other hand. She managed to get the door open as they almost fell in the entry way, while kissing again. It was a long narrow hall with brown worn carpeted stairs on the right. The walls were a light tan and there were overhead lights every so many feet. They stumbled up the stairs still kissing and embracing. They reached the 2nd floor landing and slid down the hall with his back pressed against the wall by her body. Her coat was open and he could feel the firm breasts pressing against him. They reached her door and then she fumbled with the keys trying to get the right one. It seemed like eternity, but she had it and opened the door.

    Both were panting as they entered the apartment as one. She was pulling off his coat and he was pulling off hers. While still kissing. They both just shook their arms to get rid of the coats and left them on the floor. He spied the couch but she had other plans. She grabbed part of his shirt and pulled him into the bedroom.

16

THE DOTS GET CONNECTED - 2017

Lacey was excited beyond words. She was standing over the tomb where her Great Grandfather was buried. They had uncovered the casket which was pretty well rotted by then as the worms had eaten holes in the wood. As the lid was lifted, the air became still and she felt a calm even though her heart was pounding. Her gaze shifted to the white stone tombs around her. It was a volcanic island and digging was very difficult through the rock, so a lot of the tombs were above ground. As if behind a see-through blue curtain, she could see the ghosts of the family long ago, but apart from the four of them standing together was a woman, who resembled Lacey, wearing clothes from over 200 years ago. She was looking at her Great Grandmother. The women had a warm loving smile on her face. Her eyes had the strength that so often appeared in Lacey's eyes. Lacey wanted to reach out and touch the apparition and raised her hand palm up. There was quiet suddenly and she realized the workmen were staring at her. She dropped her hand and heard footsteps coming up between the graves.

"You look like you saw a ghost." Daniel said.

She shifted her eyes and turned to look at him. A smile

broke out on her face, when she saw him. "I'm pretty sure there are lots around to see." She responded, and reached out to take his hand. He was in his work uniform and was grinning that goofy grin, he got when he was around her. "I thought that you had to work." She said giving him a quizzical look.

"Found somebody to fill in." "I didn't want you to have all the fun of digging up bodies."

"Well, you're just in time for the grand opening." They are just about to lift the lid." She nodded to the workmen and the two pried the lid off the top of the casket. There was a dirty oil cloth wrapped around something and they had to unfold it carefully from both ends.

Inside was a skeleton of a person. All the rest had been eaten away by insects or worms but the skull was intact and had some strands of what might have been hair laying around it.

Grizzly looking Daniel thought and watched Lacey for any signs of emotion.

She was smiling, which was kind of scary. But it was glee. It was knowing she was one step closer to finding her past.

Being helped by one of the workmen, Lacey stepped closer and took a piece of bone from the skull with gloved hands and placed in a plastic baggie. She took a tweezer from her pocket and used the tweezers to pick up some of the hair from around the skull. She put that in another plastic baggie. She could guess that it was a man's skull by its shape from her FBI training. She looked at the workmen and said, "Let's wrap it up and let it rest in peace."

Daniel was watching and had the strong desire to make a cute comment, like "that's a wrap or "let's not wake anybody up." But he kept it to himself, thinking this might be a solemn moment for Lacey. "What happens now?" He asked instead.

"I send it to the lab." She said. Looking back as the workmen, who were closing, the coffin and putting things back in order. "We match up the DNA samples and if everything shows that I am a direct descendent of both, then we file the claim, I guess." It only proves that I'm the legal heir and not who murdered them." Lacey asked herself mentally, what was the reason she was doing this and what was pushing so hard to find the truth? The locket around her neck started to warm up and the air went still. Again, she saw the woman that had appeared the first time and could see a very serious look on her face. The voice inside said, "It's for all of us."

Daniel took Lacey's right hand as she had the baggies in her left. They started to walk out of the graveyard and Lacey looked over her left shoulder, the apparition was gone. They walked in silence to the parking lot, where her car and his truck were parked. He stopped and turned and looked into her eyes.

She could see the gentle, calm gaze that said everything and she squeezed his hand. He bent down and kissed her gently on the lips. "I'm going to the FEDEX office and get these off to the lab." If you want too, we can meet at Latitude and have a drink and dinner."

Daniel's gaze had not changed, but a smile came to his face. "Well, I guess I can break off a few dates and meet you there." "Of course, I'll be breaking some hearts."

She chuckled. "OK, Don Juan, I'll be there in about an hour and you can pay for the evening." "Order me a dark and stormy, if you're there first."

"Deal," he said, and leaned forward and kissed her deeply on the lips." Somebody driving by honked. He pulled away slowly. He looked around and noticed they were in a school parking lot. We better go before we get arrested for PDA."

She stepped in a little closer and pressed herself against him, "or indecent exposure." She said.

His face and hers were flushed and there was enough sexual tension to start a fire. She let go of him took her keys out of her shorts and opened her door. He was just standing there panting slightly and grinning. She got in the car.

He went to close the door and said. "Until later."

She winked, started the car and backed it up.

He just stood and watched as she drove out of the parking lot.

Five days later, she was standing in her apartment on the cell phone with Marconi at the lab.

He was saying, "the Results show that you are directly related to your Great Great Grandfather and your Great Grandmother." "What do you want me to do with the test results?"

Send the documents by e-mail to me and send the originals to my Attorney by mail. His name is Jeffrey Logan and I'll e-mail you his address. In just a moment" She said "Now, what do I owe you."

There was a pause on the line, before Marconi said. "First a case of "R. Lopez de Heredia" Tondia reserve 2005 wine." "That will cover one test." "Then a passionate night drinking the wine with you will cover the other test."

"Will your wife be joining for the passionate night?" She said sarcastically.

"You know how to spoil all my fun." He said with a laugh.

Lacey said. "You better send me an e-mail with that wine, so I get the right one."

"Don't worry about the wine, if by chance you're at a restaurant with it on the menu. Try it with paella or any Italian red sauce dish. It is delicious." "I got to go, e-mail me the address."

"Bye, " was all he got in before the line went dead.

Shit she said to herself, now I have to find someone, who knows about wine.

A big smile came to her face and she started thinking that she found out more about her family and ancestors than ever before. The computer blinked with the e-mail from Marconi.

She grabbed her address book and looked up Jeffrey's address at the law office. She quickly typed an e-mail back to

Marconi with the information. She ended it with, "send me the name of that wine or I'll tell your wife. Love Lacey."

She then printed off the documents from the DNA test and noticed they were on FBI stationary. Hope this doesn't get him in trouble, she thought.

She dialled Jeffrey's office number and got the receptionist.

"Logan Law offices, where can I direct your call?" She said.

"Hi, this is Lacey and I wondered if I could speak to Jeffrey?"

"Hold on." Was the reply. The line went silent. "Lacey, he is in a meeting, can he call you back in half an hour?"

"Sure, not a problem." Lacey said. Thank you and bye." Lacey hung up and immediately dialed her mother's number. The phone rang three times and then Valerie's voice came on the line.

"Hi Lacey, what is the news." Valerie knew what was going on and had helped get Elsa's DNA sample. She also had caller ID on her cell phone. "Don't tell me, your pregnant?"

Lacey laughed, "En tu suenos, mamacita." Lacey knew that her mother could understand the expression of "in your dreams." She had used it before when asked the same question.

Valerie quickly responded, "one can only hope."

"I got the DNA tests back and we are direct descendants of the Gufstersons." She exclaimed. "We now have all the details to file a claim to the property." She was excited and wanted to share the joy. "Since you are the closest living heir, the claim should be in your name" The locket started to vibrate and Lacey felt a little confused. There was now a breeze in the room and the air felt much cooler. What the hell, she thought. It was sunny out and the leaves on the bushes and trees were not swinging with much intensity.

Valerie spoke. "No, you should be the one to file." "I will give you a Power of Attorney and grant the property to you." You have done the research and put it all together." "I don't want the property, and it would go to you anyway."

The locket had stopped vibrating the air had returned to normal and the breeze was gone. Lacey stood and looked out the patio glass doors and it appeared the kapok tree was swaying and dancing as if it were happy. She thought maybe I really am losing it. She heard her mother say, "Lacey are you there?"

"Yes, and I am sorry my mind wondered." "Anyway, think of the ramifications" We have found part of our family tree, but we haven't solved the mystery of their murders."

"Well, knowing you, you'll find the villains and put the case to rest." Valerie said.

"Hopefully' Lacey said. "So, how is Dad?"

"You know him." He is caught up in the latest PGA tournament. He still rooting for Tiger and Phil, but has some special cheers for Rory, Jordan, Sergio, Ricky, Jason and Dustin." Keeping up with the new players, keeps him occupied. Plus, he meets the regular old cronies on the course on Mondays and Tuesdays, when it is not raining." It keeps him out of the house and out of my hair."

"Don't you still play with him?" Lacey asked.

"Every Thursday morning with Ed and Sylvia." Lacey knew that Ed and Sylvia were her parent's closets friends. They lived in the retirement community and the four did everything together. The four of them referred to the gated community as "seizure world." And if an ambulance siren was heard by them. They would say, 'sounds like they are playing our song."

Valerie said, "got to run." It's Mah-jong Friday and the girls will miss me." "Love you and keep me informed on what's happening." "Bye."

The phone went dead, but Lacey still said, "Love you too."

Her phone rang. She looked at caller ID and saw it was Jeffrey. "Hi,' she said.

"So, what is up? Jeffrey responded.

"I got the results from the DNA testing and I'm having the originals mailed to you" Also the results are all positive that I am a direct descendant of both." She couldn't keep the excitement out of her voice. Her heart was starting to beat faster and she had a grin on her face.

"Great news," Jeffrey said. "This means we can move ahead with the filing." "But don't get too excited yet." We can expect some fighting by the people who have the title now." I'll put everything together and get over to the courthouse. We can ask for an expedited ruling, but civil matters don't get top priority. "So, expect some delays."

"Oh, and you're also going to get a "power of attorney from my mother and documents deeding the rights to the property to me." Lacey said. In the excitement she had almost forgotten.

"Good,' Jeffrey said. "You and Daniel should go out and celebrate a little tonight."

Lacey knew he was trying to play match maker, but there was no one else, she would like to celebrate with. She was grinning again and was anticipating seeing Daniel tonight anyway.

"Good suggestion counsellor." She quipped. "I hope you're not billing me for the dating advice."

"Just my usual cupid fee rates" First born has to be named after me. I've got work to do, so we will talk again soon." "Bye."

"Bye and thanks so much," she said. The call ended.

She hit the address book icon and scrolled down to Daniel's number. She pressed the little telephone on the screen and the phone dialled. She was giddy with excitement.

"Daniel Williams," came the voice over the phone. He was being business like and hadn't looked to see who was calling.

"Hi, big boy." "Want to get lucky tonight?" She joked.

He chuckled. "Well, I'll have to check my social calendar"

He replied. I assume you got good news and you want to celebrate."

"Very good news, and if you play your cards right you get dinner at Dream View." Lacey could see his face in her mind and was feeling very good about their relationship. He was handsome, charming and deeply in love with her. "I'll even pick you up tonight."

"That sounds fabulous" Shall we say 7 ish." He said.

"7 ish it is." "Bye."

"Bye, yourself." "Until later." He responded.

She could hear someone talking in the background and disconnected. She was still grinning and felt a warm glow from the locket. Life seemed to be right and went onto the porch and looked out on the island and the little white house with a red roof, just past the big kapok tree.

A week later Jeffrey called her. She answered the phone and said, Hi Jeffrey. It was about 10 AM in the morning and another bright sunny day. She was standing on the villas main deck after just checking the cisterns levels. It hadn't rained in a week and the last guests had just left the day before. She didn't have other guests coming for another week. She was wearing tan shorts a white T-shirt and blue flip flops. No bra and a blue ball cap that had a turtle design on the front.

He got right to the point. "We got some push back from Harry Gufsterson already. "His attorney filed a restraint to stop the change of ownership." "I can respond and ask for an immediate hearing." Also, His attorney has sent an e-mail to me requesting a meeting." "I know the attorney; his name is Horst Rumbolt and I think he is a crook and a jerk."

Lacey knew that Jeffrey was not a person to give opinions easily and his tone indicated that there was real dislike for these people. She paused and then said, "What do you think, we should do?"

Jeffrey responded immediately. "I think we should file for the hearing and also I will set up a meeting with Horst and

Harry." We want to appear that we are trying to be understanding since Harry's family has had the property for 100's of years. We don't want to appear that we are just throwing him out. "

She could feel the locket turn cold against her skin at the mention of the Harry Gufsterson name. Thinking that Jeffrey was probably right, she said. "Go ahead and set things in motion, I should be available all week for the meeting. "She thought, it is better to get this over with as soon as possible and dragging it out won't benefit anybody.

Jeffrey said, "good, I'll send an e-mail to Horst and schedule a time for this week. I'll also request the courts for an expedited hearing to resolve the matter." "if we are lucky, we should get a hearing in a couple of months. "If we are unlucky it will take about six months."

Lacey smiled. "Thank you for all your help."

Jeffrey said, "this is just the beginning, so don't get your hopes up just yet. "

She paused and said, " I hope you are keeping track of the time. I don't know if I will be able to pay you, but you never know."

Jeffrey said, "will discuss my bill later, when we know the outcome."

FRIDAY: The Meeting - 2017

Jeffrey met Lacey in the parking lot to an office building two streets back from the harbor. He was in his standard suit and tie with a brown leather briefcase in his hand. As she approached, he smiled and said "Are you ready for this"

She was in black slacks and a blue knit blouse with short sleeves and a 3 button collar. Two buttons were unbuttoned and the locket was visible around her neck.

She answered back with a smile, "Let's do it."

"Don't expect a warm welcome, from them." Jeffrey spoke

as they walked to the entrance. Just then Daniel pulled into the parking lot. They watched him park and walk up. He smiled and said "hi."

Jeffrey answered "hi", thought you could not make it?"

Daniel smiled at Lacey and said, "switched things around." "Here to give moral support."

Jeffrey said, "OK, but keep things polite and friendly." Understood?"

Daniel just nodded and winked at Lacey.

They headed for the entrance and Daniel held the door for Lacey as they walked in. They were in a lobby with wood floors and benches on the sides. The sun was over the building but the light flooded the lobby through the glass floor to ceiling windows. Jeffrey walked to the elevator bank that was on the right. He had been here before, so there was no need to check the wall mounted directory for the office number. Lacey followed pausing to take Daniel's hand.

Jeffrey pressed the button and the elevator doors immediately opened. There wasn't anyone else in the lobby, so they got on and rode to the third floor. As they got off the elevator, Jeffrey turned right and headed for a glass door with white letters three inches tall on it showing Horst Rumbolt ESQ, Attorney at Law.

Jeffrey paused at the door and said, "remember whatever is said, keep your cool." He opened the door into a reception area that was about 12 feet by 12 feet square with a dark wood reception desk and across the room were 2 chairs with a coffee table between them and a lamp and some magazines about St. Thomas on it. A woman appeared through a door on the right. She was a short brunette with a round face, brown eyes that reflected no emotion when she smiled and said "may I help you?"

Jeffrey answered, "Jeffrey Logan and we have an appointment with Horst Rumbolt."

The woman just nodded and said, "wait here." She turned and went back through the door, closing it behind her. She was back a moment later and held the door open. "Please follow me."

They followed her down a narrow hallway and she knocked on the second door on the left and opened it. She held it open and stepped aside so they could enter. The room was a small conference room with a dark mahogany table and six matching chairs. Behind the table were 3 windows about waist high. The walls were painted beige and had various prints on them. There was a door on the right side of the room.

Behind the table stood a short man with balding grey hair and bushy eyebrows. He had glasses and brown eyes without any humor in them. He had slumping shoulders and a sizeable waist. He had a white long sleeve shirt and a brown tie. Slacks looked like they went with a suit, but he wasn't wearing the jacket. He spoke, "hello Jeffrey, good to see you again and the lady must be Lacey Lockhart." Horst's eyes rested on Daniel, and this is?"

Jeffrey said, this is my brother in law Daniel Williams and a friend of Miss Lockhart."

Horst turned and said, " this is Harry Gufsterson and current owner of the property in question."

Harry said nothing. He flushed like the last time Lacey had seen him at the airport. He was breathing heavily and it was almost as if he was going to burst out with something or just pass out.

Horst said "let's sit down and can I get you anything before we start?"

Jeffrey, Lacy and Daniel all said, "no thank you."

Horst said "well let's get to the reason, we are here." "We feel that your case has little merit because Mr Gufsterson's family has had title to the property for over 200 years and you are using faulty information from whatever DNA testing was done"

The locket around Lacey's neck was getting cold and she thought she could feel it thumping against her chest.

Jeffrey said, we have given you the results from the FBI laboratory and the hospital in Chicago. In addition to the will from the original property owner deeding it to his closest living heir. We've also documented that Lacey is the Great Grand Daughter to the person who should have inherited the property originally. There is substantial documentation that the property belongs to Lacey.

"Well", Horst broke in. We realize that Miss Lockhart has gone to a great deal of expense and time to try and substantiate her claim, and we are willing to compensate for her effort as a token of goodwill. "

Lacey was about to speak, but Jeffrey held up his hand and smiled. He said "what are you offering?"

Horst spoke, "Mr. Gufsterson is willing to pay $50,000 to have the case dropped and no further litigation is to be pursued."

Lacey could not contain herself at this point. "Absolutely not. It rightfully belongs in our family."

The locket changed immediately to warm. She reached up and touched it lightly.

Harry jumped up from his chair and shouted, "you blood-sucking bitch." If you think, I'm going to let some little cunt get my family land, you can go to hell." Harry's face was a blazing red and he looked as if he was going to explode.

Daniel was out of his chair and going around the table toward Harry with his fists clenched.

Horst stood quickly and moved in front of Harry with his hands up. "Let's all settle down."

Jeffery had come around and took Daniel by the arm and pulled him back to the other side of the table.

Horst turned toward the three of them and said, "let me have a few moments with my client." He then led Harry to the door at the end of the room. Horst opened it and let Harry into what looked like his working office.

Jeffrey turned to Daniel and Lacey and said, "cool down." This is what we should have expected would happen.

Lacey looked at Daniel, "you were going to hit him to defend my honor." She was looking into the blue eyes and could see that the anger was giving way to thought.

The goofy smile returned to his face and he grinned. No, I just don't like foul language used in front of Jeffrey. He is very sensitive."

Jeffrey said "enough! "Let us see, what happens next." The island's value is in the millions, I did a little research, Harry has leveraged it to buy his condo in New York. He gets some fees from the government because at onetime there was an artillery placement on the island and there were barracks for military personnel. Then there is the boat haul out facility. So just relax, and let me do the talking.

They could hear angry voices in the next room, but not was said. The door suddenly opened and just Horst came in. He stood on the far side of the table and said. "It would be better, if we end this meeting, Jeffrey, I will contact you if we have another proposal.

Jeffrey, Lacey and Daniel stood and Jeffrey said, I will look forward to hearing from you." They all left the room and went down the hallway to the reception area. They exited in silence and walked to the elevator and Daniel pushed the button. They waited in silence.

Lacey spoke first, "I don't want a settlement, I want the family property back."

17

LOCKET TO LACEY

Josh and Valerie Lockhart had now been married 32 years and their only daughter Lacey had finished law school and joined the FBI. She took after her father, in wanting justice done and criminals to be brought before the courts to be judged. She didn't have her mother's passion for making the world a better place by influencing all of humanity.

They were sitting in their home in Alexandria, Virginia. It was not an elaborate house but a comfortable split level on a half acre lot in a quiet subdivision.

Valerie was sitting in the living room looking out at the street through the bay window with a bench seat in front of it. Beyond the window was a hedge up to the bottom of the window and then the lawn running down to the sidewalk. Just then the familiar dark blue jeep Sport pulled up and stopped. The driver's door opened and Lacey jumped out wearing jeans and a blue sweatshirt with FBI on it in white capital letters on the front. She also had a ball cap with the same letters on the front. Her ponytail was through the hole in the back of the cap and New Balance running shoes were on her feet. There was a spring in her step as she bounded up to the front door. She had just finished basic training and was ready to start the job. She opened the door without bothering to knock and those brown eyes were reflecting the joy she had within her. Spotting her mother, she quickly crossed the room and hugged Valerie, who was already standing to greet her. The warmth of loving could be felt in the entire room and both women had smiles radiating from their faces.

Breaking apart Valerie said, "so because of the exuberance I assume you passed basic." I had little doubt that you wouldn't."

"Well, to be honest, I am glad it is over. Where is dad, Lacey asked?"

"He is at the club playing gin with the boys, as always on Wednesdays." Valerie said. "There is a Redskin's preseason game this weekend and I am sure they are trying to decide the odds and point spread for a bet."

Lacey's expression changed and her face showed the same brightness but with a little uncertainty behind it. "I wanted to tell you where I've been assigned." I was going to wait till dinner, but I might as well get it out." "Chicago." Valerie's face did not reflect her feelings. She was hoping for around D.C.

Slowly a little sadness crept into her eyes. "Well, at least it is not Los Angeles." Your father is not going to be happy, because he wants to keep you close by," Valerie said.

Lacey was trying to keep the conversation upbeat, "well there are lots of flights and inexpensive fares and I will be in constant contact." Who else can I rely on for sound legal advice?"

Valerie just smiled, but her face took on the serious expression that happened when she was trying to make a decision. She finally spoke, "OK it is time for the passing of the locket."

Lacey had a puzzled expression. "What are you talking about?"

"The locked that I wear and have never taken off." Valerie continued, "it belonged to your Great, Great Grandmother and is passed down through the generations with a solemn promise. ""The promise is that the locket will be worn and never taken off until it is passed on to the next generation."

Lacey stared at the locket a moment and said, "this is sounding a little strange. "You are asking me to make a commitment to not only wear something continuously, but also having a child sometime in the future." "That is something, I have not even considered yet." Is this some trick to get me to get married?"

Valerie eyes twinkled at the mention of grandkids. "No, of course not, just following the rules of the promise as I know it"

Lacey was suspicious of the motives, "then are you alright?"

"I am fine." I just think it is time to give it to you. "

"Well in that case, OK."

Valerie unclasped the chain and leaned forward and put it around Lacey's neck.

18

RIGHTING THE WRONG. – 2000'S

It was a bright sunshine day with a great deal of work to do. One of the TV sets had gone out in the villa and had to be replaced and an air conditioning unit wasn't functioning. Getting a repair man out was difficult as they always work on island time. Meaning they show up late or whenever. Lacey was standing on the patio under a portico looking to make sure no spiders were building nests on the beams and for company she had was an iguana sunning himself on the rock wall near the pool. The iguana was young and bright green with a striped long tail and big eyes watching everything going on.

Lacey's cell phone rang and she noticed the caller was Jeffrey. It had been almost a month since the meeting with Harry Gufsterson and she knew things were going to take time. She hit the answer button and said "Hi Jeffrey."

"Hi Lacey, we have some preliminary news from the courts, all of the news is favourable." "We are to draw up a preliminary plan for the transfer of the property and submit it to the judge to determine if any of Harry's rights are going to be violated." "They do not want us, just to displace him at the time of the final decision. I got a call from Horst and he wants to have a meeting about the property again, but he doesn't want Daniel there. What do you think?"

Lacey thought for a moment before answering. "Fine as long as Horst understands that if Harry starts up again, we are out of there."

"I will relay that information and what would be a good time for you?"

"I have got guests arriving next Friday and Thursday is needed to make sure everything is okay, so Wednesday next week would be good," Lacey replied.

"Let me check my schedule, but I think that should work." "I will text you to confirm the time of the meeting." "Until then think about when and how you want to take over the property?" "You are going to need help to manage the island. Jeffrey ended with "Congratulations!"

Lacey said, "thank you for everything," and pressed the end call button.

Wednesday morning Lacey woke to the cell phone incoming call sound. She looked at the phone and there was the picture of Daniel she had placed in the address book on the phone. "Hello handsome, miss me?"

He chuckled and said "I hope I woke you."

"No, I had to get up to answer the phone."

"Are you sure you don't want me to go with you today?" He asked.

"I'm sure, it will only inflame Harry, and Jeffrey and Horst want to keep this as amicable as possible." I will have to be without my knight to defend me."

"Okay, he said, but I want a call as soon as you are done and can we have dinner tonight?"

"Dinner sounds good, but see if Jeffrey and Jane can join us." "I owe him so much for all his help."

Will do, until I hear from you, just know you are loved."

Love you too", and she hit the end button. She was thinking this relationship has moved to a whole new level.

It was Wednesday and Lacey watched as Jeffrey pulled into the parking lot. He parked and walked over to her with a serious look on his face. He was in khakis and a blue blazer, blue shirt and maroon tie. "Hi", he said as he approached, "are you ready for this?"

She smiled and just nodded. She had white shorts and a dark blue polo shirt and tennis shoes. There was no need to be formal.

He continued, "we probably will get some push back or another offer, but either way we have achieved the preliminary judgement that you are the rightful owner of the estate of your Great Great Grandfather Heinrich Gufsterson. We will hear what they say and go from there."

Lacey continued to smile and said, "just want you to know how much I appreciate all that you have done."

Jeffrey smiled, and said, this isn't over yet."

They walked to the entrance and went into the elevators. They rode to the floor in silence and went to the office door. Jeffrey put his hand on the knob and looked at Lacey for a sign. She nodded again and walked in.

The same receptionist came into the waiting area and said, Horst is waiting for you and held the hallway door open for them and they entered and walked down the hall to the same room as before.

Horst and Harry were in a conversation, that stopped when they saw them coming. Both men had serious expressions but upon Jeffrey and Lacey entering they put on phoney smiles. Harry's face looked more like a leer than a smile and there was no warmth in his eyes.

Horst spoke first, "thank you for coming today."

Lacey thought this was like the scene from "Casablanca", where Ingrid Bergman and Paul Henreid meet with Claude Rains and Conrad Veiht at the police station.

Jeffery said, "we want this to go as smoothly as possible and recognize the problems, it may create."

They all sat down on opposite sides of the table again. Harry was still leering, but Horst had taken a serious composed manner and said, "First we would like to ask if there is any offer, we could make to have the property remain with Harry or a joint ownership of some sort?"

Jeffrey face remained without expression and said, "Lacey and I have discussed this at length and there is no offer that would be acceptable." "It is my understanding that the Courts are looking for an amicable plan for transference and we would like to discuss that with you today."

Horst seemed to know that would be their answer and spoke, "in that case, we would like two months to vacate the premises and get all of Harry's affairs in order." "You realize that there are numerous items and issues that he will have to take care of before leaving the property."

Lacey felt the locket get warmer and then suddenly turn cold and start to vibrate. She reached up and touched it and a little chill passed through her body. She leaned over and whispered in Jeffrey's ear.

He nodded and said, 'we don't have a problem of the two months but would like the right to inventory the property for items that it should contain in the next week?"

Horst said," hold on a second, I would like to discuss this with Harry."

With that they both stood and walked to the door leading to Horst's working office and went in, without saying a word. Harry's expression had changed and his face was turning red again.

Jeffrey and Lacey could hear voices through the door, but could not make out the words. Obviously, this was not sitting well with Harry. Lacey's locket remained cold but was not vibrating anymore.

The office door opened and Horst came in followed by Harry. Both men had strained expressions on their faces but you could tell Harry was contemplating something.

Horst spoke first, "we agree to the inventory inspection, but can we schedule it for a week from this Friday on the 17th."

Harry finally spoke but tried to have a humbling look on his face which didn't happen, "I need to get some personal effects moved or shipped to my New York condo." He was now staring directly at Lacey. "It would be greatly appreciated."

Jeffrey turned and looked at Lacey, wanting her to respond. Lacey felt the locket go cold against her skin. She faced Harry and said, "I don't see a problem with that."

Horst then asked, "who will be performing the audit and we want to know how long it will take?"

Jeffrey broke in and said, "we are having the Glower CPA firm do it and it should take about a day." "He said, they will have about four people working on it."

Horst stood signalling the meeting was over. "Thank you for coming," he said and waited for them to leave. Harry was silent.

Jeffrey said, "I will have the necessary documents sent over for your signature."

Jeffrey and Lacey turned and left the office and headed back to the elevators. Both were silent until they reached the elevators. Jeffrey said, "that went well."

Lacey looked up from the floor, "yes it did. Maybe a little too well."

The elevator doors opened and they stepped in. The locket was back to normal temperature now. They reached the lobby and Jeffrey waited for Lacey to get out first. She turned and waited for him to exit, and spoke as they walked to the exit, "have you and Jane got plans for tonight?

Jeffrey paused in thought, "I don't think so, why?"

Lacey said, well Daniel and I were going out to dinner to celebrate and would like you to join us, our treat."

Jeffrey pulled out his cell phone and called Jane. "Hi, what's up," she said. She knew who was calling by caller ID.

Just finished the meeting with Lacey and she and Daniel want to take us out to dinner tonight", he said.

She said, "sounds OK, where and when?"

He looked at Lacey, who spoke. Old Fort restaurant at 7."

He said, "did you get that?"

"Yep, Jane said. Sounds good to me."

"We are on," Jeffrey said, as Lacey smiled at him. He said," later." And pressed the off button.

He walked to her car and waited till she opened the door. He said, "see you tonight."

She got in and looked up with a warm smile, "you know I couldn't have done this without you."

He smiled back, and said, "you are practically family now, and you haven't seen my bill yet," he closed the door and headed for his car.

Daniel and Lacey were standing at the restaurant bar having Dark and Stormys when Jeffrey and Jane walked up. Jane was wearing white slacks with a plum coloured blouse and white sandals. Jeffrey was in beige shorts a green shirt and brown sandals. They were both smiling and looking happy. Daniel hugged Jane and Jeffrey hugged Lacey.

Daniel spoke first looking at both of them, "you two look like a cat that just swallowed a canary."

Jeffrey just smirked and said, "we were just talking about the last time we got away from the kids and went to a hotel. "

Lacey immediately broke in," I don't want to hear about it." "It will only give Daniel ideas."

They all chuckled and Daniel got a goofy grin on his face. The receptionist showed up and said your table is ready, please follow me."

They followed her to a table on the patio overlooking the harbor. She put menus on the table and they all sat down. The receptionist said, "the waiter will be right with you," turned and left.

A waiter showed up immediately with a pitcher of ice water and started filling their water glasses. Having finished filling the glasses, he said, "may I get you cocktails?"

Daniel spoke up immediately, "Lacey and I were thinking of having champagne." "How does that sound to you?"

"Sounds delightful," Jane responded. "I can't think of a better way to toast Lacey's good fortune." "Jeffrey has been filling me in on the negotiations, and my goofus brother almost getting charged with assault."

Lacey looked at Daniel warmly and said, "he was defending my honor and was very gallant."

Daniel looked up at the waiter trying to change the subject and said, 'a bottle of Veuve Clicquot and four glasses, if you have it."

'Oh God, were back to the "Casablanca" thing." This is really getting corny." Jane blurted.

The waiter said, "let me check" and turned and left.

Lacey had slipped her hand into Daniel's under the table and was gazing at the anchor lights on the sailboat masts dancing in the harbour. The locket felt warm against her skin and a peacefulness came over her. A warm breeze was coming up the hill onto the patio and slightly moving the palm fronds in the trees. It was as if the trees were dancing with the wind.

Jeffrey said, "I heard from Horst and that everything was on schedule for the inventory and Harry was looking forward to giving Lacey a tour of the island."

"I don't like the sound of that," Daniel said. He didn't trust Harry, which was obvious. "

How many people are going to be there?"

"I believe there will be four people from the accounting office to document the inventory," Jeffrey said. "Lacey should have other people around all the time."

Daniel wasn't convinced by the expression on his face. "Maybe I should join you for the day, just to make sure nothing happens?" He was looking directly at Lacey.

"My knight", she said. "I will be fine."

The waiter arrived with a wine bucket with ice and a bottle of Champagne. He placed champagne flutes in front of each of them. He had a white towel draped over his arm and pulled it off and used it to extract the bottle. Showing the label to Daniel. Daniel nodded and the waiter started removing the wire basket from the top and slowly twisting the cork until it came out with a "pop." He then poured about an inch and half of pale golden liquid with little bubbles rising from the bottom of the glass.

They were all watching Daniel as he picked up the glass by the stem and sniffed the bouquet in the glass and took a sip. He was smiling because this was all a show. He looked at the waiter and nodded. The waiter then started filling the glasses.

Lacey raised her glass and said, "to all of you for helping and for your support through all of this."

They each took a swallow, Jeffrey said, "I don't want to put a damper on the evening, but you need to think how you are going to pay the transfer taxes. Any property which changes ownership in the islands has to pay a transfer tax, which in this case will be sizeable." "Since there is an income from the lease, you can probably borrow the amount."

Lacey just smiled and said, "good advice counsellor. I will call you tomorrow and we can discuss, who to talk to, and get some information." "For now, let's enjoy champagne and order some food, I'm starving."

Daniel said, "I'm starving too."

They all picked up the menus that were sitting on the table and started reading. Lacey gave Daniel's hand a squeeze and let go, so they could pick up their menus. He looked over and beamed at her with all the affection he could.

It was the 17th and Lacey was standing at the dock with the four accountants waiting for a boat to ferry them across the channel. The dock was located at an area called

Frenchtown. The area where the fishing boats came in to sell their catch that wasn't promised to restaurants, to the public. The little island with the house and shipyard was about a half mile away, across a channel that was dredged in the harbor, so the water could flow out from the main harbor. This was the same area that 200 plus years earlier that Elsa and Latisha escaped off the little island across ankle deep water. Today the water was emerald green and ran 30 to 40 feet deep in the centre. They still had to clear out the sand by dredging the channel every so often. The harbor was some of the saltiest water in the world.

It was around 8 in the morning and the sun was bright and the robin's egg blue sky had only a few small white clouds, looking like cotton balls, in it. She had on grey shorts, white polo shirt, grey light hiking boots, ball cap, sunglasses and a small dark green backpack. The cell phone rang and she could see it was Daniel. It was his 2nd call this morning. She answered, "Hi, what's up?"

"I'm just checking again I could be there in 15 minutes, if you want."

She smiled, "don't worry the accountants are here and Harry would not try anything with an audience."

He replied, "OK, but call me when your back in. We'll pick a place to meet for dinner." "How does that sound?"

"Sounds great, I will be looking forward to it." She saw a boat pulling up to the dock, with Harry on it, he waived. "Later, the boat's here." She hit the off button, not waiting for his reply.

She waived back and said "Hello." She noticed the smile again was without warmth and looked like a leer. She held the backpack with a note pad, pen and Smith and Weston .380 automatic. It was light weight and not that accurate, but great for self-defence at close range.

The boat pulled next to the dock and the driver put the boat in neutral as the current pushed it in to the rubber padded rub rail. The driver slipped a line around a cleat on the dock. He went forward and tied off a bowline to another cleat. The 4 accountants were now standing on the dock next to Lacey. Lacey introduced them to Harry and they all nodded their heads as their names were mentioned. Lacey was about to board, when she looked down into the water, which was crystal clear. It was like looking into an aquarium. She was looking down between 5 and 10 feet with large 2 to 4 foot Tarpon swimming around. The large silver scales looking like metal plates on their bodies. The driver held out his hand so she could board as the boat rocked slightly on the gentle swells.

Harry said, "welcome aboard." "This boat actually comes with the island." We keep it at the boat haul out dock." The boat was 18 feet with a white haul, a small central cockpit with a blue Bimini over it. There was just enough room for the 7 of them. The 4 accountants moved to the stern and sat on a bench seat.

The driver had untied from the dock and looked around to make sure the rest were ok. He then pushed off the dock, went to the wheel, turned it slightly and put the gearshift in forward. The boat moved slowly from the dock as the driver looked for traffic in the channel. Seeing it clear he accelerated slowly. The boat had a 50 horsepower Evinrude on the stern. The boat started to bounce across the chop in the channel.

Harry had turned to the accountants and said, "I thought we can start with the shipyard and then move on to the house. They all nodded and were looking at a prelist of items that had been made up for them by someone Harry knew.

They were now approaching the dock on the little island, which was next to a stone wall made from the blue bicht stone that was used everywhere on the island. They off loaded after the driver tied the boat up. Lacey could see the large coal fireplace which used to heat the water to drive the steam engine to pull the ships out of the harbor by chains to have their bottoms cleaned. Lacey had seen the pictures of the slaves at the historical society. She felt a clench in her heart for the slaves that carried the coal on their heads to fuel the furnace. The work must have been gruelling and many died at very young ages.

Harry was pointing things out to the accountants and introducing them to the boatyard manager.

Jeffrey had negotiated for the business. Since it did very little business and barely broke even and the equipment was old, the value was minimal. Jeffrey had also negotiated for the house furniture and appliances, so Lacey would not have to go shopping immediately for a stove, refrigerator, oven and air conditioners. She was eager to see what she was getting.

There was a corrugated shed on the far side of the property and a small trailer with windows and a window air conditioner sticking out from the side window. The word "OFFICE" over the door was painted on. The building looked weathered the siding blistered by the sun. It was already midmorning, but standing in the sun was having an effect on everyone.

Harry walked up to Lacey and said, "let's go in the office to get out of the heat." The manager and the accountants were already walking in that direction. Harry was already sweating and his shirt had stains on his back and under his arms.

Lacey replied, "good idea." She followed Harry to the office. He held the door for her as she stepped in.

The inside was typical of most trailers with a little sink and counter on one side and a couch and small pedestal table right side. Lacey noticed that someone had just cleaned or tried to clean the inside. There were marks on the counter from the cleanser used to clean. Lacey could hear the noise from the window air conditioner running. The air was a little cooler. She could see the dust particles flooding in the sunlight. There was a short hallway and what looked like an office at the end. The door was open and she could see the air conditioner unit covering most of where the window was and the gap filled in by some sort of black plastic piece.

The accountants had moved to the couch and table and were making tick marks on their worksheets. There were 2 doors in the hallway and she guessed one was for a closet and one for a bathroom.

She looked out the small window over the sink and could see 2 sailboats about 30 feet long sitting on their keels with braces on either side keeping them straight up. There was a man working on the side of one of the boats.

The manager noticed Lacey staring. He said, "we charge a rental fee and let owners do some of the work on the boats themselves." "That fellow is putting a coat of anti-fouling paint on the bottom of his boat." The boat had a dark blue haul with a white stripe at the waterline and rust colored paint down to the bottom of the keel. The man, she could see was wearing beige, tattered shorts with spots of the rust colored paint on them. He wasn't wearing a shirt and was deeply tanned. He was wearing a pair of old deck shoes and no socks. The manager continued, "we charge $75 per day for storage. They have to buy the paint from us and we make a profit from that and there are additional charges for lifting the boat out of the water and putting it back in. Would you like to see the boat lift to take them out of the water?

Lacey considered getting more information from the Manager. "Thank you, she said, that sounds interesting." She didn't want to watch the accountants making notes and now wanted some fresh air. She stepped outside and the Manager followed her. The trade winds had picked up and the sun wasn't as oppressive. As they walked, she looked across the harbor to the cruise ship dock and wondered what Daniel was doing. There was a little chop in the harbor and sun sparkled off the waves as they crested.

The Manager started talking," we can handle a pretty good sized boat." They came from behind the shed and there was a large piece of equipment on tires with large straps hanging from the 4 posts. The manager continued, "it is like a tractor with a four way hoist and we take it into the water and move the boat over the straps. "Then the straps are raised and lift the boat." We then drive it on land, put the braces under the boat to hold it and remove the straps." We are one of the few yards around that can do it and business is fairly steady, but not great because of the costs and taxes." He was looking at Lacey with a little concern in his eyes.

She said," we can discuss the future plans after the legal issues of the island are concluded." "Right now, I'm hoping you would just keep business as usual for me."

His face brightened up a little and he said, "not a problem."

Just then Harry and the 4 accountants approached. Harry spoke, "we are heading up to the house now. My housekeeper has some lunch for us."

The manager said, "I will be getting back to work, and it was nice meeting all of you." He headed back to the office.

Harry said, "this way" and started walking on a path to a white house with a red tile roof. Lacey followed a little behind Harry on his right and the 4 accountants behind her. The azure-colored waters of the harbor were 60 feet away. She was thinking this is absolutely beautiful and I could live here. She could feel the warmth of the locket against her throat and how beautiful the day was with wisps of clouds, blue skies and swaying palm trees. Of course, the downside was, what do you do when a hurricane comes? Of course, the house has been here hundreds of years. She thought that would be a good question at lunch for Harry.

They reached the house and Harry opened the front door which apparently was unlocked. The house had been remodelled over the years and glass windows put in, where there were just shutters before. The shutters were painted red and served as protection from storms also.

Lacey went in and noticed that the living room was small but comfortable. An old stone fireplace was on the right and it looked clean as if it hadn't been used. There was a dining area behind the living room with a table for six. She could tell that the rest had been remodelled with a door on the other side of the table leading to a kitchen with modern appliances and she could see on the other side a hallway leading to other rooms. There was an older woman in the kitchen preparing trays with sandwiches and fruit. Her face showed the wrinkles of time and the leathered skin of being in the sun without sunscreen.

Harry noticing Lacey looking said, "that is Maya my cook and housekeeper. She is preparing a lunch for everyone."

Lacey felt that he was being a little too accommodating, but said nothing. Mistrust was part of her life, so she felt being suspicious was only natural. The locket around her neck felt warm and peaceful as if it was happy.

Maya came in carrying trays of food and started placing them on the table. There was no attempt at introductions and Harry went to the head of the table to sit. He paused and said, "there is a bathroom after you go through the kitchen, for those who want to wash up. It is the first door on the right."

The first accountant said "thanks" and headed into the kitchen. Lacey moved around to the other end of the table, as far from Harry as possible and waited.

Harry said, "I will give you a tour of the rest of the house after lunch."

"That would be great", Lacey replied and tried to seem upbeat and appreciative.

One of the accountants started going over the list of items In the house that would remain for her.

Lunch had finished and the tour of the house was over. Lacey had noticed that the locket would grow warmer as she went to the bedrooms and she could only guess which one was her great great grandmothers. The master bedroom had been enlarged and a bathroom with an expanded walk-in closet. It was getting to be late afternoon and the accountants were finishing up some paper work. They were getting ready to go back over to the marina for a boat ride back to the mainland. Maya appeared with a light sweater on and a shopping bag and purse. She turned to Harry and said, "I have to go back with them my granddaughter has a soccer game at school."

"I understand", he said and turned to Lacey. "Can you wait till the next trip over?" I can show you the most beautiful spot on the island and the old cannon emplacement that dates back to the 1700's."

Lacey paused; the locket felt a little colder. She thought, I'm not afraid of this jerk and he wouldn't try anything with everybody knowing I'm here. "OK, she said.

"Great", Harry replied. "We can take the path behind the house that leads right up to it." "The Dutch were afraid that the British would send over ships with soldiers to capture the island. "The Dutch built the cannon battery overlooking the harbor entrance and could bombard any ship trying to enter." He had that leering smile, but seemed knowledgeable of the history.

Maya and the 4 accountants said goodbye and headed out the front door.

Harry said, "we will go out the back door."

Lacey picked up her backpack off the couch and felt inside to make sure the little automatic was still there. She was only going to trust Harry so far, and she checked for her cell phone also.

She followed him down the hallway and out the back door at the end. It was a sandy and small rock backyard with a path that led up a hill with small shrubs and bushes. She could see that at the top of the hill were the palm trees and vegetation that covered the islands. The palm leaves look like silver sword blades dancing in a blue sky. The sun was on the other side of the hill and she couldn't tell how high above the horizon it was. It was warm, but not hot and the locket was cool against her chest.

Harry was huffing and puffing going up the hill and wasn't about to enter into a conversation. They were approaching the top of the hill and she could see the path enter the tree and then continue on to a slight incline and an open space of about 30 meters.

Harry stopped at the edge of the trees and leaned against a palm at the edge of the path.

His face was red and he was breathing heavily. He said, "keep going up to the top and you will lookout at the inlet to the harbour." "It will give you the view to St John and some of the British Virgins." You can look up the Sir Frances Drake Channel all the way to Virgin Gorda."

"Are you going to be alright?" she asked.

"I'm fine just catching my breath." I'll follow in just a second. "His face was looking a little less flushed and his breath was coming back to normal.

She walked up to the summit and looked out. It was magnificent and she could see the harbor below and the islands stretching out in the distance. She didn't know their names but they were green gems on the dark blue sea. There were waves rolling along then cresting with foam. The sun was half set in the horizon and there were no clouds directly over it. Higher up there were some clouds starting to reflect the fading light, turning from white to grey and pink. Nature in all its grandeur, she thought. She was standing on hard planks which had been covered with a thin amount of dirt and rocks over the years. She heard heavy footsteps coming up behind her and turned, realizing she was on a precipice without much room to run or escape.

This is not good she thought. The locket was cold and trembling against her chest and she felt fear rising.

Harry was standing a few feet behind her. The leer was spread across his face and he was showing all his teeth. There was a wood handled machete with rust on it.

She reached into the backpack and grabbed the handle of the automatic pistol.

"It won't do you any good, I unloaded it while you were in the bathroom."

She could feel it was empty and the slide was open meaning the round in the chamber was gone. She reached in further and gripped her cell phone. He wouldn't do anything if people could hear. The cell phone case felt strange and she realized the back was off and the battery gone. Panic was beginning to grip her and her breathing became accelerated. Think Lacey she thought. Keep him talking. "How are you going to explain the wounds from the machete?" She was almost screaming.

"When you fall onto the rocks below, there will be so many cuts and lacerations that they would not be able to tell what happened. Anyway, by the time they get to you the crabs will have moved in and even made more of a mess of your body." You'll be a mass of cuts bruises and fractured bones that the cause of death will be undeterminable." I will tell them that you slipped off the ledge and I couldn't catch you in time." You didn't think I was going to let you come and take my family's property."

She had to keep him talking and look for an opening. The locket was vibrating like a tuning fork and she had to stay calm. There was a foul smell to the air. "It wasn't your families' property." It was my families to begin with."

His eyes turned cold and his nostrils flared. "Enough of your bull shit. What's mine is mine and I don't care what you think." He had shifted the machete in his hand and kept the point level with her diaphragm. It was rusted but had a sharp edge and trying to knock it away was not an option.

Light was fading and she was searching for options. The air had changed and the wind had suddenly gusted with an unnatural force. The palm trees swayed with the force of the wind and Lacey could feel her hair being blown across her face.

An object caught her eye as it crossed out of the night shadows and in to the last remaining light. It hit Harry on the back of his head with a resounding thwack. The impact was enough to crack the skull and the machete dropped from his hand and landed point up as it hit the ground. Harry fell forward with the machete driving point first into his stomach and up toward his spine. Finally punching out his back. He screamed but there wasn't anybody but Lacey to hear. He rolled on his side and blood was coming out his mouth. His eyes went blank as life slowly left his body. He was dying as the body shut down due to lack of blood to sustain it.

She was in shock. Staring at the body, she took a faint step forward. It had happened so fast and with such force. She looked up from the body and the wind was gone. The coconut that had hit him lay on the ground beside him. Its green husk had a spot of blood on it, from where it had hit his head. Her gaze slowly came up to where the trees started. There was a group of people standing there. They were dressed in clothes from many age periods and were staring back at her.

On the left side was a partially bald man with a beard, bushy eyebrows and mutton chop sideburns. He had a kindly face and held a long stem pipe. Next to him was a woman with dark hair with some grey showing. She wore a dress buttoned at the collar and long sleeves. In front of her were 2 children, a girl and a boy. Next to her was a woman with white hair and loving smile on her face. Next to her was a stocky black woman with a round face and grey hair. Then there was a large fellow in in a military uniform and next to him a woman, who was beaming. Lacey remembered she had seen them in the picture at Jeffrey's house.

She realized that she was seeing all the people who had affected her life through the years. She felt weak, but wanted to talk to them. She wanted to touch them and hug them. The locket was warm against her skin and now the air smelled like lilacs. Her eyes started to tear up and she started to cry with the overwhelming emotions and a feeling of love. She heard her name being called as Daniel came up the trail out of the trees. He was running straight toward her. She felt weak and her legs started to shake.

He was there and took her in his arms and held her close. Her head pressed against his chest as he said," are you alright?"

She was totally drained by the tension and kept her arms tight around him, so she would not fall. Tears started to swell in her eyes and she said, "I'm alright."

"What the hell happened here."

Still shaking she said, "He tried to kill me." In a soft voice, almost a whisper.

Daniel stroked her head and said, "It's alright now." Lucky you had that old machete"

"I didn't have the machete, she said. "He had it hidden behind a tree up here."

"OK, then how did he stick himself with it?"

"The coconut hit him on the head and he fell on the blade," she replied and started to pull away a little. Her breathing was stabilizing , so she started to focus better. For the first time she started to look around to see if the relatives were still there.

Daniel noticed the coconut on the ground near the body and the partially cracked skull. He noticed she was staring in the other direction. What are you looking at?"

She smiled slightly and said, "you probably won't believe me, but I have a whole group of protective angels." They seem to be mostly having a good time.

He gave her a look, then turned and couldn't see anybody.

Just then Sargent Fowler came out of the trees carrying a flashlight and sprinted toward them.

He spotted Harry laying on the ground with the macheted stuck in him. His eyes widened and he said, "Jesus, what in the world is with you?" Looking directly at lacey, "Every time we meet there are people injured laying on the ground."

"Oh, he is not injured, He is dead." She said. "You could say, he fell on his own sword."

He was staring at her and looked frustrated. "Tell me what happened?"

She began with the reason for coming to the island and went on with the whole story.

His face had softened and he was looking at the coconut and the ground around the wooden handle of the machete. Alright, I've got to have both of you come back to the station and fill out another statement and I need to get a copter out here and pick up the body. There has to be an autopsy. You understand you are not allowed to leave St. Thomas until this whole mess is cleaned up?

Looking him straight in the eye, she said." Understood."

Daniel put his arm around Lacey's shoulders, "Come on I've got my boat at the marina." The moon was up now and there were no clouds in the sky. There was enough residual light to follow the path back. He said, "are your ghosts or angels still here?"

She looked around and there were none around. "Nope, gone"

He turned toward her and kissed her deeply. "I was really worried when I couldn't get your cell phone."

"Harry disabled it." Also, he took all the shells out of the gun." He really wanted me dead, he planned the whole thing" She said softly.

He just exhaled and kept his arm around her as they walked. The moon was bright and they could follow the trail.

Epilogue:

Daniel and Lacey were standing in the police station waiting to talk to Sargent Fowler and the Captain. Since the incident 2 weeks earlier, Daniel had stayed almost constantly with Lacey. They had talked about living together and where that might lead. They had decided to fly back to Lacey's parents and see how that went. Then there was the transfer of the property and lots of legal details to be worked out. She said to him, "what do you think this is all about?"

He replied, "I have no idea, the officer that called just said they wanted to meet us here.'"

Lacey felt a tingling from the locket and again the whole group of apparitions were standing near the door to the room. They were all smiling at her and watching. They were in the main room with desks in rows and only two other officers were in the room, sitting at desks and busy writing reports or something.

The door to the Captains office opened and he came out with Sargent Fowler following. In the Captain's hand were some papers. He had a slight smile as he saw Lacey and walked toward her. "Nice to see you again Lacey" and held out his hand to shake hers. "Nice to see you too, Daniel"

He shook Daniel's hand and Daniel nodded hello.

Lacey said Nice to see you also."

Sargent Fowler nodded but kept quiet. His face had slight smile on it and there was a little twinkle in his eyes.

The Captain continued, "the reason we called you in today was to give you some interesting facts that came up in forensic in the Harry Gufsterson death. "Let me set your mind at ease, there was nothing present to say you had anything to do with the death." However, on the machete blade there were several blood spots that had dried. Of course, most of the blood on the machete was Harry's, but some of the dried blood could be identified to a DNA test of your Great Great Grandfather that you exhumed to prove your relationship.

Lacey felt the locket warm against her skin. She glanced at the apparitions and they were all smiling at her.

"This is all circumstantial" the Captain said. "But you may have added a piece to the murder of your family a long time ago. "We wanted you to know." "Also, in our search for evidence we uncovered a box beneath the cannon foundation on the hill. ""The box is being held as evidence now, but in a few weeks, we should be able to give it to the rightful owner, which appears to be you."

The apparitions were dancing across the room, outwardly laughing and hugging.

Lacey looked and the Captain with a big smile on her face. "What was in the box,' she blurted a little too abrupt.

The Captain just smiled and said, "a number of gold coins with the same emblem as your locket." It looks like you are in for an inheritance of some wealth."

Lacey had a smile that stretched from ear to ear. Daniel had that goofy smile and had an arm around Lacey's shoulder hugging her.

The Captain said, "I still want you as a member of our police force." So, what are your plans?" He was looking at both of them as he said it. He meant more by the question than just day to day doings.

They looked at each other. Daniel nodded for Lacey to answer. "Well we are in discussions about that, but we are going up to visit my parents, next week." Then we are going to pick up Daniel's daughter and have her with us down here, for another week." That is about as far as we can plan at this time." "There has been so much going on that we need a little time to let everything settle."

The apparitions were now clapping their hands.

Daniel finally spoke." If we plan any ceremonies, we will be sure to invite both of you."

The Captain was still smiling and said, "I will count on that."

Sargent Fowler also finally spoke looking directly at Lacey, "please don't kill or maim anyone in the meantime." I have been filling out paperwork for weeks."

Lacey looked at him and said, "I will try" She winked at Fowler and took Daniel's hand. They turned to leave and she noticed the ghosts were cheering. She wondered how long they would be around.

CPSIA information can be obtained
at www.ICGtesting.com
Printed in the USA
LVHW081543180422
716530LV00013B/560